WANTED

Also by

HEIDI AYARBE

FREEZE FRAME

COMPROMISED

COMPULSION

WANTED

HEIDI AYARBE

BALZER + BRAY
An Imprint of HarperCollins*Publishers*

Balzer + Bray is an imprint of HarperCollins Publishers.

Wanted
www.epicreads.com

    Library of Congress Cataloging-in-Publication Data
Ayarbe, Heidi.
  Wanted / Heidi Ayarbe. — 1st ed.
    p. cm.
  Summary: Seventeen-year-old Michal Garcia, a bookie
at Carson City High School, raises the stakes in her illegal
activities after she meets wealthy, risk-taking Josh Ellison.
  ISBN 978-0-06-199388-6 (trade bdg.)
  [1. Gambling—Fiction. 2. Crime—Fiction. 3. High
schools—Fiction. 4. Schools—Fiction. 5. Nevada—Fiction.]
I. Title
PZ7.A9618 Wan 2012   2011032650
[Fic]—dc23   CIP
                                    AC

Typography by
12 13 14 15 16 CG/RRDH 10 9 8 7 6 5 4 3 2 1
❖

First Edition

THIS IS FOR

GRANDMA GRACE AND Grandma Tjon, who began a legacy of strong women; Mom, a pint-sized force of strength; Carrie, my best friend and sister; and Andrea, my forever friend . . . because I've always wanted to be like you. And my girls, Sydney, Kyra, and Amelia—wishing you the courage to be who you are.

WANTED

THE END

THE CRUISERS APPEAR LIKE
a mirage.But a crummy one, since mirages, on general
principles, are supposed to be good and happy and filled
with tropical fruits, muscular guys in turbans, and stuff
like that. The cars rip along a shimmering strip of tarry
highway between two billboards: THERE'S PLENTY OF ROOM
FOR GOD'S CREATURES NEXT TO THE MASHED POTATOES
and NEVADA: LEADING THE COUNTRY IN BEING JUST EAST
OF CALIFORNIA. THAT AND BROTHELS (FLIP A BITCH . . .
5 MILES BACK). I'm not gonna go all *Great Gatsby* about the
billboards because they're not a symbol of anything at all.

Nothing is.

The cruisers come to a screeching halt in the parking lot, tires kicking up loose rocks from the half-melted
asphalt, modern-day Keystone Kops with wailing sirens

and clumsy, fishtail stops. When the burnout smoke settles, the cops pile out of the cars, guns drawn, crouching behind the opened doors of the cars.

I pull back the corner of a flyer advertising hand-knit Snuggies to get a better view. Four cops. The lanky one has midnight skin and talks into a radio. The next car over, two cops roll on the scorching asphalt to find better cover. Albino shades her eyes and maintains her position behind the car door. They've got to be using phrases like "clear the area," "set up a perimeter," "Starsky and Hutch will take the back while Ponch and Jon hold the front."

Well, everything but that last phrase, anyway.

Josh is wearing his golden Burger King crown. They still give them out. If you request them. It's not like something that's just there for the taking. You have to ask.

The crown sits lopsided on his head. He kneels next to me, cupping my face in his hands.

Sweat drips down my temple. I'm so cold. But my hair sticks to my forehead and the back of my neck. I'm not what Josh would consider mirage worthy.

I never have been. Not for him.

Sweat trickles to my chin, then spatters when it hits the dingy linoleum.

I motion behind the counter. Josh shakes his head.

Hemingway once wrote a six-word memoir: *For sale: baby shoes, never worn.*

I think about mine, summing up a life in six words, and

draw a blank, wishing the store owner would've done the same.

It's pretty amazing how calm I am, considering that odds are I'll be dead in time for the evening news.

1

A CROWD HAS GATHERED.

Sanctuary. That's all I text, then push send, and they come. Crystal dewdrops hang on yellowed blades of grass. The group huddles at the bleachers, clapping their arms, puffs of breaths dangling in the air.

Across the field another group gathers—dark-blue flannel shirts buttoned to the top, creased khakis. La Cordillera. I shade my eyes and squint, but they all look like blue smudges on fingerprint cards from over here.

I dig through my backpack, looking for my glasses. They're splotchy and crooked.

No one from la Cordillera is coming this way. I'll take their bets later at Mocho's place. Though I'd like to think of Sanctuary as a demilitarized zone, a place where we can all get together under a common interest. Some groups never mix, though—not even here.

I pause. I *could* go to over to them, join their circle, take their bets. But that wouldn't work. People come to *me*. Even la Cordillera.

Most of my business is done by phone, but big days, big games, it's always nice to convene—make it a little more personal. And get the cash. Right there.

As soon as I walk up, the crowd hushes. I scan the faces and see the quintessential human flaw—hope.

Sometimes I think I could probably save myself a lot of stress if I got a part-time job selling high cholesterol at the Pizza Factory instead of selling hope. Because with hope comes despair. *Welcome to life. Yep. It sucks.* Then I spend lots of time on the phone consoling the losers—kind of like a pseudoeconomic psychologist convincing them a little bit of hell paves the way to big rewards later on.

I could go back to wearing Walmart discount-rack clothes. It's not like it really matters what I wear around here, because I'll still just be me. Sometimes it's like I live in my own DMZ with problematic T-zone pimples and oily hair. No boobs. The "big-boned" girl with a weird name.

I look at their faces. Flushed cheeks, chapped lips, furrowed brows. Their eyes lock on me—expectation? Flashes of anxiety. Shades of doubt erase as expressions of self-assurance take over. It's like watching some kind of Incredible Hulk transformation when I arrive.

Here, in Sanctuary, I'm everything. Hope incarnate—a

priest, minister, preacher.

Their bookie.

Powerful.

Cashing in on hope is way more lucrative than adolescent pizza addictions.

Plus, at the end of the day, gambling isn't a whole lot different from high school. It's all about knowing the rules, the stakes, and when to quit. There's a fine line between taking a calculated risk and a suicidal one. Whenever I take bets at Sanctuary, I'm not sure whether I'm on the smart side or suicidal side. I know, though, that whatever it is, I'm alive.

I'm good at what I do. The money flows. On a bad week, I clear a hundred dollars or so—enough to dress better than any kid at this school; my clients' girlfriends hate me for it. I look at the girls, clutching their boyfriends' arms. Sanctuary's extras—generic, varsity jacket–wearing girlfriends in Payless, knockoff Coach or Uggs—almost but not quite the real deal.

I look down at my shoes. Old Gringo zipper boots. The real deal—three hundred bucks real.

I give their boyfriends something they can't. These guys are hungry to bet—to *feel* something outside this Carson City bubble. Before me, they never knew what it was like to live. Now they feel the surge of emotion watching their team win. Or lose. And a *need* to capture that feeling again.

And again.

And again.

"Ladies and gentlemen, these are Super Bowl wild-card playoffs. Ready for business?" I ask. I look at the time. "Class starts in thirty minutes. Who's on the lookout?"

A couple of light bettors—baseball, basketball, fill-in-the-blank-sport bench warmers—go to the baseball backstop and hang out. The rest of us take out tattered copies of Dostoyevsky's *The Gambler*. My bet book is cradled between the pages that hold one of my favorite quotes:

> *I deduced from the scene one conclusion which seemed to me reliable—namely, that in the flow of fortuitous chances there is, if not a system, at all events a sort of order. This, of course, is a very strange thing.*

A system.

An order.

I look at the expectant faces of my clients, who will throw their money away on chance, on whims, instead of studying the system. Few take the time to understand the way it works, the wonder of the world of betting, like they've all settled into some kind of daze of conformity, following the trends, the favorites. The world of betting is much more than money-lining the favorite. I shrug.

"I've got a special today for those wanting to cash in on something that could be real sweet: Arizona has pretty much surprised us all. If you're betting on them and have the lead after the third, then lose, you get your money back.

"And, of course, as always, anything goes. You dig your grave, you lie in it. I don't have time for hand holding."

Leonard, my guy in Reno—kind of a bookie mentor, actually—taught me some basics when I began, the first being: *Read back is final.* I read back the wagers. Client reconfirms. Done deal. No do-overs. It takes time to build a list of clients—reliable ones. Now nobody gets in Sanctuary without a face-to-face recommendation from one of my regulars. And I reserve the right to refuse.

Money changes hands, bets are read back and placed. Someone on lookout whistles. On cue I start to read from that quote. We each read a quarter of a page, some mumbling over the interminable sentences. Dean Randolph comes over and sits on the bleachers with us, staring across at la Cordillera. "What are you reading?" he asks, not really listening.

"*The Gambler,*" I answer.

Randolph nods.

I look over at a seminew client—don't remember his name. His hand trembles, cash peeking out of his clutched fist; sweat drips down his temples. *What's his name?* I stare at him until we make eye contact and I mouth, "Cool it or leave. Now." I can see his Adam's apple bob up and down in his throat. *Justin.* That's right. *Justin.* He's a junior.

Somebody's reading. Randolph listens to Alexei's first run with roulette. The guy stutters over "whence" like he's never read nineteenth-century lit before. Rookie.

"What class is this for?"

"Not a class," I say. "We're just into Dostoyevsky. We meet here all the time." I know the drill and pass him my book, dog-eared pages yellowed, highlighted, and underlined.

My bet book lies open on my lap—right in front of Randolph's nose. I move to close it and it falls off my knees. Randolph absently picks up my bet book, pages open, handing it to me while flipping through the pages of *The Gambler*. "Dostoyevsky, huh? Pretty highbrow."

"Yeah. He was persecuted in Russia for his ideas, exiled in Siberia, came back, and rocked the world with his work. *The* founder of existentialism." I smile and hold my hand out, waiting for him to pass the book back. A couple of guys cough. A blue vein streaks across junior Justin's bright red face. I glare at him and tap my fingers on the bleachers, waiting for Randolph to hand me everything, feeling the thrill, that feeling that we're so close to getting caught. But we won't get caught.

I shift my weight and try to ignore my cold, metal-bleacher–numbed butt.

Randolph nods, looking above *The Gambler* at la Cordillera. He's more interested in our friendly neighborhood gang. He hands me the book, and I close it around Sanctuary's bets, safe in *The Gambler*'s pages.

It's so freaking obvious why we're here—what Sanctuary is—that he doesn't see what we're doing. *Really. Study group?* The Gambler? *Outside? When the temp is hovering at just about ten degrees?*

I shake my head.

It's always that way with Dean Randolph and pretty much every other teacher, parent, guardian, counselor . . . whoever . . . on the planet. It's like once you hit middle age, you spend your time looking for smoke signs when your ass is already on fire.

Randolph tries to hide a yawn. He smiles at us approvingly and ambles along, skirting around la Cordillera, not ballsy enough to actually sit with them. When he's out of sight, I take the rest of the bets. Justin hands me his sweaty ball of cash. I hold his wrist. "It's cool, okay? Just be cool."

He nods.

"Or don't come back. You got that?"

"Okay."

Everything's done—the bets are placed. I close my book and am ready to head to class—with plenty of time left over to get caffeinated—when I see Nim and his girlfriend.

Not Nim. Not today.

Nim motions for Kylie "Medusa" to stay. I can practically hear him: "Stay, Medusa. Stay. Good girl." Medusa sits on the lowest bleacher, her hair a nest of tangled auburn ringlets—probably one of Nevada's government-protected ecosystems for migratory birds.

"Hey, Mike." Nim smiles. Deep dimples on ski-tanned cheeks deceivingly charming.

I've fallen for that smile plenty of times. Like eight hundred dollars plenty. I pull my gaze away. "Yeah."

"Can you hook me up?"

"I'm not a pimp or a dealer, so probably not," I say, standing up.

Nim pulls me down and sits next to me, wrapping his arm around my shoulder, nearly asphyxiating me with cologne and caked-on Degree Sport stick. He pulls me in tight—too tight. I can practically feel capillaries bursting under his grip. "You *know* what I need."

I swallow. Count. *Keep it cool.* His grip loosens and he starts to laugh that maniacal nervous laugh he gets before he goes wacko. This is not good.

"This sweet parlay will get me out of some hot water," Nim says.

Nimrod's dad doesn't know he's already hundreds in the hole. Hundreds his family can afford. Hundreds Nim can't. The irony of this entire situation is that though I'm the one who has him by his Shrinky Dink steroid balls, I'm the one trying to still my trembling hands. If he knew how scared I was of him, I'd never survive high school.

I shake my head, steady my hands to pull out the BlackBerry. "Not gonna happen. You've already used up your line of credit." Leverage. Gotta use any leverage I've got, so I squeeze a little harder. "You'd have done well this past week with Ravens."

Nimrod slams his fist into the bleacher, the aluminum

buckling. I don't think I've visibly flinched and hope to God my lip isn't quivering. He's never hit me before. But today he's desperate. Desperate people do stupid things.

The thing is, with a guy like Nimrod, you've got to take a little pity because unless he makes the major leagues or lands a modeling contract *soon*, odds are he'll end up working as a security guard for his dad's storage rental units, wearing the poop-colored polyester uniform. His only chance at post–high school glory is discovering that some deranged serial killer hides body parts in one of the storage units.

I look back to la Cordillera. A few of them are watching. Witnesses. This is good. I'll need witnesses.

As if he's reading my mind, Nimrod drops his arm and stares at the gang. Being on good terms with la Cordillera is kind of its own built-in security system.

"Please," he says. "C'mon, Mike."

Criminy. He's begging. I shrug him off. "Nope. I can give you the number of my guy in Reno, though. He's *real* pleasant. Especially when you *don't* pay your debts."

I watch Nim's dimples disappear and his face turn a blotchy red. It's kind of fun to play with him. He grabs my arm tighter. Fun's over.

"Don't be a—"

"You want to finish that sentence?" I ask, and peel his fingers off my arm.

"I'm good for it," he grumbles. Defeated.

I wait, cock my head to the side, and stare at him.

He shoves his hands into his pockets, pulling out a limp, pencil-smudged piece of paper. "C'mon, Mike. Jesus Christ, already."

"Collateral," I say.

"Collateral?"

"What? You need a dictionary?"

He flinches.

"Collateral. Give me something of yours. You lose, I keep it. You win, you get it back and we're done."

"Like my varsity jacket?" Nim nods at Medusa, who's moved so close to him, it's hard to tell where he ends and she begins.

Medusa glares at Nim and hugs it around her broomstick body.

"Um. No."

"But that jacket—"

"Means *nothing* to me. Something else. Something big."

Nim looks shocked. How could his varsity jacket be meaningless—all that leather, the letter, those pins? "Okay. Like what? My debit card?"

"With a fifty dollar–a-week limit. Please."

His jaw almost drops to the bleachers. If there's one thing Nim isn't, it's subtle. The entire student body knows his jock strap size, PIN, and mother's maiden name. Idiot.

"Shit. What do you want then? My signed

football—Peyton Manning. It's gotta be worth—"

"The title to your truck." I say. "By the end of the day."

"Are you out of your—no way. Like."

I move down a couple of bleachers. "Have a great week then."

He pulls me back so hard that the bleachers dig into my knees with an electric, cold jolt. He leans in close, so close I can smell the barely masked body odor and count his blackheads. The left side of his lip goes up as if it were attached to some invisible string, bobbing up and down, up and down. Twitchy.

How to deal with the likes of Nimrod was not addressed in *Bookmaking for Dummies*. My only hope to come out of this without ending up with my jaw wired shut and a liquid diet until we graduate is to make sure Nim wins. Unfortunately, I don't rig bets. I just place them.

He hands me a paper with his picks—a four-game parlay, all-or-nothing bet on Wild Card Weekend—money-lining each game. So rookie.

I shake my head. "Listen. Back in middle school, I did the parlay-card thing. This, though, is just green. Nobody money-lines four different games."

"I make the bet, you place the bet. Like I really need advice from a chick about how to bet."

"Gambling 101, Nim. This is pretty basic stuff." And annoying. "You can't cover the losses anymore. You're already several hundred plus in the hole. You lose, I lose, which shouldn't be the case—as you stated, you make the bet, I place it. But here's the thing. You can't cover it, and I want my money back."

I take the normal vig with all my clients, but Nimrod is *the* pain in the ass who bets too much. His losses never used to affect my take, but lately, I don't even get the juice and have gotten into a bad habit of fronting him cash I know he's not good for. No odds in my favor there.

I straighten my back, moving in close, trying not to gag on the musty smell of his cologne. My throat burns like I'm drinking tree bark and moss. "I won't front you the cash for this bet."

"It's my cash, my bet. I'm good for it." Nim pushes past me. I lose my balance and stumble backward, falling from halfway up the bleachers to the ground. My diaphragm spasms. I gasp for air.

Nimrod stands over me, framed by the heatless sun, making him look like some kind of Greek god—his perfectly waved hair on fire. He spits; thick phlegm splatters on the grass next to me and spatters into my ear.

He pulls the truck title out of his wallet and drops it next to me. "Place the fucking bet. Tonight," he says, then turns on his heel and leaves, Medusa trailing behind him. I try not to panic because it's been approximately forty seconds since oxygen has reached my brain. And you can't bookie when you're brain dead.

I close my eyes, willing my body to start respiratory

function. Sometimes I wonder if I'm like the tree falling in the forest.

If nobody sees Michal, will she exist?

"Hey. You okay?" I open my eyes. The kind-of-new guy at school, one of those instantly popular fit-ins, stands over me in all my humiliated glory. I'm still trying to catch my breath when he reaches his hand down to help me sit up. "You okay?" he repeats. He pulls his baseball cap off and pulls me into a sitting position, squatting down beside me, placing his hand on my back, dusty blond hair flopping into his eyes.

I'm caught between not breathing because, physiologically, it's impossible at this moment and not breathing because the hand resting on my back makes me feel like I did when I licked a wall socket on a dare when I was little. He squints, trying to block the sun from his eyes. "Should I call someone? Are you, like, choking on something? Can you breathe?"

I manage to nod.

"Which one? Choking or breathing?"

I hold up two fingers.

He hands me a bandana to wipe my face. "You okay?"

My diaphragm decides to cooperate and contract to let air in. I gasp for breath and rest my head between my knees, tucking Nimrod's truck title in my pocket, hoping I haven't turned that awful purple-red color. "I'm okay. Just clumsy."

Javier comes over and crouches next to the new guy.

I'm feeling incredibly exposed. Hard not to do, considering they found me sprawled on my back on the third-base line. I undoubtedly have a grass stain on my head from sliding off the bench after I lost all respiratory function. So my existence takes place in two spheres: bookmaking and humiliation.

"Josh," the first guy says, shaking my hand, smiling wide, revealing a slight gap between his front teeth, perfect for first-date lettuce disasters. "I'm new here. You might've seen me around. Specifically in your Creative Writing and Government classes."

Yeah. I've seen him. Who hasn't? "Yeah. I've seen you around."

"Hey, Mike, whatcha doing sprawled on the third-base line?" Javier says, taking my other hand in his. Together he and Josh pull me to my feet.

I brush wet grass and dirt off my jeans.

Javier's a cool guy. He's placed a couple of bets. The only time he ever won, he invited me out to Dairy Queen to celebrate, as if I were personally responsible for the Giants beating the Mariners.

I sigh, running fingers through my hair and pulling it back into a ponytail.

"Binder placing a bet?" Javier points to Nim's looming frame in the distance. He and Medusa are working it in some spontaneous feel-up moment—probably the only time they'll get until after school. "He do this to you?"

Josh points to where Nimrod was standing. "*That* guy pushed you down? And *spit* on you? What the . . . ? That's just wrong." The small scar across Josh's left eyebrow practically glows white in his red-flushed face.

"Save your indignation for when you lose. You here for Sanctuary?"

Javier turns back to me. "Yeah. Josh wanted in on something."

"You're late."

"We mixed up meeting places. My bad." Javier scuffs his shoe across the grass. "Listen. I'll let you two figure it out. I've got to finish some calc before Mrs. Hensler gives me infinite detention."

I laugh.

We watch Javier head toward school. "Wild Card Weekend. I'm not really into new clients," I say. "I'm not interested in consoling beginners—or losers."

"Not a beginner." Josh flashes a smile. "I don't lose."

"Cocky. So how much are you throwing away?"

"You'll take my bet."

"I don't have all morning." I shrug, waiting for the typical *I want to put twenty dollars on the Raiders winning.* After which I'll have to explain the Raiders aren't even playing.

"First scoring play. San Diego Chargers."

I push my bangs out of my eyes and nod. "Nice."

He hands me a hundred dollars. "Want in on it? You can match my bet and we'll make loads more." He's smiling, a half-moon toothy smile that makes him look utterly dorky or adorable.

"I don't gamble. I just make my money off of those who do."

"It's a good high," he says.

I shrug. "So is having a nice bank account." Which I would, if it weren't for the fact I have a few credit cards I need to pay off. I look down at my Old Gringos. Maybe three hundred was going overboard. But they're pretty sweet.

"You like the sidelines, huh? Don't play the game."

"Watching you guys suffer is entertaining enough." I don't know if this is a challenge, an observation, or him just being a total *pendejo*.

"Suffer with me."

"Are you for real?" I head to the building, Josh matching my stride. "What is that? Suffer with me? I mean, hello. Did you get that from some soap?"

Josh bursts out laughing. "Yeah. Can't blame a guy for trying."

"Trying?"

"Anyway, we can watch the game together this weekend. At Bully's."

I shake my head. "Nah. I'm good."

"Wish me luck, then."

"It's bad luck for a bookie to wish somebody good luck."

We walk into the building, a wave of heat with the familiar sweat socks/school caf burritos smell blasting us.

"See you soon," Josh says.

"Yeah," I say. "Like in ten minutes in Creative Writing." I watch him walk down the hall, talking to practically everybody he walks by. He turns around and sees me watching him—too late for me to turn away. He nods and shouts, "Play the game."

It bothers me that he already knows about my sideline life.

2

Doping: High School Sports and That Chick Who Smells Like Testosterone in Geometry Class

Valuing Diversity? Yeah. Right. Our Fragmented Student Body

I TUCK *PB & J* UNDER MY ARM. It looks like Seth and his underground paper are back in business. Seth walks by and nods, shoving *PB & J* into everyone's hands, slipping it in lockers. He's probably already papered everybody's cars in the parking lot. I hope it doesn't snow.

PB & J had to go *way* underground for a couple of months because around November, Seth wrote an "unconfirmed" article about an unidentified fungus in the locker room. The Health Department made the school rid the locker rooms of fungi that may or may not have been there.

It cost the district about five grand.

Kids call Seth "WikiLeaks."

I weave my way through various crowds of students. The theater group is doing a scene from *One Flew over the Cuckoo's Nest* in the courtyard in the alleyway that links the two buildings of classes. From an architectural point of view, the place looks more like an oval-shaped, two-story mall than a high school. They're trying to promote their spring production, as if high school alone weren't dramatic enough.

I inhale. I smell like Clearasil. Maybe I should invest in a good perfume. It's hardly likely Josh, or any other guy for that matter, will find Clearasil sexually stimulating.

Josh: not even the same league. Good six-word memoir.

When I open my locker, an avalanche of books falls on top of me. I pull out my wrinkled Government report and try to iron it on my thigh. The bell rings. The hallways begin to clear out. Mocho heads toward me, disbanding from the sea of blue and khaki, looking almost normal alone, instead of like a cliché—the way he looks when he's with the pack.

We practically grew up together, living in the same trailer park. Pre-Cordillera, Moch wanted to be a pro baseball player or be like Sy Hersh—some Pulitzer Prize–winning journalist. We had an aluminum can–collecting business. Moch bought a mini tape recorder with his earnings to conduct lengthy interviews with the people from the neighborhood. I usually just bought candy. I wonder if he still has those tapes.

Funny that Moch and I both went illicit.

Mocho helps pick up the pile of papers, books, and magazines. I blush when he flips through my dog-eared copy of *Cosmo* that was inconspicuously tucked into my Government book. He hands me the magazines. I shove them into my locker, pile the books, and keep them balanced until I can slam the door shut without all of them falling out again. "Thanks for helping me out." The books thud against the locker door. "I could've been buried alive."

"Uh-huh," he says. He looks away, absently picking a Yoda sticker off some kid's locker.

My back and ribs hurt from falling off the bleachers this morning. I pull out my Creative Writing folder and write my two memoirs along with one about a sideline life. Falling off the bleachers and oxygen deprivation have made me downright prolific. *Just call me Proust.* I kind of laugh to myself.

Mrs. Brooks is on a memoir kick. Every day we're supposed to write six words that sum up a feeling, a moment—anything that tells her what our day has been like. Every day I scramble to write six words that will get me a passing grade. Today I'm compelled to write:

Oops. Got off at wrong life.

But I don't think that'd get me a passing grade and would probably get me a trip to see Mrs. Valencia, the feel-good counselor who has made everybody read *The Secret*. "Attitude, attitude, attitude, sweetheart. What you seek is right before your eyes."

It feels like every time I look for something, it's back at

what could've been if Mom were around.

I write: Wanted: Happiness. Lost in Great Basin.

Moch is picking the sticker out from under his nail.

"Were you out there this morning?" I couldn't see across the field without my glasses, so the entire group looked like a smear of blue and tan—smudged chalk.

"Yeah."

"So when somebody pushes me off the bleachers, you just sit tight. Is that what happened when Pacho got his jaw broken by Garbage Disposal? You just sat tight?" I say. "Thanks a lot, Moch."

He cocks his head to the side, thick eyebrows drawn together in a deep scowl. "I never leave a *hermano*."

I know what he's saying is true because last week, after Pacho was beaten badly, Moch came to school with bandaged hands. But it bothers me that I don't count. Pacho does.

Mocho glares at me with glassy eyes. I shift my weight from foot to foot. Silence falls over us, like we're in a bubble.

It's been a funky morning. I feel a lump in my throat.

Moch bites down on his lower lip and grunts.

I swallow back the ache. "Moch," I say, looking around the hallway, "you know it's totally okay to string words together in a coherent sentence. It doesn't make you less scary."

He glares for just a second, then cracks a smile. His teeth have more gold than the Vatican, but he still looks ten years younger than he probably wishes he does. "Don't say that kind of shit, Michal. You could get real messed over for that." His scowl is gone and he looks worried. "You okay?"

"I'm fine. Thanks." I can feel Nimrod's thick fingers on my shoulder.

"Walk to class together?" Moch asks.

I nod. Moch, though he tries to hide it, is one of the best in Creative Writing. He writes six-word memoirs about everything you wouldn't expect. He writes about papaya sunsets and shaved coconut snow, childhood mud pies like bubbling pots of mole—a spicy chocolate life.

Then one day he wrote about the way blood congeals on the floor. Mrs. Brooks hasn't called on him to share since.

Plus he's gone a lot lately. A lot. I refrain from reading the obituaries most days because I'm afraid before long he'll be there and his poetry will be gone, too. Most of us could write his memoir: Bang! Wasted life. Anger turned cliché.

"What are you doing hanging with Ellison?" Moch asks, interrupting my thoughts, doing his limp-walk, swagger thing.

I wink at him. "Do you have some kind of hip dysplasia or something?"

"Michal, c'mon." He stands a little taller, though. His eyes are smiling. It's nice to see he's still Moch somewhere under there.

I liked him a lot better when we collected aluminum

cans but don't think this is the right moment to take a walk down memory lane. I've already pushed my luck to the limits this morning.

"Josh Ellison? He's a client. He's in our Creative Writing class. Nice."

"Rich," Mocho says.

"He drives a Prius, yeah. Probably not destitute." *And just placed a hundred-dollar bet.*

"He could buy Nevada and sell it tomorrow. His dad's the one who brought in Ellison Industries," Moch says.

"*That* Ellison? Save-Nevada-from-bankruptcy Ellison? Job-creator, tax-paying model-citizen, next-governor Ellison?"

"He's just a trust-fund tool, probably getting an airplane for his eighteenth birthday."

"So what?" I say. I don't imagine Josh and his family have ties to the Carson City gang scene. And Josh doesn't look like a meth head.

Before the bell rings, he says, "Ma asks about you. Come by the house for dinner this week." There's something behind the invitation, something he's not telling me.

"You okay?" I ask.

Moch shrugs. "Come by. Okay?"

"Okay."

We walk into the classroom. Josh is sitting where he's sat ever since he came—three chairs from the back in the third row.

Yeah. I've noticed.

He smiles when I pass him. I nod in his direction.

Moch glares at Josh, then me, returning to his monosyllabic gang persona.

Mrs. Brooks asks who wants to share a memoir, her hand hovering over the seating chart to pick at random. I look around the class, a little desperate for somebody to volunteer. Mrs. B's bony finger circles the paper, then descends like a vulture. The entire class is waiting in dread anticipation. There's no telling who'll be crucified. "Seth Collins," she says. "Six words. Go."

Seth exhales. He's a light bettor, mostly to get the scoop on sports for *PB & J* and *Carson High Tribune*—the "legit" paper he edits. I'm a little surprised he didn't go this morning. He clears his throat and says, "'Sanctuary. Pleasure. Pain. Cash up front.'"

Mrs. B taps her chin. "Cash up front?" she echoes. "What a rich phrase—so open to interpretation."

The class is laughing, heads buried in their notebooks.

I can feel the heat rise to my cheeks and slump in my chair. A few others volunteer, satiating Mrs. B's need to tap into the affective domain before plunging into an activity on meaningful thesis statements.

I close my notebook, hiding my memoirs—glad Mrs. B doesn't ask me to read out loud because I don't want Josh or Moch or anybody else to know I don't have poetry.

Others' bets. Others' lives. Silent observer.

3

JANUARY 11 IS ALWAYS A sucky day. It doesn't make sense to celebrate somebody's birthday when they're already dead. But I'd rather remember my mom alive than dead. Kind of silly missing someone after all these years. I hardly knew her anyway.

I brush the thought away. It's probably a mix between Josh and Moch and Nim. The tingle of the morning bets and almost getting caught by Randolph was long gone by the time I had to turn in my Creative Writing memoirs.

I stand in the middle of the hall, holding my books, and watch as everybody streams around me, undisturbed, like I'm a giant stone in the middle of a river. The river changes course.

I stay the same.

The halls clear out and I'm still standing there—untouched. Invisible.

I watch the parking lot clear out. I sit at the tables in front of the media center to finish all my homework so that I can take care of business at home—have the weekend free.

For what?

I should feel alive with a backpack full of bets and Wild Card Weekend coming up, four games and a list of hopes—yards run, yards thrown, sacks, winners, losers, you name it. But I don't.

I don't care who wins or loses—ever. It's Deism. I set the bets in motion and sit back to watch how things turn out. It's like having control because it doesn't matter how the game ends—I've already stacked the bets the way I need them to make the money I need to make. So I watch my clients—how they suffer, cry, feel like they're invincible because of one day of good luck.

That's the thing. I watch.

My life feels vicarious.

"I'm home!" The house smells like burned cheese and melted plastic. "Lillian?" I follow the smell to the kitchen, where Lillian is scraping charcoal off generic-brand toast, plastified cheeselike substance dripping from the sides of the bread. "I got fish tacos from Super Burrito," I say.

Lillian stops midscrape and looks up at me over her thick-rimmed glasses. Her THE PERSONAL IS THE POLITICAL T-shirt, threadbare and faded, slips off her bony shoulder, the collar stretched out into an amorphous top.

I blush, a little embarrassed she leaves the house like this. I set the table with the rarely-been-used dishes I got for Lillian for Christmas and wipe off the layer of dust. I place a half-burned candle on the table.

"You don't need to be spending your salary on food for us. You need to be saving for college next fall," Lillian says. She thinks I get my spending money by working at the school financial office in the afternoons. She doesn't know I have four bank accounts.

"It's TTIF (Thank Tacos It's Friday), two for one," I lie and look at the sink, dotted with the burned cinders. "Thanks for making dinner, though. It's nice to eat together."

At least she made an effort. When I first moved in, she set two alarms, one to wake me up, and the other to let me know when I needed to go out and catch the bus. After living just a couple of months with her, I was in charge of washing my own clothes and making my own breakfast, lunch, and usually a microwave dinner.

I was eight.

Lillian was in college majoring in biochem—the first girl in her family to study in the U.S. When she got pregnant with Mom, her parents pretty much disowned her because good Catholic girls, good Mexican Catholic girls, get married.

She didn't. She said good-bye to her family and Mexico.

She finished a nursing degree at night, started working

at clinics, and never looked back. Over the past thirty-five years Lillian has left Mexico behind; she took the trill out of her *r* and has spent her time fighting for women's rights—specifically, sexual rights. My mom kind of got forgotten in the midst of Lillian's politics, picketing, and pamphlet pushing. It's easier to love a cause than a person. Causes are perfect. People aren't.

I light the candle while she disposes of the cremated sandwiches.

"What's the occasion?" she asks.

I shrug. "I guess I could ask you the same."

We both look at the calendar. A faded picture of Mom and me is tacked up on the bulletin board next to it. Lillian had it taken right before Mom left with the One Mind, One Body religious group for a spring-break retreat.

The fish taco lodges in my throat. I take a long drink of water to wash it down, then spend the rest of dinner playing with the tortilla chips on my plate, listening to Lillian rage about some new law being pushed through the legislature that could limit medical access for illegal immigrants. There have also been vandalism and attacks at the clinic—supposedly a local neo-Nazi group. They can't afford extra protection and are worried that somebody's going to come in and steal the meds. She's going to start taking night-watch turns with some other staff. "Will you be okay here? On your own?"

"Sure. Of course."

"You could invite a friend," Lillian suggests.

"I'll be fine."

I sometimes think Lillian would love me more if I were one of her patients, struggling to make ends meet, dodging the INS, working sixteen-hour days for nothing instead of being her bastard granddaughter.

When Lillian finishes, I wrap up the leftovers and place them in the fridge. I blow out the candle. "Happy Birthday, Mami," I say under my breath.

Dusk weighs on us, smothering the light of the sun. I shiver and head toward my room. I've got a lot of work to do tonight.

When she thinks I'm out of earshot, I hear Lillian say, "I miss her, too."

That's hard for me to believe. You can't miss somebody you never even wanted—never even loved. I think if there's love, for real, it's not something you ever have to say behind cardboard walls. It should be shouted.

For Lillian, love pre–*Roe v. Wade* came at a high price. And her daughter, Roe, was born the same month the involuntary servitude of motherhood became unconstitutional.

When Mom died, I became unwanted generation number two.

I ease my door shut and ignore the nettles of pain that have settled in my chest—like spiny fish bones poking holes in my flimsy heart. My arm hurts, blue-black bruises dotting my shoulder's olive skin where Nimrod embedded his steel-grip fingers.

I stare at the blurred computer screen through fish-bowl tears. I blink and they spill down my cheeks. I pull on a sweatshirt and hold a copy of the picture of Mom and me—the one we have in the kitchen. The only picture of us together. Ever. She's slight, wiry, with ropes of dark, wavy hair. Her eyes are infinite—pools of deep brown kindness splayed with more lashes than I have hair.

My throat aches; a flutter of pain settles in my chest. We look nothing alike.

I try to remember her voice, how she smelled—if only I could have one of Mocho's memoirs. His Mexico is so alive, not buried under some feminist agenda.

My Mexico smells like fish tacos and burned grilled cheese. I put the picture facedown and open up my bet book to the last pages. *My* bets, but ones I never place. It's always been out of curiosity—just to see how much I'd make.

I look at the running column of losses and wins.

Since September, I'd have made over three thousand dollars—all on pretty modest bets.

Three thousand dollars.

I even place vicarious bets.

Three thousand dollars.

Play the game.

I think about Josh. *Play the game.* I look at his bet.

Maybe thirty dollars. A small bet, just to get my feet

wet. Just to feel something. Anything. I can call Leonard. Place a bet with him. He might give me a no-vig first-timer deal.

The shrill of my telephone rips me from my trance. Number unknown.

I don't answer and click it to vibrate, turning my bet book to the worn pages where I wrote down this morning's bets. Tomorrow I'll go to the bank to deposit the cash I got this morning.

Play the game.

The phone rings again, dancing across the tabletop until I pick up. "Hello?"

"Hi, um, hi."

Silence.

"Mike?"

"Speaking."

"Mike. It's Josh. I'm in your Government and Creative Writing classes, though you didn't notice me the past month until we officially met this morning. Javier told me you'd kill him if he gave me your number, but I was kinda worried about you and wanted to know if you're okay. Totally not Javier's fault. He said he'd call for me, but he doesn't have any minutes so he can't call, which, I said, would totally defeat the purpose of checking on you because to check on you, we'd have to call. Okay. Now I'm sounding like a total asshole. Here. Javier's right here."

"Mike, it's cool. Josh is cool. Your number is safe with

him." Javier sounds bored. "He's a nice guy." He emphasizes *nice*, probably meaning "this is a pity call."

There's a rustling sound and Josh is back on the phone. "So, um, you're okay?"

In the living room, Lillian turns on the TV, watching seventies and eighties reruns. "Gotcha," the funky disco theme song from *Starsky and Hutch*, fills the air. Our house sounds like some kind of bawdy sex show. The phone nearly slips from my sweaty palms.

"Yeah. I'm okay. Thanks a lot for calling."

Silence.

"You don't sound that happy about it. You sound pissed," Josh says.

"I am. Happy."

I run through my mental inventory of things to talk about and come up blank. Luckily Josh doesn't. He says, "Javier says you're real good with math, and we have some killer calculus homework from Mrs. Hensler."

"On a Friday?" I ask.

"Sure. Friday-night math marathons. Wanna come over for pizza and homework? We'll buy the pizza if you're willing to help out with the math."

"Math. I'd love to help." The barbs are back, crawling up my throat. I swallow, trying to control the quaver in my voice. *Math. Of course.* "I can't, though. I've got to write some six-word memoirs for Creative Writing tonight."

"On a Friday?" he asks.

"Sure. Friday-night memoir marathons."

"Yeah. Sure. Okay. Glad you're okay."

"I'm okay."

"Okay."

"I don't think I've ever used *okay* this often in a conversation before. Statistically speaking, we're off the charts here."

Josh laughs. "Memoir it."

"I don't think *memoir* is a verb." I pause. "Is it?"

"Well, it should be," Josh says. "Shit, we say 'Google it.' Why not 'memoir it'?"

I laugh. "I like that. I'll start to use it at least once or twice a day."

Silence.

"Thanks for calling," I say.

"Can I keep your number?" he asks.

"Yeah. This is the number to call when you want to place a bet. I send out notices for winners and losers within twenty-four hours of the game, match, race . . . whatever. I'll save your number for the next time Sanctuary convenes, will send you a text. Javier knows the rotation."

"What about a number to call when I want to talk, memoir, or whatever?"

I'm silent.

"Like, what if I don't want to place a bet and want to call?" he asks. "Can I *do* that?"

"Um. Sure." I give him my social cell-phone

number—one that has seemingly limitless minutes.

"Okay." He hesitates.

"Okay." I turn off the phone and turn on the computer. I flip through my bet book.

I compare the spreads on my favorite sites, figuring out where I'll get the best payouts, calculating my vig. It'll be a lucrative weekend.

I place the bets. Hesitate, put thirty on the Chargers. First score. All I have to do is press enter. My stomach tightens.

Not today.

Lillian shuts off the TV, wanders around the house— the floorboards creaking by the bathroom. I listen as she pauses outside my door. She goes to her room and closes her door.

I stare at the blinking cursor on the screen, then finish my Creative Writing homework. The perfect way to spend a Friday.

Charred sandwiches. Lingering regret. Faded memories.

4

parking spot—Carson High looming in front of me looking
more like the Mall of America than a sanctuary of education
and knowledge. Every time I drive up to school, my stomach
tightens. Other kids make everyday life look so easy.

It was a big weekend; lots of games, lots of payoffs.

Josh won.

I look at the numbers in my notebook—an overall suc-
cess for most of my clients and a few hundred dollars to pay
out during the day. Being the messenger with a winner is
fun. I love to see how their faces light up, counting the bills,
like it's the best ride they've ever had.

What does that feel like?

I'd have won, too. I think about my sideline life. *Play
the game.*

I'm starting to feel like Ray Kinsella in *Shoeless Joe*. Just voices echoing in my head. Maybe I'm going insane. Sure. One man's insanity is another's baseball field for dead players.

Play the game.

Oh for crying out loud.

I'm playing the game. My way. My vig was over a hundred dollars this weekend.

So what if Josh made way more, like four hundred dollars more? His was a risk. Mine's the sure thing.

Whatever.

There's a smattering of teachers' and administrators' cars in the parking lot. Inhale. Exhale. It's good to arrive early—alone, invisible. I check my phone again—to make sure the battery hasn't died, or that I haven't set it on no-vibrate, no-sound. Maybe I've got some weird call blocker that interferes with any incoming calls.

Nothing.

If he'd wanted to call, he would've by now. I guess Josh was being nice—making sure I didn't die after my Nimrod encounter. Which was a pretty decent thing to do, worrying about the death of somebody he doesn't even know.

It's funny. But after the possibility of something different, I feel lonelier than I did before meeting Josh. Maybe I can escape to Grassroots Books in Reno after school and buy a couple of romance novels—just to have a chance to talk to Cory or Andi, whoever's working.

I barely have my car door closed when Nimrod rushes toward me. "All bets are off." Medusa is standing behind him, his letterman's jacket hanging from her wire frame, swallowing her up in stiff white leather and midnight-blue wool. His class ring dangles from a chain around her neck. She probably has his belly-button lint saved in a jar beside her bed.

I bite down on my cheek, steady my hands, and turn to him. "Uh, Nim, over the weekend four of your teams played—one lost. You money-lined instead of playing the spread as I suggested and blew the parlay. So this whole hindsight-is-twenty-twenty doesn't really work in the world of gamblers. I guess that wasn't covered in your Gambling for Dimwits class."

"Bets. Are. Off." The words clip off his tongue. He swats his hand in the air and turns around, ready to blow me off.

I yank on his arm. "You lost, Nim. You now owe me near eight hundred dollars. Just so you remember, last Friday, when I was cleaning up your phlegm splatter off my cheek, you said, quote-unquote, 'Place the fucking bet. Tonight.' So I did. Friday night. Over the weekend, your teams played. Over the weekend, *you* lost."

"Well, *I* changed my mind."

"What are you, in second grade? You don't just change your mind. You placed a bet, you pay it." I can feel the anger bubbling up.

"I don't have to pay shit. Like who are you to tell me what the fuck I *have* to do? Lard-ass trailer trash."

Medusa glares at me, mustering the strength to cross her scarecrow arms in front of her chest. "He's not to do business with you anymore. So you can stop the pseudo-stalker thing and move on. He's *not* interested."

"Oh, I get it." I clench my fists to keep from trembling. "You have to get permission to play. Well, when Medusa here writes your excuse note, let me know. Until then, you don't back out. Nobody"—I step forward—"ever backs out of a bet. Ever." My voice doesn't even waver.

Cars trickle into the parking lot, doors slam, my classmates do the ultimate juggling act balancing what's-the-point skinny lattes and books while talking on iPhones, texting, and creating ways to demean and crucify each other in the age of social networking.

Nimrod stands before me, jaw clicking, leaning into me, pushing me against the car. He clacks a Tic Tac between his teeth, which does little to cover the stench of bacon bits and fried onions. "I bet you like this, huh? This little one-on-one we're having here."

I wiggle, trying to make the metal of my car door miraculously open and suck me away from him. Nimrod leans in harder and heavier, grinding his pelvis against mine. "Bets are off."

I try to move away, but all I can feel is his dead weight on me. Everything starts to go gray when I see a blur of color slam into Nimrod and crumple to the ground. It at least jolts him, so he moves back. I push away from Nim, shoving my backpack in front of me as some kind of lame barrier, sliding down my car door, sitting on the still-wet-from-frost asphalt.

Nimrod and Medusa walk away. He turns back and says, "I think we're clear here, aren't we?"

I pick up my glasses, twisted and crooked from Nim stepping on them. I try to focus through one decent lens and see Josh lying on his back, a trickle of blood coming from his nose.

"Hey. Are you okay?" I ask, trying to keep my voice steady.

"That's one big fuckin' dude," Josh says. "It was like running into a monolith."

We sit in silence until I think I can talk without bursting into tears. "Thanks, um, for coming to the rescue."

"Are you okay?" he asks.

I swallow and nod and feel helpless and stupid and scared and alone and small—teeny-tiny small, like an ant about to be squashed.

"Don't know what you would've done without me," he says, and winks, pushing my hair off my forehead, his fingertips electric on my skin.

My lip trembles.

"Hey," he says. "It's okay."

When I manage to blink back the tears, I hand him a

Kleenex. "Your nose. It's bleeding."

He shoves the Kleenex against his nose. "Have you ever considered the line of work you're in is, for lack of a better term, *terminal*?"

"Yeah. Nim's an anomaly. Sort of like an evolutionary glitch . . . on steroids. Most of my clients place bets, pay debts, win a little cash, whatever. You did well, by the way."

"Told you I don't lose. I waited for you at Bully's."

I can feel blood rush to my cheeks.

Josh stands up and helps me to my feet. "This is getting to be a habit." He rubs his shoulder and readjusts the Kleenex on his nose. "You gotta admit. That was pretty valiant. Me going after him like that."

"Are you trying to flex?"

He clears his throat. "A little. Okay. A lot. I'm just scrappy, you know, lots of lean muscle—not a lot of bulk."

"Still flexing?"

"You can't tell?"

I squint and clear my throat. "No?"

"They used to call me Noodle at my other school." He drops his hands to his sides. We laugh together, and I feel a release of tension, laughing harder. When I snort, he pauses for a second, then doubles over.

I try to stop, control myself, but can't, and snort again.

"So," he says, "I'm your big hero?" He attempts flexing again, then just shakes out his arms. "Forget it."

"Didn't even faze him, did it?"

"Didn't budge. Unbelievable. Valiant or not?"

"Valiantly stupid."

Josh winces. "Why stupid?"

"You're pretty new."

Josh nods. "I've been here for almost a month already."

"That long?" *Of course* I know it's been that long. Who wouldn't?

"Nice to know I slipped under your radar, there."

"Don't be snarky. I'm serious."

"Serious. As a heart attack?"

"As a colonoscopy."

"Ouch. *Not* pleasant."

I stop to tie my shoe. "Go on ahead of me."

"I'll wait."

I shake my head. "These are the last few months of high school—months you don't want to spend—"

Josh laughs, interrupting my monologue on being a school untouchable—she with only one photo in the yearbook. "Spend with the only chick who laughs for real, not doing some lame *tee-hee-hee* thing. Spend with a bookie. A bookie? A high school bookie. *That* blows my mind. No way. You're a keeper."

"I'm not a novelty." I hate that my voice is quavering, so I inhale and fumble with the zipper on my backpack. "What do you want?" I ask.

"I could use a friend."

I shrug. "You have friends—an entire entourage now."

"I thought you hadn't noticed me before."

That stings. We're silent.

"Wow." Josh kicks at an empty Coke can. It skips across the gravel lot and bangs into the curb. He pulls the Kleenex away. "So that's it?"

I rub my throat, trying to push back the ache. "Thanks again," I say. "You go ahead. I'll be right in. I'll text you with Sanctuary to let you know when to meet up for the winnings."

Josh faces me, his backpack slung over his shoulder. He bends over to scrape blood spatters off his jeans, his lanky frame looking a lot like a question mark. "Know the last time I gave a shit about what anybody said or thought about me?" His jaw is tense. His eyes look like they're ready to shoot sparks.

I shake my head.

"Neither do I." He cocks his head and turns toward the building, crushing the Coke can under his shoes. He pauses and turns. "See you around."

I swallow. "See you."

5

AFTER I FINISH LUNCH, I PACK up my antiecological, plastified cheese-and-crackers packs. I'm not sure what's more plasticky: the cheese or the container. Nim and his friends walk by; he's talking about how he can get away with anything in this school, this town. He holds up a ticket, flashing it. "Number twenty-seven. I can park wherever I goddamn please in this shithole town." He crumples the ticket and tosses it my way, smirking, then sneering at me like I'm a cockroach.

I pick crumbs off my sweatshirt, stacking the empty cheese-and-crackers containers one on top of the other, shoving the crumpled paper in my romance novel, trying to keep the cover out of sight. Cory at Grassroots Books says that I need to learn to "own the cheese."

Personally, I don't need Nim to know I crush on scantily

clad, muscular figments of Nora Roberts's imagination.

A couple of girls I don't know—maybe new—are in the hallway, and Nim stares past me at them.

He turns to his friends. "Did these little border bunnies lose their way? Maybe we should make a few calls, huh? Help them find their way back under the barbed-wire fence where they belong." He holds out his hands out, saying, "Green card? Green card?"

Everybody giggles like in some sit-com laugh track. I can just see the Tweets and texts now . . . LOL, LMAO, ROFLMAO, LOL LOL LOL.

God.

He looks behind him, though, knowing that if he ever said that in front of Moch or la Cordillera, he'd probably be jumped before the day was through. Both girls stare down at the ground. I can practically feel the heat coming from their bodies and wish I had some of Lillian in me at the moment. She'd come unhinged and probably sue him for something.

Lillian's big on lawsuits. She's good at indignation.

And I place bets. Sometimes I feel so shallow.

Nim and his friends walk away. I turn to the girls and say, "I'm sorry—sorry he says that stuff." More sorry, though, that I don't say anything back.

One of the girls looks up and shrugs. "What can you do?" she asks.

"Maybe some kind of *pendejo* intervention. Do you think it's possible that people are born with a DNA glitch that makes them incurable *pendejos*? Like the thirteenth chromosome is the terminal butthead one, so with a little genetic modification . . . Who knows?"

The girls smile.

"Do you want a Coke or something? My treat." Coke could do a whole new ad campaign: *Wash hate away with a swig. Carbonated love in a can. Cheers!*

Six words.

The girls are staring at me, big-eyed. Sometimes I wonder if I'm talking out loud or if looking at me the way they do is just the way I'll always be looked at. Nim and his crowd are walking down the hall. He turns back and winks at me, making my stomach feel all queasy.

"Is okay," one girl says, squeezing my arm. "What you can do 'bout him?"

I stare at the crumpled parking ticket. I have the title to his truck, which he'll need if he ever gets pulled over or some police officer asks him about those tickets.

The queasiness turns to anger. "A lot," I say. "A lot." I buy them Cokes. We sit down in the courtyard. I'm surprised they join me.

"You from here?" one asks.

I nod. "Yeah. Sorry. I'm Mike. You?"

"Sofia. This is Laura. We in nine grade. New."

I whistle. "Tough place to be new."

I feel bad for them. New here, for lack of a better word, sucks. I remember after living with the One Body, One Mind

49

religious group for eight years, the real world was a pretty cruel awakening. "Kumbaya" was replaced by "I see Paris, I see France." Meditation was replaced by masochistic games like dodgeball or red rover, where it's perfectly okay to hurl rubber balls at or clothesline your classmates.

And under no circumstances should I have brought my Bible Battles Trading Card collection for show-and-tell.

I spent eight years in a New Testament world—love everyone, turn the other cheek. The real world tends to work according to the eye-for-an-eye teachings. Just make sure you gouge first.

"So what you gonna do?" Sofia asks.

I smile. "A little smiting."

She looks at me weird. Her friend, Laura, who hasn't said a word, mutters something to her in Spanish.

"It has to do with the paper?" Sofia asks.

"A piece of paper can mean everything to somebody," I explain.

Sofia nods. "You don' have to tell me."

6

I WIPE OFF A SMUDGE FROM my one good lens. My head hurts having spent an entire day bleary-eyed. I'll get my glasses replaced this afternoon—another hundred bucks down the drain.

I look up to see Nimrod and his friends head from the field to the locker room. Medusa and her gang follow close behind. "Okay." I take a deep breath. "Here goes. Wish me luck."

I look around. *Who am I talking to?*

I make the call from the school's only pay phone, hoping to sound desperate and worried and pissed about some dumb teenager recklessly driving in the high school parking lot—taillight busted, skid marks and all. I keep the call under a minute, then hang up.

I run to Nimrod's truck: a shiny, green, double-cabbed

machine of masculinity. It's impeccable.

Now or never. Never is starting to feel like a better option, but I'm tired of the safe way out. Sure, I have U-Dub, University of Washington tomorrow. But why does today and every day until then have to totally suck? And if it sucks for me, it'll suck for all the kids like Laura and Sofia.

Plus, I have to send a message out to my clients.

I circle the truck and break the right taillight, picking up the little pieces of plastic and putting them in my pocket, pulling out the key I lifted from him in government class. Growing up in a tough neighborhood had its advantages. I reserve pickpocketing and other skills for emergency situations.

I climb into Nim's truck, turn on the engine, then take a big breath because if I blow the fenders off this thing, I can kiss solids good-bye until the Second Coming. I pull the break, slip the truck into neutral, and floor the pedal, holding the brake with all my weight and stop just as soon as the acrid smell of burned rubber fills the air. The truck shudders to a stop when I turn it off, and I lean my head against the steering wheel, trying to catch my breath, then slip out of the truck.

I plunk myself on the bench facing the parking lot, feeling like this is a pretty bad idea right about now.

"Whatcha doing?" Josh plops next to me on the bench. I jump about ten feet in the air. "Can I sit here?"

"Sit where you want."

"That's what I'm doing."

I nod.

"Why do you make it so hard to be your friend?" Josh asks. "Like it's some kind of privilege granted after crawling through the nine circles of hell."

I organize the word search of thoughts in my head and pick the wrong ones. "Why do you care?" I ask. "It's not like people are rushing to buy BFF necklaces with me."

"Maybe because you make it so goddamned difficult. You're about as approachable as the antichrist."

"Hey. He can strike up some pretty good deals. Haven't you heard of Charlie Daniels?"

There's a strained silence, then Josh says, "'The Devil went down to Georgia, he was looking for a soul to steal . . .'"

I try to muffle my laugh but end up snorting anyway.

"Mike?"

"Yeah?"

"I'm sitting where I want to be."

I look over at him. "Freezing your butt off on a bench outside Carson High School staring at a parking lot—"

"Next to you," he finishes my sentence. "So whatcha doing?" he asks.

"Waiting," I say.

"Waiting for what?"

Blue-red lights flash on top of the police car that turns into the school parking lot, cruising up and down the lanes until it stops behind Nimrod's truck. An officer comes out, walks around the back of the truck, staring at the broken taillight. He crouches down and brushes his hands across the fresh skid marks, smelling like burned rubber. Exhaust lingers in the air. The officer talks into his radio.

Nim and Medusa walk out of the school ahead of the others, her fingers laced in his: blemish-free, wearing school colors, walking hand in hand, their best friends frolicking behind them, tossing a Frisbee back and forth. They're probably singing the school fight song.

They look like a freaking brochure for high school happiness.

Josh looks from Nim to his truck to the police officer to me. He smiles. "Kinda wish we had popcorn." His arm brushes mine, and I try to pretend that Josh's arm rubbing mine doesn't send my stomach into some kind of delirious butterfly-wing revolt. I hope my face isn't turning that unattractive, blotchy crimson color.

I clear my throat. "I don't think they serve snacks at experimental theater."

"Looks more like reality TV. Want to tell me what we're watching?" he asks.

"Vengeance," I say.

"Oooh. Like eternal damnation and that kind of stuff."

I laugh. "Small-scale vengeance—just making a point today. I'll save eternal damnation and the heavens raining locusts for another day."

Principal Holohan joins the scene. His hair looks like the flames of a campfire—tufts of red and white gravity-defying wisps tangle in the wind. He's followed by Dean Randolph.

We hear the policeman say, "Unpaid parking tickets. Kid, you're gonna have to make a call, because we've got to bring you in." A tow truck arrives and gets to work booting Nim's truck.

Nimrod rushes the poor tow-truck worker, whose face loses all color. The police officer grabs Nim and throws him against the truck, clicking cuffs around his wrists. Beast immobilized.

"Well," I say. "That turned out a lot better than I thought."

"You want to tell me how you pulled *that* off?" He looks at me like I just parted the Red Sea.

I feel a frisson of fear and excitement. My stomach does flip-flops. "Nim did it all, you know. I just made a call, put the wheels in motion."

This doesn't erase the fear. But it gives me the power back. It keeps my business safe. It sends a message. Leonard would be proud. Sofia and Laura won't know about this, but that's okay, too. Silent justice.

Maybe that's what Lillian feels she does—like she makes a difference. If this is it, I get that. It's nice to step outside myself—do something for somebody.

Nimrod's face is smooshed against the passenger door of his truck. Medusa and the others wear shocked, just-been-Tasered expressions on their faces. I'd like to see *that* in the yearbook.

"So what does a bookie do after exacting revenge on a client?"

I look at the time and shrug my backpack over my shoulder. "Go home."

"You want to do something later?"

"No thanks."

"How about this? When you *do* want to do something, call me." He clasps his hands behind his head and stretches out his legs.

I watch his expression, waiting for the change—the slight nuance that reveals the truth behind the words. The mockery. His eyes are hidden under the brim of his baseball hat, though, so I can't read his expression.

"Thanks for the company," I say.

Josh tips his hat. "Thanks for the show. See you tomorrow, Michal Garcia."

I pause. Nobody calls me Michal. It sounds nice: *Mee-kal.* He even pronounces it right. I can't remember the last time I wasn't Mike. Michal. It makes me feel different, like I matter.

Stupid. It's just a name.

Josh holds his pinky and forefinger to his ear and mouth. "Call me, Michal."

Michal.

On the sidelines. Sure. Doormat. No.

7

Sanctuary Wednesday 7am courtyard.

THERE'S A BIGGER CROWD for divisional playoffs. I look at the faces and inhale, breathing in the scent of anticipation. Three guys are huddled around a paper. I glare at them. They should be paying attention. It's my show now.

"Sorry, Mike," Javier mutters and hands me Seth's *PB & J*—his one-page headlines edition. Seth hands them out between big issues to drum up interest and cash for printing the paper. Javier points to the third headline down. I skim down the first two about gang violence and a food drive, my eyes focusing on the one Javier pointed out.

Bringing Down Goliath: No Stones. Just Parking Tickets

I clear my throat and say, "So?"

"Nothing." Javier smirks. "Just thought you might have the inside scoop to *that* story." The group laughs.

"You guys here to bet or chitchat?"

They settle down. I can feel the heat creep up my cheeks and try to keep my cool. *This is my show.* I scan their faces. Ready to win. Most will lose.

Josh isn't here. Such a tool, feeding my story to Seth. No wonder he wanted to hang out with me after school.

We open *The Gambler.* Nobody has to sit on lookout because the courtyard is teeming with teachers. I sometimes wonder if they think I'm selling Do-Si-Dos or something. Whatever.

I read from the book, picking a passage to mirror Seth's headlines.

> *Is it not a beautiful spectacle—the spectacle of a century or two of inherited labour, patience, intellect, rectitude, character, perseverance, and calculation, with a stork sitting on the roof above it all? What is more; they think there can never be anything better than this; wherefore, from their point of view they begin to judge the rest of the world, and to censure all who are at fault— that is to say, who are not exactly like themselves.*

Most of them look up at me, brows furrowed, confused. *They're hopeless.* They don't move, though, and wait expectantly for me to say more. It's fun to be in the place everybody wants to be. I'm still buzzing from Monday's vengeance, and reading about it makes it all the more real. I can hear Leonard's nasal voice in my head, though: *Take the bets. Get a good spread. Come out ahead.* Basic bookie law.

It's kind of the point of it all.

No wonder everybody's been talking about Nim's truck being impounded. Everybody knows it was me. Message sent. Meaning received. But there's a fine line between glory and stupidity. I need this job. I need the cash. I need to keep my clients in line. I *didn't* need some stupid headline to advertise it. I'm all about invisibility. How can I expect some trust-fund pretty boy to get that? What a tool.

I close the book and give them my daily special. "Between the Chargers and Falcons I'm offering a no-juice line. One-time deal—almost unheard of in playoffs. Any takers?"

Silence.

"Do you guys even know what that means?"

Javier speaks up. "Not really."

I sigh. "Never mind. Who's betting what?"

The guys place their bets. They like when we meet in the courtyard. It makes it more dangerous—alive. There's a rush when we pass money under the noses of the esteemed faculty—some of whom place bets with me, too. Well, just Mr. Myers, the Driver's Ed teacher.

Nim shows up with all the other bettors. "You have something of mine," he says when the crowd clears.

"You have something of mine."

He hands me the cash and I count it. "It's all there," he says.

"That it is."

"So?" he says. Nim snatches for the paper I hold in my hand. His knuckles are bruised and chafed.

I pull the paper away, staring at his hands. "What happened to your hand? Those bruises look pretty fresh."

"Garbage Disposal," he mutters.

Garbage Disposal. Everybody knows about them. But Nim? Nim's part of some who-knows-what-supremacist group? *Nim?* I look around for Moch but don't see him. It's not uncommon, since he skips every other day of school anyway. But last time Garbage Disposal hit the streets, Pacho ended up with a broken jaw and Moch had two broken ribs.

Garbage Disposal and la Cordillera are things people talk about—things that I don't want to believe are real beyond some lame dress code. All talk. No action. But lately, there's too much action. I hate to think of Moch as a gangbanger. I hate that Garbage Disposal is real—with guys from my class in it. "Garbage Disposal? Are you serious?"

"Listen, you want to hang out with Cheech and Chong, that's your deal. At the end of the day, we're just doing the good *citizens* of Carson City a favor. Look around you." Nim motions to the kids walking up and down the courtyard. "They're like fucking cockroaches."

"*They?*"

"Let me correct that. *You*," Nim says.

When Nim needs me, I'm white. When he wants to demean me, I'm Mexican. And it's always like that—I'm not enough of one or the other. I wonder what happened to the melting-pot theory of America.

"You people take our jobs." He tugs on my shirt. "My money is earned."

Earned? A set allowance from his parents is *earned*? I stare at Nim and try to imagine Garbage Disposal—a group of guys who get spray-on tans, don't have accents, and eat beige food have decided how America should look and sound and taste.

"Why do you hate so much?" I ask Nim.

"None of your business." He shoves his bruised right hand in his pocket, gripping the title with his left, raking it from my hand, giving me one awful paper cut. Nim whispers, his voice an angry growl. "If you ever mess with me again, you're dead."

"Likewise," I say.

He doesn't hear the last thing I say because I'm barely speaking above a whisper, sucking on the thin line of blood across the palm my hand. The buzz of Monday and taking bets is gone, leaving me with an empty, sick feeling in my stomach.

The bell has rung. Students pass and swirl around me,

making me feel like I'm the center of a whirlpool—that abyss of nothingness. Ten minutes ago I was on some kind of vengeance high. Now all I want to do is swim my way out and make sure Moch hasn't been left for dead somewhere.

There are two places where time is eternal—heaven, from what I've read, and Carson High School, from what I've experienced. Ninety-minute blocks are spent in a twisted time warp, and no matter how much I look at the clocks, the hands don't advance. I feign concentration, only thinking about getting to Mocho's house. He wanted to talk. He asked me over the other day. I didn't figure it was anything, and now I don't even know if he's alive. *Garbage Disposal.*

After school I run to the parking lot so I won't get caught up in the lineup on the way out.

"Michal!" Josh *Tool* Ellison catches up to me just as I get to my car. I've managed to avoid him all day. "Can we talk?" he asks.

I shove one of Seth's preview papers at him. "I think you've talked enough." I should've known he'd be like the rest of them. I wriggle my key in the door. Figures right now would be the time it decides to get stuck. *C'mon, Little Car.*

Josh watches as I struggle. "Can I—"

I hold up my hand. The Buick makes it virtually impossible to have a dramatic exit. Locking this car, in fact, is probably a monumental waste of time. It's not exactly robber bait. The lock finally budges and I pull up on the metallic handle with all my strength. The heavy door swings open, and I throw myself in front of the steering wheel.

Josh stands between the door and me. "I'm sorry. Really," he says.

I shrug. "Whatever."

"Please, just give me another shot. Let me make it up to you somehow."

I stare at the line of cars streaming out of the parking lot; I've missed the window of time to get out of here before everybody else does. "I've gotta go," I say, closing the door. I look at Josh in my rearview mirror and can't help but think he really is sorry.

When I drive up to his house, Mocho is sitting out front on an old lawn chair, its plastic weave frayed at the ends. Mocho's cousins run around the yard, playing whack-me-with-an-aluminum-tube game. I feel a surge of relief and wave like a maniac through the window. There's a three-legged table propped up against the side of the trailer house, and two recliners without their backs. The brown tufts of grass are barely visible underneath patches of dirty snow, old tires, and what looks like an impromptu car-part garage sale. I don't know what Moch wants with all that junk.

Before I have a chance to get to him, Mrs. Mendez is waving me into the old trailer house. I see Mocho say something to her, and she swats him with a dish towel.

Mrs. Mendez gives me a warm hug when I walk up the crooked aluminum steps. "Where you been, Michal? You never come by no more. How's Liliana?" She's wearing a maid's uniform—some retro-aproned gray dress, like she's just stepped out of a TV sitcom.

Mocho walks in behind us. I flinch at his swollen face— bluish-black cheeks and split lip, a bruise shaped like a class ring on his jaw.

"Are you—"

"Fine," Moch interrupts.

I follow his eyes, scanning the kitchen: peeling wallpaper; a cardboard box covering a broken window; linoleum, worn and yellowed with time, bubbling in one spot so everybody stumbles on the same bump in the floor except his mom, who sweeps around the crammed kitchen gracefully.

It bothers me he pays more attention to some peeling wallpaper than the smells coming from bubbling pots, the kids running around the neighborhood, the laughter coming from a back room. The place is alive with its broken window and peeling paint. I sit next to Moch on the couch and watch the soccer match between Barça and Celtic.

"*¡A comer!*" Mrs. Mendez hollers, and the kitchen fills with bodies of all ages. Chairs, stools, and wooden crates covered with towels are shoved next to two card tables. I'm placed at the head of the table, squished between two kids who I understand to be Mocho's niece and nephew—both recently arrived from Mexico. They giggle every time I try to say something in Spanish.

"You never learned your Spanish." Mrs. Mendez *tsks*.

I'm a little embarrassed. Lillian left Mexico behind and never spoke Spanish at home because she did all she could do to put a sea between us—first Mom, then me—and Guadalajara. It's weird not to have roots in a place that's full of what I could be. Lillian washed the Mexican away.

The only thing that lingers in our home is a candle she lights to the Virgin of Guadalupe some days. It's the barometer to her stress, and when it hits the fan, the candle comes out on the kitchen counter with a small statuette. "Old habits," she says.

Mr. Mendez smiles when he sees me, patting me on the shoulder. "It's been a long time. How is Lillian?"

"Good," I say. "Thanks."

Mr. Mendez wears a tired smile and kisses Mrs. Mendez on the forehead, washing his callused hands in the sink before sitting down. He smells like car grease and petroleum jelly.

"Dad's got a new job," Moch says. "It's kicking his ass. They've got him hauling heavy machinery—stuff he shouldn't be doing at his age. *Salud* to Ellison the Great."

I wince and feel embarrassed and defensive at the same time. Josh isn't all that bad.

Mr. Mendez shoots Mocho a look, narrowing his eyes just a bit, then cracks a smile—two missing teeth on the left side of his jaw, making him look almost cartoonish. "My job puts this food on the table and in those pots. Be grateful."

Moch turns away, his anger clouding his six-word memoirs, covering the aromas of chocolate and chilies, grilled meat and plantain. The cousins start to giggle, and the tension dissipates.

I'm passed steaming plates of shredded meat, spicy green salsa, and thin homemade tortillas heated on the stove. They warn me away from a plate of hot chilies and all laugh when my eyes tear just by smelling them. Even Mocho.

Everybody talks over everybody, and I catch some words in English, none in Spanish, and the rest of the time feel like even though I'm not understanding ninety percent of things, I'm part of it—part of this table.

Mrs. Mendez stands to sweep the dishes off the table, pauses, and sits.

"You okay?" Moch looks over his glass of water, his forehead a washboard of worry.

"*Borracha*," she says, "but without the tequila. Better get a pregnancy test," she says, and laughs.

"Ma!" Moch says.

Mr. Mendez looks pale, like he needs to sit down, too. Except he's already sitting.

She looks at us, her mouth a straight line, smooth

chestnut face glistening with sweat.

Time stops.

"Just kidding. You's funny. You need to look at your faces right now. So so funny." She dabs her forehead with a tissue, her laughter filling the small kitchen. It's almost as if the walls seep up the laughter and happiness, giving them texture and life. "*Embarazada?* Ha!" She winks at Mr. Mendez, who turns from pale to crimson in about two seconds.

"*Por dios,* Ma." Moch rolls his eyes.

I laugh so hard, Moch's cousins jump in their chairs. "What would Lillian say to that?"

"Ahh, Liliana," Mrs. Mendez laughs, sweeping the dishes off the table.

I rush to the sink. "Please," I say. "Let me wash dishes. Sit down."

She bumps me away. "Come back next week." She pinches my arm and *tsk tsks.* "You girls all want to be skinny these days. *Flacas.*" She wrinkles her brow and shakes her head.

I swallow a laugh. Skinny I am not. But I revel in the fact that somebody out there thinks I could use more calories.

"You come back to eat. You wash dishes. Bring Liliana."

"I'd like that," I say.

She motions to a plate and I pass it to the table. We cut the sweet empanadas in half and a burst of flavor fills my mouth—sweet raisins, cinnamon, and a twist of lime in a flaky crust. Mrs. Mendez slaps Mocho's hand away from the last one on the plate. "That's for *Abuela* Liliana."

I wonder what Lillian will taste when she bites into the empanada: home, family, a sense of place—or just a pie.

Mocho nods and doesn't look all that mad about it.

"Thank you," I say, wrapping the empanada in a napkin. "I guess I'd better be going. I've got a lot of reading to do tonight."

"I've gotta get going, too," Mocho says, standing up.

A heavy silence falls over the room. "I thought you was staying in tonight," Mrs. Mendez says.

"Were, Ma. Were staying in."

Mrs. Mendez blushes.

"I've just got some stuff to do." Mocho puts on his face—the one he uses at school. The Mocho he was at the table—the aluminum can–collecting Moch—is gone again. "I won't be late."

"*Dime con quien andas y te dire quien eres,*" Mrs. Mendez says.

Mr. Mendez translates for me. "You are who you spend time with."

"At least I've got some pride. Yes, *señor*. No, *Señor Gringo*, thank you, *Señor Gringo*." Mocho's anger consumes the room.

I keep my eyes glued to the empanada crumbs on my plate.

Mr. Mendez puts his hand on Mrs. Mendez's forearm

and squeezes. His voice sounds strained, as if each word is a needle scraping across his throat. "You think I don't have pride. Every job I do, I do with pride, to put food on this table, so that you—" Mr. Mendez is pointing at Moch with a trembling finger. "So that you can do better. You think being in a gang is pride? Under this roof, at this table, you respect your mother, this family, and our guest."

Moch stands up.

His father points at him until he sits down again.

Mocho's cheeks burn.

"You may be excused, *Hijo*." Mr. Mendez's arm drops to his side.

Moch shoves his chair back and leaves, slamming the flimsy aluminum door behind him. It makes a clanging noise and doesn't shut all the way, tapping the frame, again and again, until the house is stuck in silence. His car squeals out of the driveway, throwing gravel against the side of the house like thick patters of rain.

Mrs. Mendez stoops over the sink, her hands absently wringing a dishcloth. She looks out into the dark neighborhood, streetlights dimly illuminating the other trailer homes; a street with chewed-up asphalt; cats scrounging around garbage cans; the heavy bass of reggaeton coming from a house three doors down.

And for just a moment, I see what Mocho sees.

Mrs. Mendez squeezes my arm. "*Flaca*," she repeats. "I expect to see you here more."

"Thanks, Mrs. Mendez. I'd like that." I swallow and say in a lame attempt to get back some of Mexico, *"Muchas gracias."*

Mrs. Mendez smiles and hugs me, wrapping her arms around me. "This is your home, too. Always."

When I pull up to the house, I look at the yard, shoveled walk, cleaned-out flower beds. We need to trim down the bushes Lillian keeps around the house—bright purple geraniums that bloom year after year. She's had the geraniums ever since I can remember.

I watch Lillian's silhouette through the window. She sits alone at the table, stooped over her dinner, a soft glow of light coming from behind the shade. She stands when she hears me turn off the car. I watch as she pauses, looking outside, then sits back down at the table.

I go inside, give Lillian the empanada. By now, though, the dough looks gummy and tough, the cinnamon scent and steaming flavor is lost to the grease that seeped in while the empanada cooled. She bites down and chews on her Mexico—leftover and cold. "Thank you, Mike," she says.

I nod and go to my room to do homework, writing in my Creative Writing notebook:

Heart bursts with words not said.

8

AFTER LILLIAN GOES TO BED, I sneak out and drive to American Flats, cutting down an old access road nobody ever uses. I follow tire tracks in dirty snow patches, a trail of trampled sagebrush bushes, until I see Mocho's car. I need to talk to him, to make sure he's not—

Not what?

Not who I'm afraid he's becoming. Not who Nim is.

I hate this place.

My phone rings, making me jump so hard I bang my elbow against the door; dizzying waves of pain shoot up my arm. Josh. *Now* he calls. I click it to vibrate.

As soon as I park, it feels like something is squeezing on my chest. It's hard to tell between real and fantasy at the Flats—it's this area's urban legend: ghosts, neo-Nazis, devil worshippers, poltergeists, spirits, raves, séances, and death. Always death.

I hike down the hill to the abandoned cyanide mill; the skeleton buildings are bare, graffiti-painted ruins—Nevada's version of the Acropolis, without the Yanni concert, complete with cyanide residue to make you sick.

And ghosts. I'm pretty sure there are ghosts because even at night, there's an eerie light out here. Like the place glows. Unless that's cyanide, too.

Welcome to Weirdville, USA.

The knot that was in my stomach has grown and filled up my entire torso—like I'm a solid chunk of ice inside. I clap my hands against my arms and try to rub off the chill, pulling on my gloves, wishing I'd brought a hat.

Altitude. It's higher here.

But the chill isn't the normal kind of cold-wind chill. The crunch of my footsteps on packed-down snow echoes in the concrete corridors. Fear rises in my chest. "Moch?" I whisper.

Maybe I can talk him out of what he's going to do up here. That's reasonable. I can just plead with his rational side. I practice, keeping my voice as low as possible. "Moch, please stop all your illegal activities and—"

The wind answers—a shrieking sound that rips through the canyon and burns my face. I walk halfway up the exposed staircase in the main building, slip on a layer of ice, grasping a crumbly step so I don't fall down. It doesn't lead anywhere—just half-crumbled, icy stairs to nowhere. I listen. I shine my flashlight on some graffiti. FUCK YOU.

"Thanks," I mutter.

Moch wouldn't set a campfire to call attention to himself. Maybe he's just out here to think about stuff.

He'd want to be inconspicuous since it's BLM (Bureau of Land Management) property. He'd be fined, possibly sent to jail, then deported if he were caught here. I'll just be fined . . . and maybe sent to jail.

I can hear voices—muted, lost in the wind. It's hard to follow where they're coming from in the emptiness—as if voices are all around me, like I'm stuck in a drum. I turn off my flashlight and follow the path to where Moch used to set off pipe bombs with his friends, hoping he's there.

I circle around the main building, hiking down a chewed-up ramp that was probably once a staircase, trying to keep my footing when I slip, fall down a few stairs, tearing my jeans. A jagged piece of glass sticks out of my knee. I bite my lip, wincing with pain, pulling out the glass.

Have I had a tetanus shot? I can practically feel my jaw starting to spasm. *Stop it.*

I pull out the glass and whimper.

"Who the fuck's out there?"

The voice isn't Moch's.

I'm right below them. The moon is bright—full; its light spills down the canyon, glowing blue on drifts of snow, illuminating the face of the main building of the Flats. I tuck myself into the shadows sitting in a puddle, pushing myself against the side of one of the outer buildings, holding a filthy pile of snow to my throbbing, bloody knee.

"Who's there?" the voice shouts again.

"Can you keep it down, man?" Moch's voice.

"You alone?" Whoever the guy is, he sounds really nervous.

"I could ask you the same," Moch says.

"Like who else would wanna come to a place like this? This place creeps me out."

"Afraid of the dark, huh?"

"Fuck you, man. You got it?" Silence followed by the sound of a plastic bag being opened. "Wow. This is *mad* good."

I hear Moch's monosyllabic grunt. "Yeah, insanely good. You keep dipping, though, you'll smoke all your profits."

"C'mon, dude. We all dip."

Silence.

"Don't go all pious on me. Like you *don't?*" The guy sounds on edge, like he's maybe taken from the cookie jar one too many times. Moch is quiet. There's a quiet clicking sound of someone opening and closing a metallic lighter. *Click click click.* He breaks the silence. "You watching the divisional playoffs this weekend?"

"Pass. Not a big fan of ass grabbers in spandex. Cash?"

A ruffling noise and the sound of a zipper.

"It's all there."

"*Chulo*," Moch mutters. "Only a total *pendejo* wouldn't count."

"Where can I reach you?" the guy asks.

"Nowhere. I'll contact you."

"When?"

"When I'm ready."

The guy leaves, the moonlight casting eerie shadows, fingers of blackness that stretch over snow-covered sagebrush and stones, zigzagging through the moonscape like phantoms.

"Moch?" I whisper.

"Who's there?" I hear the cock of the hammer of a gun.

"Moch, it's Mike."

He scrambles off the concrete platform and finds me in the shadows. "What the— What are you doing here? Are you totally *loca*?"

I turn on my flashlight. My jeans are soaked in blood. "What are *you* doing here?"

"*Joder*. You'd be killed if anybody knew you were here. You want that?"

"And you?"

I stare at him and watch how anger has chiseled his face into something unrecognizable. But his face softens. "Mike, you're bleeding all over the place."

He takes my hand in his and pulls me to my feet. I hobble beside him, leaning on him, and we hike through wet snow to get to our cars. "Moch—"

He holds up his hand, shakes his head. "What do you think I do, fix up cars and sing 'Greased Lightning'?"

I drop my gaze and shake my head.

"We're not ten anymore. Things change. We changed."

"But this?" I think of everything Moch can be. Moch: baseball player. Moch: community reporter. Moch: drug dealer. Moch: dead. "This is . . . wrong."

"When I was a little kid, somebody forgot to tell me that I don't count. I've lived here since I was two. I was a Cub Scout. But, you see, I don't exist according to the nice people at the Social Security office. I'm a space taker, oxygen waster, persona non grata—"

"Drug dealer."

"What am I s'posed to do? Break my back every day working in some kind of indentured servitude? You're sitting pretty comfortable—heading to U-Dub next fall. You ever been to the Carson River? Seen the shantytown there? Open your eyes, Mike."

"So what do you do with the money? Some kind of college fund? A CDT?" I swallow back the fear that's bubbling up inside me. I figured la Cordillera was just a thing he did to let off steam. Kind of like my gambling, a means to an end. But what's Moch's end?

My breathing comes quicker. I wrap my arms around my chest, hoping Moch doesn't see I'm shaking. "You're such a cliché—poster boy for a life in a gang. You're so—"

"You got a better way to do things? Show me," he says. "*Joder*, Mike." He slams his hand on the hood of his car. "When are you going to see the world for what it really is?"

"What is it?"

"A dead end." I can't see Moch's features in the shadows. But I can feel the tension, how his entire body bristles. He moves toward me. "Don't come back here. Ever."

My breath stops in my esophagus and remains, like it's frozen with the rest of my insides. Crystal-like ice particles have formed and closed my throat. I try to swallow, inhale, exhale, but everything feels cryogenic. I move toward my car door and open it, backing in, afraid to turn my back on somebody I thought I knew.

I ease the door shut and lock it, leaning my head on the steering wheel, willing the air to reach my lungs.

Moch steps away from the car and lights up a cigarette—the orange ember like a firefly in the blackness. He watches me back out as I clumsily reverse my way to the main road. Part of me knows the old Moch is there, making sure I get to the road okay. I can see the dwindling light of his cigarette, the outline of his body leaning against his car. I drive toward Carson trembling.

Alone.

Hopes of future lost in present.

9

THERE ARE FOUR MISSED CALLS, the last one a little past midnight. He's such a tool. I stare at the phone—the blinking missed calls—and listen to the voice mail.

"Just calling to make sure you haven't been buried alive in a shallow grave in central Nevada because you got involved in some kind of Mafia scandal or have become the target of a federal investigation. That, and, um, sorry about Seth. We were just talking and, damn, that guy is good about getting information. I'm. So. Sorry. Really. I so owe you. It was like my brain-to-mouth filter had a glitch the other day. I've already called Seth to retract." *beeeeep*

I pull over to the shoulder of the road and when I feel like I can calm my voice, I call.

"You pick *now* to return my call? Is this the beginning of what I anticipate to be a very painful payback for me opening my big old mouth?"

"You said—I have it right here on my phone—'I *so* owe you.' Would you like me to play it back to you?"

"It's true. I do. I didn't specify time of day for said payback."

"Did I wake you up?"

"I would never be sleeping at, uh, two in the morning. Why would you think I was sleeping?" He says this through an exaggerated yawn.

"This is dumb. I'm sorry. I just—" My voice catches. *Stupid stupid stupid.*

"Hey. Are you okay?"

"Have you ever noticed you ask me that a lot?" I try to keep it light, keep the tears away.

"Maybe because, it seems to me, you . . . aren't."

"Do you happen to have some gauze and iodine at your house?"

"Okay. Now I'm awake. And worried."

"I just kind of need company right now."

"With gauze and iodine? Like that's normal."

"I'm a bookie. How's that normal?"

Silence.

"Never mind," I say.

"Follow Ormsby until you run into what looks like a concrete water tower. I'll wait for you outside."

"Your parents?"

"I'm already on my way downstairs."

I drive around Ormsby until I see the gray cylindrical water tower–like house. I've driven by it before and never realized it was an actual house for actual people. Total postmodern Gothic. Enormous. My trailer house would look like a lawn ornament here.

Wrought-iron gates open and Josh waves me in front of one of the garages; there are seven. He's at my door and opening it by the time the car is off. He stares at the blood on my leg.

"What did you do?" he says.

"I fell on some broken glass," I say. "Really."

He cocks his head to the side.

"I snuck out. So I don't really feel like going home to have Lillian patch me up. I'm not in the mood for an inquisition."

"Understood." He pulls me up and wraps my arm around his shoulders. I can hardly put weight on my knee by now. Maybe I need to go see a doctor.

We walk through a fifteen-foot-tall door. "Expecting Goliath?" I ask.

"No," Josh says. "Sasquatch."

I smile.

The house is . . . weird. It's a hollowed-out cylinder with a glass ceiling, so the courtyard feels totally open. One side is completely cemented and the side facing east is a hundred eighty degrees, floor-to-ceiling windows, with a view of the mountains. There's a winding concrete stairway from the first floor to the second floor, hugging the inner circular wall. It doesn't look like it's been furnished yet—but I have a feeling that's the point. Sleek-looking couches and odd-angled chairs are placed deliberately—no stained couch cushions in sight.

It has the look of just-moved-in. Polished lemon-scented wood floors and some really beautiful floor tiles—not the kind you peel and paste like our bathroom floor linoleum.

"Can you make it upstairs?"

I hobble upstairs to Josh's room—the only place in the house, from what I've seen, that looks like it could be inhabited by humans. In fact, too human. "Can you open a window?" I ask. "Just for a little air." The whole male-adolescent stink really can be gross.

Josh blushes. "Sorry. I wasn't prepared for company." He throws a blanket on his bed and says, "You probably should sit down, put your foot up on my chair."

I hoist my leg onto his chair.

"I think I'll have to cut your jeans off," he says. "Sorry."

"Sorry if I bleed on your stuff."

Josh cuts my jeans off just above the knee, his fingers grazing my thigh. I wonder if I can attribute my light-headedness to blood loss at this point.

"I think it's more bark than bite," he says, looking at the cut. He washes it with warm water, then pretty much dumps an iodine bottle on it, bandaging it up. After, he brings up an ice pack and cold pizza from the kitchen. It disappears within minutes along with Cokes and a bag of barbecue chips.

"Your room's as big as my trailer," I say. I lean back and stare up at his ceiling—the only place in the house that doesn't look like an HGTV makeover room. It's covered in newspaper clippings, torn pages from books, comic strips, a hodgepodge of movie tickets, raffle tickets. I like looking up there—as if every mystery about Josh could be revealed if I just had the time to read through it all.

Josh lies down next to me and starts to point things out on his virtual tour of delinquency: "That newspaper clipping—front-page news about a hole drilled in downtown Boston." Josh grins. "My friends and I did it. All we needed were traffic cones and orange vests, and we rented the drill. And that"—he points to Saint Frances High School— "was my sweetest good-bye. It was determined that I was unfit for such an esteemed academy so, on parents' day, I streamed porn into the Sunday-mass TVs."

"That?" I point to a depilatory cream, hoping it doesn't have to do with some model he dated.

"Ahhh . . . that cream was *sweet*. I put hair-removal cream in the lacrosse team's shampoo bottles—picture day."

His ceiling is a collage of his schools and why he got kicked out of each one. He tells his stories like a warrior who has returned from battle. "My last shot of getting into a quote-unquote 'good college' is Northwestern, because that's where my dad went. Dad is overly generous with his alumni association checks. The physics lab in the engineering college is named after him: the James Michael Ellison Physics Lab."

"Wow," I say. "That's huge."

"It's only a plaque," Josh says. "Kind of shabby looking, too."

"Not the college. You. Your collage of delinquency."

Josh smiles.

"Why do you do it, though?" I ask. "What's the point?"

"I've formed my own antibullshit division."

"This oughta be good," I say, and close my eyes. "I'm listening. I just kind of need to close my eyes a second."

Josh has a smile in his voice. "It started with the depilatory cream. There's some freak thing about guys needing to haze each other so they can be friends. Fine if you're a tool and want to buy into it. But the hazing included one of my best friends, Maria. They held her down and shaved her head. As you've witnessed, I'm not a particularly effective badass, so I formed my antibullshit division that day. But it doesn't stop at school. Look around this place."

I don't have the energy to look around and am glad Josh keeps talking.

"My mom thinks it's nice we live in a catalog. In the entrance, we have an umbrella stand—with umbrellas with ivory handles. Ivory as in elephant tusks, endangered-animal poaching, and whatnot."

I shrug. "Well, not the most Greenpeace-friendly household."

He laughs. "How much does it rain in Nevada?"

"Not umbrellas-with-ivory-handles much."

I feel Josh get up from the bed, and I miss the warmth by my side. He strides around the room, pulling brand-name clothes from his closet, tossing them to the floor with Turkish rug–dealer flair. "Everything my family does is for show, with just the right amount of political activism to give us the good Ellison name. It's like the adult version of high school: say the right things, join the right clubs, and you're in. It's just bullshit. So when I make an entire team go bald in patchy spots, inciting an asbestos and other toxic elements investigation in the locker room that costs the school thousands and thousands of dollars, it's like getting back at the establishment, just nailing them where they're vulnerable. It makes them more human," Josh says. "And it makes everybody else feel a little less lame, I guess. Maybe I'm just trying to level the playing field." Josh looks at me. "Like why you did what you did to Nim."

"Nah," I say. "That wasn't leveling the playing field. That was revenge."

"There was more to it than revenge."

He's right. But I'm doing fine, just getting through today to get to tomorrow. I'll go to college soon and leave it all behind. I'm not into the causes—Lillian is.

I sit up, my entire body screaming for sleep. "So on a mission to end the bullshit, huh? It sounds pretty heroic. I suppose I can forgive you for leaking my story to Seth, then."

"Michal, you have no idea how lame I felt today."

I shrug. I'm almost dizzy from tiredness and look at my watch. "It's late. So late. I just got comfy and warm and . . . tomorrow's gonna be a nightmare."

"I'll bring coffee."

Josh helps me downstairs. I'm still hobbling, but I don't feel as bad as I did earlier. He walks me to my car, opens my door, and lays a towel on the bloody driver's seat. "You okay to drive?"

"Absolutely." I inhale, exhale, shivering in the cold car. My car wheezes to life and I put the heater on max, my leg bobbing up and down, waiting for the heater to actually heat. "Thank you," I say. "Antibullshit division and all."

"You're as far from bullshit as they come."

I laugh. "Flattery on someone who's lost a pint of blood will get you everywhere."

"I'm serious. You're real."

"I don't know how else to be."

"You know, I've been 'the new guy' five times in three years. Suckage Central for most, but I've always made a couple of friends, played a prank or two, coasted by. Here, I can tell, it's gonna be different."

"What's different?"

"You." He says it so matter-of-factly.

Doesn't he realize I'm drowning here? Treading water just to get by?

"See you tomorrow, Josh Ellison."

"See you in a few hours, Michal Garcia."

"Thank you," I say, and drive home in a haze of tiredness. I don't even remember opening the front door and getting into bed, falling asleep in my clothes.

Unexpected friendship in an antibullshit package.

10

MY HEAD FEELS LIKE SOMEBODY ripped it off my neck, bowled it for ten frames, then put it back on. The snooze alarm goes off again, and I slam my hand onto the button, then pull myself out of bed and into the bathroom.

I stand in the shower and muffle a scream when ice-cold pellets stream out of the eco-showerhead. Now is not the time to think about water conservation, so I get out, wrap a towel around me, and sit on the toilet until the entire bathroom is cloaked in steam. When I step back in, hot water streams over me.

As crappy as I feel, as scared as I felt last night, it all feels okay now. I sit on the edge of the tub, water beading on my arms and legs, feeling weightless. My knee is bluish and swollen. But it doesn't look like I'll need to amputate the leg. I wash it and wrap it in fresh gauze.

"Hey, Mike!" Lillian bangs on the door. "You okay in there?"

I nod, then think better of it because nodding feels like somebody's taking a mallet to my frontal lobe.

"Mike?"

"Yeah. I'm good." I pick up my crumpled clothes and shove them to the bottom of the laundry basket. I'll throw my jeans away later. Luckily I'm still the one in charge of laundry, so it's not like Lillian will notice bloody clothes.

A pot of coffee percolates in the kitchen. Lillian pushes a cup across the table, looking up from yesterday's paper—the one she gets from the clinic. News is news, but it's kind of weird that we're always one day behind, like perma life lag.

I cup the coffee mug in my hands, sipping down the bitter liquid. "Thanks for the coffee. I guess I slept in this morning."

She motions to the clock. "You're running behind." She puts a plate of half-cold scrambled eggs in front of me, burned toast on the side. "You were out late," she says through the paper.

I take a forkful of egg and just about gag on the congealed grease. I grab a piece of the charred toast, spreading it thick with butter and jelly, pushing the plate of eggs away. "Sorry."

Lillian watches me. "You do anything stupid last night?"

I shrug. Witnessing a drug deal probably isn't a smart thing to do. However, witnessing one and living is miraculous.

Lillian does this thing where she raises one eyebrow, and it turns from an arc into a pointed gray triangle, as if an invisible string is about to yank it off her forehead and flap it around in the wind, marking the spot where all happy thoughts surrendered.

"Just went out. With a friend."

"Anything else?"

"Like what else?"

"Like anything else that's stupid? Other than sneaking out, which is *totally unacceptable*." When Lillian's angry, her accent sneaks up on her.

"I'm not my mom."

Lillian nods.

"Or you," I say, pushing myself back from the table. "I'm gonna be late." When I leave the room, Lillian's turned to the weather page in the *Nevada Appeal*, and I want to scream at her because the weather *does* change from day to day—maybe nothing else, but the weather does.

Yesterday's paper. Today gone until tomorrow.

11

IN THE COURTYARD THERE'S a short line of kids waiting to buy tickets to the class ski trip. I look at the poster: PEARLY GATES HEAVENLY SKI TRIP: RIP DOWN POWDERY SLOPES. SAINT PETER IS WAITING. There's a pretty hokey drawing of Saint Peter on skis, his robes fluttering in the winds marked with "The North Face." Underneath the picture, there's a string of things that are supposed to justify spending sixty dollars on one day, including all-you-can-drink hot chocolate, transportation, equipment rental, all-day skiing, and a day of unforgettable memory making. (Perfect for yearbook photo ops before it goes to press!)

This year's yearbook committee chose No Borders, No Boundaries as our theme. But they're just words. Boundaries Abound would be more appropriate. Maybe that's why I hate the yearbooks with pithy quotes and most likelies and cameo shots of pep rallies and school dances . . . now this—a ski trip. It's a montage. The accumulation of some-one else's memories—a collage of lies that transform our stories, stealing our truths. So when we go back to our twentieth reunion, we'll take down the dusty book, see the smiles, and think, "Yeah. That was a good time." We become generic—our history is a template to fill with new faces and dates. Copy. Cut. Paste.

I much prefer *PB & J*, named after Seth's favorite sand-wich, with just the right mix of irony, sarcasm, and pretty decent reporting.

Josh plops into the spot next to me. "Latte? Two shots of cinnamon dolce, extra shot of espresso." He hands me the coffee. "How's your knee?"

I've been sitting in the courtyard, watching the stream of students, waiting to see if Moch shows up. I cradle the coffee in my hands and inhale the sweet smell. "Thank you."

"You're welcome. Who're you waiting for?"

"No one."

"Have something to do with last night?"

I clear my throat.

"Sorry. Just curious. It's not every night a bloody-kneed damsel in distress comes knocking on my door. I'm feeling pretty heroic today, as a matter of fact."

I place my hand on my forehead and swoon. "My hero." He'd probably be insta-repelled if he knew I was really swooning. Like blood-deficient, wishing-he'd-kiss-me-right-here-right-now swooning.

Seth walks by and tosses me a paper. He winks at me and I can't help but smile. "Friends?" he asks.

"Friends." I nod.

"Cool."

"That guy is fearless," Josh says. "His story?"

"Seth is sibling number four of, like, seven or something."

"Seven kids?"

I nod. "Very biblical. Anyway, King Hand-Me-Down but wears his clothes with style. When he was a freshman, he refused to shower until his parents stopped making him go to seminary, and the school, after four weeks, wouldn't let him in the doors. I asked him if he really didn't believe in the Mormon doctrine or just wanted to sleep in, and he said, 'I need time to think about it. Just not every morning at five forty-five.'"

Josh nods. "Cool dude."

I skim the headlines of *PB & J* and read his editorial, a rant against using student-body funds—extra cash earned from the sale of student ID cards—to pad the ski trip to Heavenly that nobody can afford.

The Student Council Synonymous with Bourgeois (and Most Likely Doesn't Know What Synonymous and Bourgeois Mean)

Elitist Dictionary for Dummies: Word of the Day: Pecksniffian

The Bumpy Road to the Super Bowl: Upsets and Surprises

"He's right. I mean, everybody had to buy those cards and now they're using the money for an exclusive ski trip."

The bell rings.

Callie and Trinity, the student council secretary and treasurer, are selling all-you-can-drink hot chocolate coupons for tomorrow's trip—a last-minute "Heavenly" special. They finalize the last purchase and close the metallic box filled with money from the sales, a pretty thick pile of tickets remaining.

Exclusive. Subsidized by student-body ID card sales. They put the ski trip to a vote and said they won by a hefty margin. I don't even remember voting on it.

They walk by, the box latch clanging. "Tomorrow morning will be awesome," Callie says. "I'm wearing my new Columbia jacket."

"Columbia?" Trinity scoffs. Like an actual scoff. "That's cute."

Callie deflates, then rebounds like some kind of bouncy ball, returning to her singsong happy voice. "It'll be so fun!"

It's like watching perky blond clones.

"Tomorrow will be *the best*," Trinity agrees. "Like . . . *the best*." She swings her head around, her ponytail practically knocking my new glasses off my face. She flips around. "How about a little spa— Oh. Hey, Mike. Are *you* going on the ski trip?" she asks. "Or maybe it's not your thing. I mean, growing up, I'm sure your family couldn't afford this kind of stuff. And it's hard to start skiing with your full figure, balancing that extra weight."

Callie looks away, and I think she's probably embarrassed. Pretending Trinity is anything less than the spawn of evil is like going along for the ride.

I stare at Trinity and get that burning feeling in my stomach. I try to look at her for who she really is. I try to see beyond the lacquered, shiny coat to the dry rot underneath.

Trinity's pristine smile falters.

"Hey. We'll be late for class," Josh says.

Trinity smirks and says, "Hello, Joshua Ellison. I thought you'd never ask."

Josh scowls and puts his hand on my arm. "Michal?"

Trinity looks from Josh to me and gives Callie a look like she's seen Elvis. Her cheeks get bright red dots in their centers. She spins on her heel and walks down the hall, Callie trailing behind.

"Hello?" Josh waves his hand in front of my face.

"Yeah. Thanks. I'm in Zombieland today." I stare at the poster.

"Are you thinking what I'm thinking?" Josh asks, eyeing the box tucked under Trinity's arm. He points to the article.

"You're the antibullshit president. Not me."

"You sure about that?" he asks.

Yeah. I'm sure.

Josh and I walk to Mrs. B's class together. I search the hallway for Moch, wondering if it's too late, if everything he was, everything he could be, has been swallowed up by drug deals and gang warfare.

I hate feeling like there's nothing I can do. I hate feeling like I'm just watching everybody's life pass by like some parade.

When we walk in the door, my stomach knots. He's sitting in his chair, hunched over his desk, scribbling in a notebook, blue hoodie pulled over his head.

"Talk later, then?" Josh asks.

"Definitely," I say.

I sit behind Moch and tap his shoulder.

"Hey," I say.

The anger I saw the night before is gone. "You look like shit," he says.

"You, too."

He squeezes my hand. "Cool?"

"I don't know. Who are you?"

Moch rolls his eyes, his mask back on. He coughs, smelling like a distillery.

Mrs. Brooks asks if anybody wants to share a memoir. Her finger lands on Moch's name. The class inhales, waiting for another memoir about congealing blood and waxy cold skin. I'm waiting for one about drop sites and meth labs. Instead, he reads, "No country. No nationality. Mex-American exile."

Mrs. B exhales. She wipes at her nose and smiles at Moch, getting *that* look in her eye—the look teachers get when they want to save someone from himself and believe they've found a way.

I hope she's right.

Her watery eyes home in on me. I scrunch down in my chair and pass as invisible. She holds up her bony, yellowed, tobacco-stained finger, and it lands on another name. "Trinity Ross. Why don't you read what you've got?"

Trinity glares in our direction, then flashes Mrs. B her ten-thousand-dollar headgear, braces, retainer-straight, laser-whitened smile. All those years of being a human satellite dish paid off. I make a note to call her "Crest" in my mind.

Mrs. B crosses her arms in front of her thin body. "We're waiting, Trinity."

Trinity opens her notebook, the corners of her mouth turned up—a smile that doesn't reach her eyes but stays frozen on the lower half of her face. She says, speaking right at Moch, "No papers. No English. No service." She pauses. "Go home."

Mrs. B is gobsmacked.

Trinity's words hang in the air like pogonip—an ice fog that won't dissipate. I can practically hear them crystallize above our heads, leaving us under a film of ice. The class settles in an uncomfortable silence. I watch Trinity, the sneer on her face, the look of entitlement, like she was branded when she slipped out of her mom's body—*American.* Moch doesn't even look up at her.

Look at her. Look her in the eyes.

He sits huddled in his chair. Defeated. Like he doesn't belong here.

"That's eight words, Trinity," I say, feeling like fire is radiating from my stomach up through my esophagus.

"Technicality," she says.

"Technically, then, I have to quote Pat Paulsen on this. 'All the problems we face in the United States today can be traced to an unenlightened immigration policy on the part of the American Indian.'" I try to keep my voice as even as possible, keep out the anger and the quiver. Keep it in control and look at her like she's just another bet to place—a bet that will lose. "I guess the Native Americans forgot to put up the KEEP OUT EUROPEAN BUNGHOLES sign."

Josh bursts out laughing—the class follows. But it's not natural laughter, just that awkward, get-me-out-of-here laughter.

Moch stands up, gathers his books, shoving them in his backpack. The laughter stops.

If you leave, she wins.

Mrs. B snaps out of her trance. "Ms. Ross, your attitude here is absolutely unacceptable. Mr. Mendez, take your seat." She looks Moch in the eyes and he pauses, not sure whether to stay or leave.

Stay. Stay. Staystaystay.

Trinity's voice sounds like an LP on the wrong speed—screechy, frenetic. "Freedom of speech, Mrs. B. Ask my dad. He's the one who went to law school, passed the bar, pays your salary and *his* education with taxes on money he *earned*. Those who can, do; those who can't . . ." Trinity crosses her arms in front of her.

"Well, then, you can just head to Dean Randolph's office and wait until I get there. I'm sure you'll be talking to your father before I have a chance to arrive. Just tell him that those who teach, suspend. Explain to him why I'm proposing your in-school suspension and, by doing so, expelling you from any school activities until the end of next week."

"But." Trinity's face contorts and turns a weird shade of red.

Mrs. B holds up a hand. "Leave. Now." She turns to Moch. "Mr. Mendez, I will *not* tell you again. Take. Your. Seat. Where you belong. And take off that hood. We are in class."

Right on, Mrs. B.

I will Moch to sit down in his chair. He pauses, then sits.

Trinity grabs her things in a huff and is already texting on her BlackBerry. Mrs. B says to the class, "In no way, shape, or form is any kind of racism, classism, ageism, or prejudice okay here. No way. Shape. Or form. Period. Excuse me just a moment." She makes a hushed call from her desk. "Okay, then, let's talk graphic novels, my love- lies." Mrs. B does a Wicked Witch of the West cackle and heads to the back of the class, squeezing my shoulder as she passes.

12

I DON'T KNOW WHAT NEWS traveled around the school faster: news that Mrs. B took a stand and suspended Trinity Ross—the untouchable; news that the administration undermined Mrs. B's decision—they let Trinity off on a stern warning and sent her back to class with a smile pasted on her face; or news that Moch and a couple of friends got caught ditching with cans of spray paint in the parking lot and suspended for what looked like intent to paint.

I'm not saying Moch wouldn't have done something like spray the hell out of Trinity's car, slash the tires, key it, and do oodles of damage. That's a given. It just all seems like a bunch of crap on a cracker.

So by the end of last block, the plan had gelled.

◆

My legs wobble from crouching in the stall for the past two hours. This could be a new exercise. Bathroom-stall yoga—bend in ways you never thought possible. It's not only the crouching, hiding, keeping my feet up out of sight, but it's also the not touching. I mean, there are only so many clean-looking places in a stall.

My brain feels like somebody has clubbed all the creativity neurons—the inside of this door is an English teacher's worst nightmare. I've spent the last two hours reading about love, cheating, comparative penis sizes, misspelled expletives, and GPS messages. Mariela has been here . . . a lot.

My knee throbs.

It's already dark. The sounds of bouncing balls, ten pairs of shoes squeaking across the gym floor, and echoing whistles have disappeared. Basketball practice, wrestling practice, and all club activities have ended. I listen to distant footsteps in the courtyard—stragglers. Heavy doors slam shut.

I wait until the only thing I can hear is my own breathing.

My knee almost gives out on me when I stand up. I shake it, then peek out the stall door. I listen and put on a Carson High hoodie, pulling it over my head, tucking my hair in.

Inhale.

Exhale.

A tingling travels up my spine—a buzz of nerves connecting, accelerating my heart and breathing. My hands feel slippery. I wipe them on my jeans and creep into the empty hallway—more light here than in the bathroom. It's already too dark to make out colors. It's the time of day when everything is cast in varying shades of gray. My ears hurt with thunderous silence; every footstep I take ricochets off the lockers, amplified by a thousand because of the emptiness. I slip off my shoes and pad down the halls in my socks.

Just as I'm about to turn down the science hallway, I hear voices and heavy footsteps. I backtrack to the drinking fountain and crouch underneath it—too late to realize that this is about as effective a hiding spot as if I pretended I was a human statue.

They reach the hallway and turn the other way. I think they're the basketball coaches. They're talking about some guy's prostate. Their voices grow fainter until I can barely make out the words, everything sounding like a muted grumble.

I make my way down the halls, hugging the walls, keeping my backpack in front of me and my face down in case there are security cameras I've never noticed before but now's not the time to look for them.

I feel the blood rushing to my ears, pumping through my body, my heart pounding, filling every inch of space around me with noise. I rifle through my backpack and take out my Leatherman. I'm not sure if it's a good thing I know how to open locked doors. Just most of the kids in my neighborhood did. There's a certain skill set needed to be . . . what am I?

I shake my head.

Focus. Basic stuff. My glasses fog. I take them off, wipe them, put them back on, the rim slipping down my nose. I unscrew the doorknob and pull, pushing the other side in. Metal crashes to the hard tile floor, piercing and sharp, the noise reverberating in the school. I feel like I'm in the epicenter of a catastrophic earthquake and visualize the arcs and circles that they'll draw to radiate from the boom.

I don't move. Listen. Wait. I'm ready to push open the door when I hear, "Hey. What are you doing?"

I freeze, pressing my head against the door, feeling the cool metal against my flushed cheek. The only sound I can hear now is my heart throbbing in my ears. But I've got to find an excuse for being here—a reason.

"Michal?"

I turn and slump to the floor. "Josh?" The blood rushes so fast to my head, I feel a little fuzzy.

"What are you doing?"

"What are *you* doing?" I ask.

"Following you," he says as if it were an acceptable answer.

"You practically gave me a heart attack. Like right here, right now, my heart ceased function and for a second

I thought I would enter the realm of—"

"The pearly gates?" Josh asks, and grins.

"Geez," I say. "Get in the office."

I fumble with my glasses, push them on, and follow Josh.

"I have to put the knob back on. Can you give me some light?" Absentmindedly, he flicks on a light and the place is flooded with blinding whiteness. I practically dive to turn it off, the fluorescent bulbs sputtering on the ceiling.

"Sorry," he says. "Stupid."

I toss him my flashlight and fiddle with the knob, doing a pretty decent job of putting it back together. It's loose, but it'll do. I tap my fingertip to my lips and listen. The wind howls outside, but the windows don't rattle, absorbing the beating, moaning just as the gusts leave, as if relieved. I listen to the distant traffic, the *tick-tick-tick* of the heating system, low hum of a generator, and the way the lonely building takes noises and throws them back and forth between its metal lockers and open spaces.

"Why are you following me?" I ask.

"Nah. I think you owe me an answer first." He crosses his arms in front of his chest and cocks his head to the side. "Well?"

"I'm just—" I think for a second. "I'm just leveling the playing field. Now. Your turn."

"I *knew* you wouldn't let things be the way they were this morning. I *knew* you'd do something. What's the plan?"

"You leave. I finish here. And I owe you. Big-time."

Josh shakes his head. "We're in this together now. You can't just blow me off like that. I'm in."

I roll my eyes. "Well, make yourself useful and find the ski trip stuff."

We search through the office, trying to keep everything as organized as possible. Mrs. Martinez, the student council advisor, has shelves covered in photos—years of dances and pep rallies. The bottom drawer of her desk is locked. I search for a key and find one in the top drawer.

It doesn't fit.

I get a heavy-duty paper clip and am twisting it to get it to the right size. Josh interrupts me, squeezing my shoulder. I nod. There's a light clack of heels on tile. The footsteps get louder until they're right outside the door.

My head pounds in the place right above my right eye. Like somebody's striking it with a ball peen hammer. A phone rings. "Hello? Yeah. Just came back to make sure the office is closed. Uh-huh. Yes. It's closed. The kids are so excited. The ski trip is tomorrow. They've worked so hard. Uh-huh." Mrs. Martinez laughs. Keys jingle.

Josh motions to her desk. He crouches underneath, then I do, miraculously folding myself into his lanky arms and legs, my knee screaming in pain from the position. We soundlessly pull her chair toward us.

The door opens. I can hear how the knob is wobbly. Mrs. Martinez keeps talking. "Yep. It was closed. My

OCD moment. Totally. Okay. I'm on my way."

Her perfume floods the air—a kind of woody, floral scent. She flicks on the light, pauses, still "Uh-huhing" on the phone.

Please go now. Please, please, please go away. Please. Now. Please.

"Hello. Yes. I'm on the way." She closes the door, jiggling the handle to make sure it's locked. We listen to her convince whoever she's talking to that she's not obsessive. Her voice fades into nothingness, and the only thing I can hear is Josh mumbling something incoherent.

We lean forward, foreheads touching. "Okay?" I ask.

"Okay." He touches his watch. "I don't know how we're gonna get out of here without triggering the alarm."

How does he know about the school alarm system? I look at my watch and shrug. "First things first." I jimmy the lock on the desk drawer and take out the metal box that says HEAVENLY.

We count out over twenty-five hundred dollars. *Do these people know about banks?*

"Are we gonna take the cash?"

I nod. "And we're going to do one better," I say. "Feel like going skiing tomorrow?" I grab the unsold tickets, taking out the ticket registry list, shoving it into my backpack. "It looks like tickets have gotten an awful lot cheaper."

"Ahhh, somebody'll want a refund." Josh smirks.

"But who'll know who bought the tickets?" I take out

the registry list, hoping they don't have one saved on a computer somewhere. I doubt they do. I point to the sign on the inside of the cash box: CASH ONLY. "Did you buy a ski pass?"

Josh grins. "Yes. As a matter of fact, I did."

"Fancy that," I say. "So did I."

We close the lid, placing the box back in the drawer, and organize the office, wiping off surfaces with Kleenex from Mrs. Martinez's desk. I have an urge to leave a message—tell them they all suck. But I can't think of anything more creative than "You suck." I have more style than that.

"Now. Let's find a way to get out of here," Josh says.

Antibullshit division reborn. Mission totally possible.

13

I CAN BARELY CATCH MY breath. I squat down on the curb, ignoring the pulsing in my swollen knee. I inhale and close my eyes, feeling the jolt of excitement, letting the rush wash over me. Josh sits next to me. Silent. I wonder if he feels it, too.

"Michal, shall I escort you to my stealth getaway car?" Josh points down the street.

"I kind of have to get into my own, which I parked over at the Starbucks." I look down Saliman Road and sigh, wishing I could teleport to my car.

"One: Your Buick is anything but stealth. Two: I'll drive you. I parked over here, off Pinto."

"So you weren't just following me. You had something in mind yourself."

"Great minds. Plus I spent the last two hours hiding

out in the janitor's utility closet. When I got out, I saw you and . . . *voilà!*" Josh pulls me to my feet, his warm hands wrapped around mine. He doesn't unhold my hands as soon as I'm on my feet; he laces his fingers in mine. "You're going to have to teach me your technique—breaking into an office without breaking a window. You're much more polished."

"Thanks." I blush and pull my hands away, shoving them into my jacket pockets.

"I'll drive you to your car, but only if you let me invite you to dinner."

"Why?" I ask. Suddenly I am so so tired.

"Wrong question, Michal. You should always ask 'Why not?'"

There are always more reasons *not* to do something than to do it. That's why being a bookie is so easy—it's easy to watch people place the bets and take the chances while I sit back and wait. I've always been okay with that. But now I'm not and I don't know why.

"A celebration." He holds out his arm and links mine through it.

"For making it out of the school by climbing through an open boys' bathroom window the size of a postage stamp, jumping two fences, running across a field through a herd of cattle before I collapsed into a not-quite-frozen patty pile?" I feel happiness bubble up and fill me, then start to laugh. "I stink. I think if anything, we'd better get takeout."

Josh's eyes crinkle and fill with tears. I have to lean up against the fence to keep steady. Our world explodes with laughter—belly-aching, can't-catch-my-breath joy. "I can't believe we just pulled off an actual heist." He pulls dried grass from my hair, tucking a loose piece that fell from my ponytail behind my ear. I feel like my scalp is on fire, prickling where he touched me.

"Nothing unlike your past exploits," I say. "Hard to top those."

Josh shakes his head. "You know, changing schools so much is like hopping into parallel high school universes—the only distinguishing mark is the school mascot and colors.

"There's always a Nim. There's always the in crowd, the band geeks—they can't help that. I think it has to do with the polyester uniforms—institutionalized nerddom. There's always the overachieving student council president-slash-debate club captain-slash-basketball point guard-slash-valedictorian-to-be. There's always a Trinity."

It's unsettling to think I'd be the same in every school— the girl who wore jeggings for a year because she felt too bad to tell her grandma she spent thirty bucks on something totally uncool. I think I just wanted to wear something Lillian had bought for me, something she had picked out; she had taken the time to think about me. That doesn't happen much.

"But," Josh says, stepping closer to me, "you're the first."

"I don't know what that means," I say. "The first what?"

"You have purpose. You're the one," he says.

And now I feel like I'm going to be a virginal sacrifice, recruited to work in the CIA or . . . I can't let myself hope for the *or*. That happens in movies. Not to Michal Salome Garcia in Carson City, Nevada. I clear my throat. "Stealing ski trip passes and catering to my peers' vices aren't purpose. According to your line of thinking, I should open a brothel."

Josh laughs. "Nah. You'd never do something so legal."

His intensity is gone and I feel like I can breathe again. I picture myself dodging between the cows in the pasture and cover my mouth to keep the snorts muffled.

Josh pulls me close to him, wrapping his arm around my shoulders. "We've got some ski passes to distribute. At least let me take you to coffee."

"Deal," I say.

At Starbucks we debate about what to write on the invitations, then decide simple is best. "But who should the invitations be from?" Josh asks, tapping away on his iPad.

I shrug. "Anonymous?"

Josh shakes his head. "Anonymous is cowardly. We want to stand by our work. Give it a name."

"Like we really need a name for delinquency," I say.

"This isn't delinquency. This is big, like *Dead Poets*

Society big. Hey . . ." He pauses. "Dead Poets?"

I sigh. "I think that's been done. Plus we don't read poetry."

"Or hang out in a cave."

"Or go to an all-boys school."

"Thank God," he says, and winks.

"We just steal ski trip tickets."

"*Just* steal ski trip tickets? Please. We've done more than that. We're exacting social justice for—"

"For kids like me," I say, swallowing a little of the perma-shame that comes with being considered substandard. PWT.

"And Moch," he says.

I'm grateful he says that, like he knows what Moch means to me. "To the exiled," I say.

"Exactly," Josh says. "To the exiled. Plus tonight we get to play Santa Claus."

"How are we gonna pass this stuff around and *not* get caught?" I ask. "Hell. We're gonna get caught."

"Not if we didn't in the office when Mrs. Martinez walked in, turned on the lights, and didn't even look our way. Not us."

Since when did I become an *us*?

I believe him. Like by being with Josh I'm covered in lucky fairy dust. He splits a chocolate graham cracker in two, handing me the bigger half. "Living in the land of exiles isn't so bad after all, right?"

"Depends on who you're talking about. I don't think Napoleon was too into Elba or the Jews were particularly fond of Babylonia."

"Nah. But our little Babylonia isn't so bad." He raises his eyebrows. "Right?" he says through a mouthful of graham-cracker crumbs.

I nibble on the chocolate cracker. "No. Not too bad."

"That's it," Josh says. "Babylonia."

"What about it?"

"That's us," he says. "Babylonia."

"Babylonia," I say. He's right.

Dear Valued Member of Carson High Student Body,

You are invited to the Pearly Gates Heavenly Ski Trip. Show up to the ski bus tomorrow at seven a.m. sharp, appropriately dressed for the best ski day ever!

Put the ticket in your wallet, pocket . . . wherever.

Trash this letter as soon as you read it.

It will not self-destruct. It will not turn into a toxic poison that melts your skin off. It is a simple piece of paper that is evidence of our wanton disregard for trees (in the name of justice). And an invitation.

Cordially,

Babylonia

We take the file to Kinko's and print out the invitations. I feel a shudder of excitement. Josh and I Google a list of

Carson High students, then pop their names into Spokeo on my iPhone. We map out a reasonable route and pass out the letters and ski passes, making sure we leave one for Seth. He won't go. But he can write about it. I hope.

Josh pulls up next to my car, still parked outside Starbucks: the least ecologically friendly machine on the planet; an eighties throwback; an embarrassment to American car makers everywhere. But I have grown to love the splotchy maroon Buick beast. She's trying to hang in there like the rest of us. I just need her to make it to the end of the school year and through the summer so I can do my one and only road trip with her to the Great Basin National Park. My graduation present to myself. My chance to say good-bye to Mom.

"Here we are," Josh says.

"Yep." I'm not really sure what the protocol is for saying good night to someone you committed larceny with. I can feel Josh looking at me, and I tuck my hair behind my ears. "Thanks. This was—"

"Magic." Josh smiles. "See you tomorrow morning, Michal Garcia."

"Bright and early," I say, opening my door. The blast of cold air practically takes my breath away. The scent of snow lingers in the air. Clouds shroud the mountaintops. *Nice.* Fresh powder for tomorrow.

"Will you be there for the show?"

I look over at him. "Wouldn't miss it." I get into the

Buick and tap its dashboard. "C'mon, Little Car." I turn the engine and pump the gas until she growls to life, the heater blasting me with icy air that smells like a musty basement. I shiver until the air turns tepid. "Thanks," I whisper to the car. Josh waits until I pull out of the parking lot.

The streets are pretty empty. I drop a ticket off at Moch's place and drive home. Lillian looks up from her book. "After nine? On a school night?"

"A new study group for the AP tests this spring," I say casually, trying to mask my limp. I don't need Lillian to kick into parental guidance mode right now. "Good night," I say, closing my bedroom door behind me.

My memoir notebook is open beside my bed. I pick it up and write:

Remember when yesterday and tomorrow disappeared?

14

But this is too big, too important.

I surf for a while, trying to drum up good ideas on how to spend the twenty-five hundred dollars. It's student body money, money the whole school should be able to enjoy.

I flip through the yellow pages.

Fly-Me-a-Message.

It's almost ten. I doubt anybody's there. I call the number. Someone answers. He doesn't sound happy until I offer double the normal rate. Cash.

"Gotta get FAA approval."

"Okay. I'll give you two and a half times the rate to speed up the approval process."

"I'll need the cash first thing tomorrow morning."

"Done."

"What's the rush?"

"It's a last-minute gift to the school," I say. "From the student council."

He laughs. I'm relieved that he doesn't ask any more questions.

I spend the rest of the night organizing the Commandments.

It takes me forever to decide whether or not to text Josh with my plans until I finally decide to talk about it the next day instead. If we get caught, they'll go through our texts and connect the dots, and then good-bye, U-Dub. It's three in the morning by the time I get everything organized.

I fall asleep and wake up before my alarm goes off. My head feels heavy, my thoughts fuzzy. I can't tell if the tingly feeling I have is from sleep deprivation or excitement. I'm afraid I won't make it through first block without slipping into a coma. Time for caffeine overdrive.

"Good morning," Lillian says. "You're early."

"Good morning," I say, grabbing a cereal bar, skipping the coffee to avoid any kind of prolonged exposure to her inquisition stare. "Study group. Gotta rush!"

I get the pamphlets printed out, drive south to Minden, then shove them in the door slot of Fly-Me-a-Message's offices with the money he asked for, and pray nobody sees me. I am back at school a little after seven, just in time. Thank heaven for twenty-four-hour Kinko's and a relatively police-free morning. I can't afford a speeding ticket.

At school a crowd has gathered around the ski bus. Student council even took the time to decorate the bus with cloudlike powdered slopes and skiing cherubs. Mrs. Martinez paces around the patchwork crowd of students. Seth is weaving his way through the crowd, trying to get the inside scoop.

I feel a twinge of guilt, because I can tell some kids *really* wanted to go. Some probably saved up awhile to buy those tickets.

Josh is waiting for me on the bench, facing the parking lot. He nods at me, holding up a supersized coffee. *Thank God*. The crowd grows. More kids. More tickets. Mrs. Martinez is on full-blown fluster now and has been joined by Mr. Holohan, Mr. Randolph, and a few other teachers. A police car pulls into the lot.

Oh crap.

Josh whispers, "We're cool."

Icy, more like. My leg bobs up and down and Josh presses his hand on my thigh, the warmth like an electric shock. I feel like I'm being branded, the palm of his hand searing my jeans, and I do all I can to not pull my leg away.

By the time the first-period bell rings, everybody's heard about the robbery, the letters. The hallways are electric. Everybody wants to talk about Babylonia. First block, most teachers end up doing holiday-style work because nobody's listening. The news is short-lived; at lunchtime the buzz has died, and most kids don't even care about Babylonia or ski trips. I can't keep my eyes from the clock. *Come on. Come on.* I need this to happen *now.*

I hear the faint sound of an airplane motor and see the first glints of gold paper drift to the ground.

The lunch bell still hasn't rung. We've got five minutes.

"Dude, you guys have gotta see this." Some kid points outside.

That does it. In about two minutes, the entire student body is gathered in front of the school, staring at the plane, reading the banner. I'm impressed. They even made it with a little bit of gold glittery stuff in loopy letters.

Thou Shalt Not Use Student Funds for Elitist Events

The bell rings. Nobody cares. The golden papers pass through kids' hands. Someone hands me one. "Check out the Commandments. That's just *sweet.*"

I try to find Josh in the crowd, but it's impossible. Everybody's talking about the Commandments. Some kid laughs out loud. "'Thou Shalt Revere Napoleon Dynamite as Our True God.'"

"I don't get it," another kid says, pointing to the ND reference.

"You wouldn't."

"Dude, this one about not cussing in pig Latin, gibberish, or Klingon kills me."

The Commandments, the message . . . everything works.

Perfect timing.

We're finally herded to class after Principal Holohan screeches at us in his megaphone. In last block, Government, Mr. Sullivan talks to us about student manifestations and the power of movements—how misguided they can be. He reads us a story about the Third Wave, an experiment where a history teacher used his students as guinea pigs, getting them to believe in a made-up movement.

But Babylonia isn't made up or invented. It's real. I can see the excitement in everyone's eyes.

The last bell rings, and I exhale. I've been waiting for the office to call me down since I arrived. Nobody's called. Nobody's looking for me. Nobody knows who Babylonia is.

We weren't caught.

Seth comes up to me. "Can you believe today? It's like newspaper porn." He holds the Commandments in his hands. "Other than the banner, I particularly like 'Thou Shalt Consider Study Hall the Sabbath and Nap.'"

I laugh. "'The Student Council Is Synonymous with Bourgeois.'" I point a finger at him, smiling.

"Don't look at me," Seth says, holding his hands up in surrender. "But this is something big. Real big. There's going to be a special *PB & J* next week. You up for funding?"

"Absolutely," I say.

"Catch you tomorrow, then, at Josh's place. Divisional playoffs party."

That's news to me.

I swallow back that left-out feeling, thinking that as soon as this day is over, I'll probably sleep until Monday. It's probably a guy thing—watching the games at Josh's house.

I stand in the middle of the hallway. Kids stream around me. I'm untouchable—even after today. Totally invisible.

Then he bumps into me. "Are you trying to defy mob laws of physics?" Josh asks.

"No. No. It's, um—"

"Standing in the middle of this place will get you killed." He pulls me to the side of the hall. We lean against the gray lockers. "You're a genius. I could kiss you."

Do! But I resist the urge to pucker. "I didn't have time to ask you if it was okay," I say, trying to keep from turning to a puddle of goo in his arms. The hallways have cleared.

"Genius," Josh mutters. I silently swoon. "And the Commandments. Fallen Commandments. You're brilliant."

"I dunno. I kind of feel bad because some kids actually saved money to go on the ski trip. A girl in my physics class was pretty bummed. Sixty bucks down the tubes. They're getting screwed here."

Josh shrugs. "They played into the elitism, you know. They could've protested and said they wanted something for everybody." He's so sure of everything. So *right.*

"Most probably weren't thinking like Gandhi. We're only in high school."

"So that's an excuse to *not* think?"

I can't help but believe that we've made a difference—a change. We've shaken up the natural order of things, and the world will now be different because of Babylonia. *Babylonia.*

"Anyway, tomorrow. My place. Noon. Division play-offs. Small group," Josh says.

Exhale.

"Cool. Tomorrow. I'm in."

Stragglers head to the doors. It's eerie how the school doors open to such brightness—like watching people cross over in one of those ghost-talkers shows.

"Movies, tonight. My place. We'll talk Cardinals versus Rams and how many yards we think Morrison will throw to win the game."

"Do you know how unlikely it is to think the Cardinals will win? They shouldn't even *be* in the playoffs. Wild-card luck."

"I'm lucky. We bet on the Cardinals. To make it interesting, we'll bet on a running game. They win on the ground, not by Morrison's gun. Come over. We'll debate about it."

"I'm *so* tired. Don't you sleep?"

He shrugs. "It's an Ellison thing I picked up over the last couple of years, sleeping like five hours a night. My dad's the same. Three extra hours a day over the course of, say, seventy-five years adds up to over eighty-two thousand hours, which is like three thousand four hundred more days—all in all, nine more years. So when I'm seventy-five, I'll actually have lived eighty-four years. Nine years. A lot of quality time."

"So what about dozing off in Mrs. B's class?"

"For somebody who never noticed me, you certainly observe a lot."

I blush.

"Catnaps. Just to keep me going. So. What about tonight?"

"How about this: I'll come over tomorrow. I, unlike you, need sleep."

"Deal. I'll pick you up."

"You don't have to."

Josh walks down the hall. "Insurance. I'll be at your place tomorrow at eleven thirty."

"Fine," I say. He stops when he's about ready to leave the building. My phone beeps.

Place the bet. Cardinals. A hundred on Cuccaro; sixty rushing yards.

"You're insane," I mutter. That's as far-fetched as they come. It's not like Cuccaro is Walter Payton or Emmitt Smith. He's good. *But sixty yards?* I should've taken him up on Morrison's passing game.

I drive home on autopilot. I've never so looked forward to getting to my room and bed in all my life. I organize my bets, making sure I read through them twice before placing them.

Lillian heats a couple of pot pies in the oven. We wash them down with watery Kool-Aid. There's a strange comfort in the expected—our routine—since the past week has been everything but. "You look tired," she says.

"I am," I say, and stand up to clear off the table.

She sits me down and cleans the dishes, back turned to me. "Is everything okay?"

"Everything's okay," I say. *Jumbled and messy and crazy. But okay.* "Just tired." I talk to her back—straight and strong, as always. I wonder why we never talk to each other; why there's always a paper, a wall, her back, or mine between us. "Good night, Lillian," I say.

"Good night."

Missing predictable comforts. Emotions bubble inside.

15

"PSST! PSST!" *TAPTAPTAPTAPTAP.*

I jerk awake, my heart pounding, and flick on my bed-side lamp. It takes me a second to realize I'm at home. In bed.

Taptaptaptaptap.

This is the point in the movie when everybody in the audience screams, "Don't go there! Don't look." I stay in bed. Years of watching late-night horror movies has taught me well. Whatever is tapping at the window will go away if I stay here.

Crap. My lamp.

I turn the light off and cover my head with blankets.

My phone buzzes on the bedside table: Look outside. Stat. Josh.

Josh? I ease out of the covers and move toward the

window, pulling the curtains back to see some guy standing outside with a ski mask on. I muffle a scream.

Josh pulls off his ski mask. "It's me. Don't be freaked
out."

I mouth, "What are you doing?"

"C'mon." Josh waves me out.

I shake my head.

He falls onto his knees, palms together. "Please, please,
please." It's so cold, I can almost make out his icicle words
in the air.

I tap my wrist. "Too late," I say. "Tired." Like dead tired.
I feel like I've crammed a lifetime into twenty-four hours.

Josh starts to dance the Charleston, his noodle limbs
flapping at his sides.

I muffle a laugh.

"C'mon!" Josh says. A dog starts barking, setting off
a canine chorus of howls. It's embarrassing how cheesy a
trailer park can be.

"Nice," I say.

Josh waves toward the front door.

I get dressed and tiptoe down the hallway. I open
our door to see Josh standing on the porch in a kind of
curtsy. "Good evening, Michal," Josh says, then looks
up. "Listen, I'm a skinny shit with absolutely no muscle
tone. Thirty more seconds like this and my legs start to
do this embarrassing trembling thing. So I invite you to
exit before the wobbling begins, which would be right

about . . ." He stands up, shaking out his legs.

"What are you doing?" I ask, stepping out onto the porch before he collapses into a pile of bones.

"Wrong question," Josh says. "What are *we* doing?"

"Let me guess. We're going to change the world, making it a happier, better place by doing a job at one of the big casinos in Reno, enlisting nine others. We'll call ourselves Ellison's Eleven."

Josh shakes his head. "Can't be all work. It's time for a little R and R."

"There's an all-night free spa for thugs, thieves, felons?" I say. "Wow. That could've saved me lots of tension headaches had I only known."

"Shhh." Josh puts his finger to his lips. "We're more than *that*. We are Babylonia." He says it like it means something and pulls me out of the house, the screen door banging against the frame. "C'mon. Trust me."

I follow him to his car. He opens my door with a flourish. The heat is blasting. Colin Hay is on the radio, singing: "I tried talking to Jesus, he just put me on hold; said he'd been swamped by calls this week and he couldn't shake his cold."

"'My my my, it's a beautiful world,'" I sing along.

Josh smiles. "Indeed, it is."

We drive around the deserted streets of Carson. No one is out tonight. Probably because they're sleeping like normal people.

"We're here," Josh says, parking on a no-streetlight street. Josh gets out of the car. "Let's go."

I follow him across the street, waiting in the shadows. I press my back against a wooden fence and wonder how everything got so complicated. I'm standing in some perfect stranger's front yard, the ground covered with prickly pine-cones and needles, waiting for Josh to find a way into the back. He opens the gate with a quiet click and waves me in.

Josh already has his shirt off and is pulling down his pants. "Michal, I give you our very own private spa." Josh slips the cover off the hot tub and eases into the water. "This is amazing," he says.

"No way," I whisper. "There's no way I'm stripping down. Like, ever in a bazillion years."

Josh looks up at me. "Why not?"

"I just won't, okay?" I take off my shoes. "I'll just soak my feet. And I probably can't get my knee wet, anyway. It'd get invaded by aggressive skin bacteria. I don't want to be one of those weird cases on Discovery Home and Health."

Josh scoots toward me and grabs my hand. "Just come in. Just *be*. And leave one foot out, like this. You've earned this." He drapes one of his feet over the side of the Jacuzzi.

"Turn around, then."

He closes his eyes.

"I said turn around."

"Fine. Fine."

I take off my sweats and T-shirt and slip into the

bubbling water, keeping my knee out, practically yelping from the heat. A motion detector goes off and floods the backyard with light. We slip down, dipping our heads underwater, the tips of our noses out, my leg hanging over the edge of the Jacuzzi. The lights turn off. We sit up again. The moon is almost full, so pretty soon I can see more than blackness and shadows.

I look down at my drab bra and wish, for the first time ever, that I had cute underwear. I wonder what color goes with blotchy skin prone to acne breakouts. That's probably not covered in *Teen Throb's Tips on Summer Beauty*.

"This is the life," Josh says. "Hey." He jabs my shoulder. "Relax, will you? You must learn to live."

I'm vaguely aware of the fact that moments like these are the ones we'll talk about together in twenty years, laughing, saying, "Remember that time . . . ?" This entire week has filled me with that gift.

Remember that time . . . ?

Josh has his eyes closed. I can't seem to enjoy the moment because I can't breathe, since I'm trying to keep my stomach sucked in.

As if he reads my mind, Josh says, "Every moment like this erases a bad one—but to do so, you have to purge yourself of the bad memory forever." Josh stands up, beads of water dripping off him. "I'll go first." He clears his throat. "When I was twelve, I was about four feet tall. Not really. But you get the idea. Anyway, before school one day—I used to go early to get homework done and stuff—a group of freshmen jumped me and Saran-wrapped me to a tree in the school entrance. They forced me to drink about a Super Big Gulp–sized water laced with crushed Lasix pills. By the time school started, I had pissed myself. Kids showed up to a nice welcome with me there. I was called Enuresis the entire school year."

How can somebody say those things so openly? It's like he doesn't know how to hide anything, hold anything back. He's fearless.

"That sucks," I say. "I'm sorry."

"This is one advantage of moving schools so much."

"Yeah. You can reinvent yourself every place you go."

"Not reinvent. Geography doesn't change a person; I guess I have the advantage of arriving without a past," he says. "Mysterious."

"Mysterious?"

"C'mon. A little mysterious, anyway."

"It's hard to tell. Carson High is so big, it's like we all get swallowed up."

"You don't," Josh says. "Everybody notices you."

How can he not realize I've been a shadow for the past nine years?

Passing cars' lights stream through the fence, casting shadows across Josh's face. His eyes are closed. I lean my head against the back of the Jacuzzi. I like the idea—the systematic replacement of bad memories with good memories.

"Okay. My turn?" I ask.

He nods. "If you choose to purge."

I should have a card catalog for all of those bad moments I've always been ashamed about. I hesitate, move to stand up, then sit down.

I inhale and stand up, keeping my knee as dry as possible. "It was my thirteenth birthday. Lillian doesn't remember birthdays, usually. Nobody had remembered. So, basically, it was a total cow-dung day until I was called to the office fifth period and was handed this gift. It had store-quality wrapping. You know, the kind of wrapping that uses double-sided tape—so you only see the shiny paper. And there was this lime-green bow on top. Perfect, really. The secretary wished me happy birthday and sent me back to class. They all started chanting, 'Open it! Open it! Open it!'

"It felt so good to rip open the paper in front of everybody, like I mattered, you know. There was a gold box with a beautiful lid. I opened the lid and pulled out four cans of dog food."

I sit back in the water and don't realize I've been holding my breath until I exhale.

Josh rubs my cheek with the back of his hand. "It's gone now," he says. "These memories, this afternoon and tonight, take its place."

I nod and swallow, a little piece of hurt breaking away and dissolving. *It's gone.*

"To the exiled," Josh says.

"To the exiled."

We lean our heads back, staring up at the stars, my bad leg ice-cold in the air, but it's worth it—worth every second.

We hear a voice. "Anybody out there?"

Josh and I slip lower into the hot tub.

"Hey! Anybody there? I'm calling the police!" A heavy door slams.

"Move move move move move!" Josh jumps out and grabs my hand, half pulling me out of the water.

We snatch our stuff and scramble through the gate, across pinecones and needles, my feet screaming as they slap on the pavement; we jump into Josh's car as he peels out onto the black streets, turning off his headlights until we're down Timberline past Western Nevada College. I pull on my sweats, thankful I didn't bring anything that could be left behind. I touch my glasses. Still on my face. I nurse my knee. It's bigger than it was yesterday and an awful blue-green color. I think I might have to show Lillian.

Josh drives into a construction site, parking in front of the skeleton of a house. "I think, Michal, the spa is closed," Josh says.

We sit with the windows ajar, listening to music. My heart stops racing and thumps in time to a quiet song. I mutter, "R and R? You consider that R and R?"

Josh and I exchange a glance, then burst into laughter. We fog the windows with what is as close to tangible happiness as I've ever seen. The pit in my stomach is dissolving. Happiness.

Josh turns on the car. "C'mon. I'd better get you home for your beauty sleep." We pull up in front of my place. His car slips into silent, electric mode. I search for any lights and exhale, seeing that the place is dark. Luckily, Lillian took off after dinner. She's got the night shift at the clinic today. It's hard to remember which day is which; they're all spilling over into each other. "I'll pick you up tomorrow. Eleven thirty."

I nod and step out into the dry cold. Before I shut the door, I say, "Why me?" and immediately regret asking.

"Why you what?"

"Me? There are nearly three thousand kids at school—"

"You're different," he interrupts. Josh looks at me, not a trace of irony or silliness on his face. "They're jealous of you because you're different."

"Well, now that we've committed larceny together, I guess you don't have much of a choice."

"Apparently you haven't figured it out yet. Michal, you are my choice."

I can feel the heat rise to my cheeks. I try to control the quavering in my voice. "Thanks for today, yesterday . . . just thanks."

Just when I think I'm safe, he says something like that, making me believe I'm not a second-generation glitch, the result of faulty judgment, bad timing, a broken condom;

that I matter. I close the car door and carry his words with me into the house, wanting to trap them in a jar and keep them forever.

I stare at the memoir notebook and write:

Pro-choice. His choice. Life has meaning.

16

"MIKE, MIKE, I'M DISAPPOINTED. What's this dabbling all about? You've got a good thing going." Leonard has a nasal voice; I think he's got a deviated septum. He's a skinny, bald, thirty-something, carton-a-day smoker who has this nasty tic of sucking the food in from the back of his teeth, making weird smacking sounds in his mouth.

I don't have time to argue with him today, though. I slept in way too late and need to place the bet and get ready.

"Leonard, I don't need the fine print-speech. Give me a little credit. Three hundred dollars' credit, to be exact." I just need to cover one hundred and fifty, which is easy enough since Nim paid me back and I will have enough to cover most bets and winners this weekend. The problem with the online sites I use is that they only deposit once a month into my account, and if I do an early transfer, there's a fee; when there's a fee, the bank calls Lillian because she's technically the "adult" on the account; and Lillian wonders why in God's name somebody wants to transfer $789.43 to me from a place called Bodog.

I can't afford to have Lillian get involved after all these years.

Leonard makes an awful whistling sound with his nose like pan-flute background music. I wait. I don't beg. I don't have to because favors will always end up being paid off in one way or another. Just a matter of time.

"Yeah. All right. You've got until the end of next week, no interest. But Mike, this is the last time. You're gonna have to start banking some of your vig, set up your own accounts, and get off the sites. They're tying you up."

Yeah. But I can't bank my vig because of credit-card debt. I've got to stop buying crap.

"Thanks, Leonard." I hang up the phone and stare at it, wondering what's happening to me. I get that old feeling like I'm being set up—like this is some elaborate plan to turn me into the school joke. I need a jar of words—proof that things were said, that I'm not inventing all of this.

I shower, blow dry my hair, and get dressed. I inhale and turn around, staring at myself in the mirror. If my goal was to look like a cashmere eggplant, mission accomplished.

A pile of new clothes lies on the bed next to five fashion

mags, all with articles that claim to find the *just right look for your body shape.*

None of the articles addresses eggplants.

I try to give my hair "body"—and have even shampooed with one of those special European deals that's supposed to make my hair look like a TV commercial model's. Unfortunately, though, the perma-limp wins out, and I still look like the "before" picture on the bottle. And kind of smoky-mesquite smelling.

I should cancel. This is stupid, a stupid football party. Plus I don't think I can face Josh and everybody else he's invited looking like an eggplant. Nobody should ever have to look like an eggplant. Yesterday's Babylonia victory is blotched out by my hideous purple sweater.

I can just order pizza and watch the game from here. I dial Josh's number and hang up. I look at the time. Eleven fifteen. Kickoff's at one thirty.

Why did he say eleven thirty?

I dial again, then hang up.

Again.

He insisted on picking me up. It's like a trap. If I could just go in my own car . . . I wouldn't go.

I peek from behind the curtain. Lillian drives up. She walks in the door balancing grocery bags in her arms. I grab one and take it to the kitchen, digging into the day-old raisin bagels that go gummy in my mouth.

"You're dressed up," she says. "Plans?"

I swallow. "Divisional playoffs. There's a party at a friend's house."

She raises her eyebrow. "New sweater?"

I nod. "Yeah." I stare at my reflection in the window, tugging on the sweater. If Lillian's geraniums were in bloom, I could stick a couple in my hair and pass for an Anne Geddes Where Are They Now? poster child.

"It looks nice." She touches the soft cashmere.

So I buy expensive clothes and cut out the tags at home so Lillian won't see them, because she'd go through the roof.

But it's something I do for me and only me. I get the grades. I got a full ride to the University of Washington. Lillian has never once had to do *anything* extra for me and has made a point of making sure I know that room and board is burden enough. All her "extras" go to her causes— Planned Parenthood, Clinica Olé, Oppressed Person of the Month. It's like playing Name That Cause.

Admirable. Sure.

I know I sound petty.

But when you're nine years old and want a cake for your birthday—even a Hostess Cupcake would do—and your grandma, who refuses to be called "Grandma," thinks your birthday is better spent handing out brochures in front of the legislature building and holding a picket sign that says I WAS A CHOICE, you can get a little jaded.

It sucks being a leftover from Lillian's big mistake—my

mom. And it sucks feeling guilty that Lillian doesn't have clothes as nice as I do.

I shrug her hand off my arm. "It was on sale. I'd better go finish getting ready."

I apply makeup according to the step-by-step process outlined on page forty-three. Just as I remove the mascara wand from my eyeball for the fourth time, I hear a knock on the door. My goal was to be on the lookout and dash to his car as soon as he drove up, but I'm too late. Lillian's already invited Josh in.

I rush into the living room. Josh looks around our trailer house, and his eyes land on me.

I feel like a stain—this overdressed, over-made-up Rorschach blotch of purple ink on the décor in our home, which you can best describe as contemporary trailer trash.

"Hi. Um. Josh. This is Lillian. Lillian, Josh." They shake hands and we all stand weeble-wobbling back and forth from one foot to the other.

I will my deodorant to kick into overdrive because the last thing I need are dark purple rings. "Wow," Josh finally says.

"Wow what?" I ask, probably a little too much on the defensive side.

Josh cracks a gap-toothed smile at me. "You're so pretty."

Lillian scowls. She's probably already looking at Josh as if he were the evil carrier of sperm—the reproductive germ that turns the women in our family into undereducated indentured servants. Then she looks at me as if I were the carrier of bad judgment.

"You look nice," Josh says.

"I'm probably overdressed," I say. "I can change."

"Don't," he says, gnawing on his bottom lip, avoiding Lillian's gaze. Lillian, though she can't be five-three, has a way of making everybody look up at her. She's this giant, scary person who makes everybody feel unsettled.

I feel bad for Josh, being stared at like that. Josh looks up at the faux fireplace mantel, pointing to the smattering of framed pictures, most of them missing the glass. "Are any of those you?" It feels like Josh is reading our weird family history through a collection of random images—like he's on some kind of archaeology dig, sweeping away the dust, hoping to reveal the truth.

He points to some of Lillian's political rally pictures. "Is this the real deal?"

"The real deal," Lillian says, the iceberg melting. Just a little.

"As in Woodstock, sit-ins, marches on Washington, and all that stuff?"

"Yes," she says.

"Lillian is *the* 1960s poster child," I say. It's impossible to keep the accusation out of my voice.

Lillian scowls. "Back then we believed in more than new clothes and extravagance," she says, staring at my sweater. "Nice to meet you, Josh. If you'll excuse me for a moment."

This is our cue to leave. Run. Flee. Never look back. But Josh studies the photos on the mantel. "She still do stuff like this?" he asks when she leaves the room.

I motion to a pile of boxes. "She works at Clinica Olé and is really involved in Planned Parenthood. We fold and pass around brochures every weekend."

"How amazing your grandma actually does stuff . . . like, she walks the walk, you know?"

"The real deal," I say. "But don't say 'grandma.' It's 'Lillian.' I think it's a way for her to divorce herself from the idea that I'm a direct descendent of not *her* mistake but that of a nation that hadn't yet passed *Roe v. Wade.*"

Josh puts the picture back. "No wonder you're so cool."

I have never considered myself to be remotely cool or remotely connected to Lillian. It makes me feel uncomfortable.

There's a picture of Mocho and me pulling our wagon piled high with aluminum cans. Josh laughs. "Who's this?"

"Mocho."

"Wow," he exhales. "So he's one of those from-the-beginning-of-time friends?" Josh sits on the edge of a rust-colored recliner that doesn't recline anymore. The tips of the arms poke out of the threadbare fabric. He stares at the picture of me and Moch.

It bothers me a little bit because he only knows the

today Moch. Josh looked at Moch's clothes, tattoos, and limp and decided who he is.

Maybe he's right, though. "Yeah. That was back in our running-through-sprinklers-together days. Not anymore, I'm afraid."

"Why?" Josh asks.

"People change," I say.

My leg is bobbing up and down. I'm hoping we can get out of this place before Lillian passes me some colorful packets saying *Condoms: Essential wear.*

"Let's go," I say, and jump when I see Lillian. She's leaning against the doorframe in the kitchen.

"Just a second. Could you tell me where you're going again?" All of a sudden, Lillian's gone PG. "It's not like Mike to go to a party."

"Lillian." I can feel the color flood my body. "Geez." I. Could. Die.

I turn to Josh, expecting him to look horrified, but he just smiles. "Sure. My parents have a place in Genoa. Near the golf course."

That seems to satisfy Lillian. It's not like Josh is going to say he's taking me to a crack house.

"Okay," Lillian says. She leans toward me, like she's actually going to kiss me on the cheek, then stops. We stand, facing each other, in a weird, uncomfortable, almost-tender moment. "Have fun," she says.

"I will."

I follow Josh to his car and slip into the front seat. Lillian hollers, "Mike! If the mm-mm fits . . ."

Oh my God. Lillian thinks joining the XX and XY chromosomes in the same room will result in inevitable reproduction. "It's a football game," I say, hoping Josh hasn't seen *that* condom ad.

Josh's car beeps like a garbage truck when it backs up. He pops in a Ryan Adams CD and says, "Ready to win?"

Win?

"Our bet. Did you place it?" He smiles.

"Oh. Yeah. That. I did."

I'd like to focus on the bet but all I can think is:

Purple grapes, eggplant, cashmere Barney—me.

17

WE'RE AT JOSH'S PARENTS'
vacation house in Genoa Lakes. Instead of being the kids
relegated to the basement—like at most parties—we drive
to a whole new house thirty minutes away, complete with
cooking and maid service and everything.

Javier is here with Matt Prince and Marilyn Fuller—
kids I've gone to school with since I've lived in Carson City.
Kids I've never really known. I never tried, I guess. I'm
always amazed that people know how to act in a crowd
of peers. The whole mingling, socially adept thing—well, I
missed that day. Even Seth is here. It's nice to see him, and
I'm kind of hoping this doesn't turn into a raging party
with half the student body. I'm relieved to hear Josh say,
"Cool. Everybody's here!"

We drink soda in red plastic cups; the divisional playoffs

buffet is complete with pizza, jalapeño poppers, and pretty much every other fried food you can possibly fathom. We all sit in the den in front of the home version of an IMAX screen.

Seth starts talking about Babylonia, wondering who it is. He and Javier debate about John Cale and Lou Reed. I don't figure either would be up for a cool discussion about Johnny Cash's "A Boy Named Sue."

I've always liked that song. Maybe since I'm A Girl Named Mike.

When it's been decided the Velvet Underground wouldn't have been the Velvet Underground had it not been for Cale, the discussion ends. Javier and Josh tap their glasses against each other and say, "Exploding Plastic Inevitable."

I raise my cup and say, "'Because you're mine, I walk the line.'"

The room goes silent and I feel the familiar prickling sensation of heat creeping up my body, hitting my cheeks. I am a furnace.

"What?" asks Javier.

Josh says, "'I keep a close watch on this heart of mine.'"

Then Josh and I break out into the chorus. I try to do the low, gravelly Johnny Cash voice. Josh practically spews his Coke all over us.

Seth jumps up where we leave off and sings "American Pie." All ten minutes of it. The room explodes in applause, and I can't help but laugh and snort and feel a bubbly sense of normalness. "Who's next?" Seth asks.

My phone is vibrating. I've got six new messages for late bets even though I closed bets last night. It's too hard to juggle stragglers, and they're the ones who are most likely *not* to pay. I go to the back of the room to send off my Sanctuary closed message. "You gonna work, Mike?" Seth asks.

Everybody turns to watch me. "No. Bets are off."

Javier jumps up. "C'mon. We want to see the famous Mike Garcia in action."

"Not today," I say. Five messages are from Nim. One with: please please please.

I respond: No.

"Kickoff. Ten minutes," Josh says. Everybody in this room has placed a bet—everybody but Seth. We gather in front of the TV like it's our temple.

"You're not going to write about this, are you?" I ask Seth.

"Umm, and betray my capital investors?"

"Ooh, have we bought your silence?"

"No. I just don't think a gambling ring is as interesting as, say, the other stuff that goes down at school."

"Like what?"

"Like Babylonia."

By halftime, those who bet on the Rams are already spending their winnings. "Game's not over yet," Josh says.

I feel my stomach tighten. I'm doing math to see how to cover the $150 I blew, how I'm going to get the cash to Leonard and make payments on two credit cards. I can't believe I'm wearing a fifty-dollar sweater that makes me look like fruit—a sweater that won't be paid off until the end of the year.

By the end of the third quarter the Cardinals and Rams are tied. Not only do the Rams have to win, but Cuccaro has to rush another twenty-three yards, minimum, for us to win the bet. And today, of all days, Morrison's decided to play a passing game.

It feels like someone shoved my intestines through a meat grinder.

Stupid. Stupidstupid.

I go to the bathroom to splash water on my face, practically tripping over the cleaning lady, who's on her hands and knees scrubbing the tiles. "Excuse me," I say. "I'm sorry."

She looks up and her face brightens. "Michal!"

"Mrs. Mendez. *Hola*," I say in my Dora Spanish. "What are you doing here?"

She stands up, wiping her chafed and red hands on the apron. "Me and Martin work for the Ellisons. Nice people."

I want to ask her if she gets paid well; how she manages to get all the way to Genoa to work; if she's feeling better; what's going on with Moch. But I just ask, "Did you make the food?"

She nods.

"It was great. Thank you."

"*De nada, Hija.*"

I love when she says that.

"When you come back for dinner? With Liliana?"

"This week," I say. "We'll bring dessert."

She laughs and waves me away. "Liliana is good at many things. Cooking, no."

"You're telling me. I've survived on pot pies, mac 'n' cheese, and an assortment of Hamburger Helpers through the years. Did you know there are fifty-four varieties? Enough for six weeks of different dinners."

She *tsks*. "You come over. With Liliana. I'll make you some of my fire tamales. Liliana forget her home." She leans against the wall and rubs her stomach. "Okay. Maybe this American food make my stomach funny. I don't eat the fire tamales no more neither."

She looks tired—dark rings under her eyes. "Are you sleeping okay?" I lead Mrs. Mendez to a chair at the end of the hallway and bring her a glass of water.

"With Moch as a son, nobody sleep."

I nod.

"So. How are you?" I ask.

She tells me about Mr. Mendez, their plans to open a restaurant—the Tamale Palace. Just a little hole in the wall off of Highway 50. They're pricing rentals now—just a few thousand away from making it work. That's what she's always wanted. She's always talked about it.

"Hey, Michal!" Josh comes into the hallway. "Fourth quarter's started." He turns to Mrs. Mendez. "Great food, Laura. *Gracias*," he says with a grating flat *r*.

I cringe. She shouldn't be Laura. She's Mrs. Mendez.

"You two know each other?"

I open my mouth and feel Mrs. Mendez pinching my leg. "We used to be neighbors. She's Moch's mom," I say. "Thanks so much for everything, Mrs. Mendez."

Mrs. Mendez winks. *"Te espero en la casa."*

I stare at her. Embarrassed. What the *hell* is she saying? Why did I take German? I've got to be the only Mexican American in German class. Like where will I ever use my German except for with the exchange student, Heinrich, who everybody calls Maneuver? We so lack imagination.

I go back to the den. We're five minutes into the fourth quarter. We're pretty much divided between the two teams. The room's quiet except for Seth, who crunches on Kettle chips. Every time he crunches down on another chip, it's like he's stuck his hand down my skin and is ripping out my spine.

Third down. Cardinals have possession of the ball and need to get to the four-yard line to make the first—twelve yards away. Cuccaro needs to rush another twelve. *Just. Twelve. Yards.*

Ten seconds.

Ten seconds in football can be like ten minutes. The Cardinals have called a time-out. They have the ball and are within field-goal range. If they kick and make the field goal, even though they win, we lose.

Cuccaro has to run it and keep the play running even when time runs out.

Cuccaro needs to run to get the touchdown.

Josh and I need those twelve yards.

Twelve yards.

No team would *not* punt at this point in time. I mean, punting they'll tie it up. A touchdown, though . . .

Crap on a cracker.

I really wish I hadn't eaten those taquitos—deep-fried meat-stuffed tortillas that people try to pass off as Mexican food. Poor Mrs. Mendez. She must cringe when they ask her to make such abominations. We're not a mole crowd.

We've all crept closer to the TV. The whistle blows and the teams take the field. A quick huddle and the Cardinals line up.

No punter.

No punter.

Morrison gets the ball. We can't see who has it, but then we see Cuccaro is running middle field. Everything in the end zone is a blur of color and the ball is lost under a pile of human bodies.

The camera zooms from the pile of bodies to the ref back to the bodies until one by one they peel off each other like layers of an onion. The ref stands there, then raises his arms in the air.

"Touchdown!" Josh screams.

"Touchdown! Touchdown! Touchdown!"

"No freaking way," Javier moans. "That's just wrong—berserk wrong."

We stare at the screen, waiting for the main ref to confirm.

"TOUCHDOWN!" My entire body fills with warmth. Seven hundred and eighty dollars! Three hundred and ninety each, minus the one fifty we bet. One fifty I didn't have. That'll pay off most of this month's credit card. And that's just on the game. We'll get an extra hundred or so with the proposition bet on yards rushed.

Almost out of debt.

It's so easy.

So easy.

Josh, Matt, Marilyn, and I huddle and sing, "'We are the champions . . .'"

Somehow the Kettle chips have been spread all over the room—littering the floor. Matt and Marilyn dance on them—grinding the salty crumbs into the rug, making ugly grease spots.

Who will pick that up?

Seth watches us and rolls his eyes. "So, how much am I getting for *PB & J*?"

"How much do you need?" Josh asks.

"Maybe a hundred dollars."

"I can pitch in forty."

"I'll match it," I say.

Matt and Marilyn each say they'll each give twenty-five. That gives him an extra thirty. The good thing about *PB & J* is that it gets photocopied. So by the end of the week, even though Seth puts out two hundred copies, there'll be a few hundred floating around. Everybody does their share.

"Party's over," Javier groans. "I'm gonna go home to watch the other game. It's just too depressing here."

Matt and Marilyn follow. I start to pick up the crumbs.

"That's cool," Josh says, motioning to the hallway. "We've got a vacuum."

Mrs. Mendez isn't a vacuum.

He comes back in with an actual vacuum and I exhale. The carpet that looked new a few hours ago has some pretty greasy spots on it. We clean up the room and take the dishes to the kitchen. Mrs. Mendez shoos us away. "Laura," Josh says, "we'll take it from here. It's Saturday. You should probably go."

Mrs. Mendez smiles and says, "I finish here, Mr. Ellison." She looks into the den. I watch as she puts baking powder all over the stained carpet; then, after vacuuming what we just vacuumed, she gets on her hands and knees, scrubbing out the grease with a mixture of detergent, water, and vinegar. I squat next to her to help and she glares at me. "I will finish."

"I can help."

She doesn't smile. "I will finish. Alone."

Seth, Josh, and I leave the room. I can't stop thinking about Mrs. Mendez stooped over the stupid chip-stained carpet and feel embarrassed.

We sit in the kitchen, quiet. Waiting. Mrs. Mendez comes in, her hands chafed. "Anything else, Mr. Ellison?"

Josh shakes his head. "No. Thank you. I think Mom would've had my head if you hadn't saved the carpet in the den. Thank you."

She smiles, her spark back. "Good evening." She picks up her purse and walks out the door. She doesn't look at me again. *How does she get to work?*

"Do you guys want to watch the other game?"

Seth shakes his head. "Man, I've got a paper to write— as in newspaper. Plus Mrs. Hensler is *killing* me with calc."

"I've got to figure out my bets," I say. "I should get home to hang out with Lillian. Have dinner or something."

"Let's go." Josh locks the house up. The sky is that slate color. Flakes of snow drift to the ground in erratic fits— the kind of snow that make things cold, not pretty. We drive toward the main road when we pass Mrs. Mendez, walking.

Josh stops. "Hey, Laura? Can I take you somewhere?"

Mrs. Mendez shakes her head. "Is okay."

"C'mon. Get in the car. It's too cold to walk." I get out of the car and hold out my hand. "Please."

"I not walking to Carson. Martin will come when he finish work."

"Call him. Tell him we've got you."

Mrs. Mendez pauses and shivers. "Okay. Thank you."

We're quiet on the drive home. Seth is probably mentally composing the entire paper. I'm curious to see the news on the ski trip. Josh plugs in his iPod. Music shuffles from Train to Rascal Flatts to Frank Sinatra. He drops Seth off first, then asks Mrs. Mendez where to go, driving past the airport to their trailer park.

I can't stop that aching feeling in my stomach; everything's felt off this whole week. Too many ups and downs.

Mocho is sitting in the same worn lawn chair as the other day. Comba, his friend, sits next to him. It's gotta be near zero degrees, but they sit outside under the dim streetlamp. After Comba's sister was killed last year in a drive-by, he dropped out of school and nobody's seen much of him.

At first Mocho doesn't even acknowledge us. Comba wears mirrored sunglasses that cover half his face, a gold chain hanging with an even golder pendant from his neck. He sits, elbows leaning on knees, tattoos snaking up his arms, twisting around his neck, his ribbed white tank top hugging his body.

They've got to be freezing.

Moch and Comba look up at the same time. Comba takes off his sunglasses and looks from Josh to his car and back at Josh again. I'm a bit concerned that he wants to turn it into scrap metal. Comba's got scary eyes—dead eyes—like nothing matters. He's got nothing to lose. He watches Josh totally detached, like Josh is nothing.

This was a bad, bad, bad idea.

Josh bristles.

Bad bad bad idea.

Mrs. Mendez jumps out of the car, saying a quick thanks. She squeezes my hand and tries to cut Moch off at the pass, but it's too late. Moch rushes past her, yanks open Josh's door, and drags him out of the car, slamming Josh against the hood.

"Moch!" I shout and jump out of the car. I pull on his arm. He throws his hand back, hitting me in the jaw, sending me sprawling. The metallic taste of blood coats my tongue.

"*¿Quién trajó este cabrón aquí?*" Moch is drunk.

Mrs. Mendez goes to him and slaps him across the face. Hard. "*Ingrato chamasco, ¿que crees que estas haciendo?*"

"*No soy ningún lambiache,*" Moch says, words slurring. He turns to me. "*Usted. Si, usted se agringó.* Mike, do you need me to translate that you're a kiss-ass gringa from your name-brand clothes to your name-brand friends?"

"Yeah. I'm gringa. That's exactly what I am, and why is that so bad? You grew up here, too. You're just as gringo—one that eats tamales and chilaquiles. So what you eat makes you so much more Mexican? Or is it because you talk different now that you're part of la Cordillera? That's what makes you more Mexican? A contrived accent? A couple tattoos?"

He stumbles away from the car. "*¡Vete a la verga!*"

He opens his mouth, but I interrupt him. "Yeah. You go to hell too."

Josh peels his face off the hood of the car. We stand in a semicircle, waiting. Waiting for the ugly words to get sucked away in the gloom of the sky; waiting for some miraculous time reverse to happen, to take this moment away.

Moch punches Josh's car. I listen to the sickening crack of bone on metal. Mrs. Mendez drops her head in shame. "I so sorry, Mr. Ellis—"

"Don't fucking apologize for me, Ma. *Just don't.*"

Mrs. Mendez turns on Moch, swinging at him with her purse, punching him, hitting him, screaming at him, "*¡Qué vergüenza!*" over and over until it looks like her arms won't be able to lift her purse again. She drops her arms to the side, wipes her tears, and walks in the house. Yellow light comes from the kitchen window.

Moch turns into Comba; his face loses all expression, like he's become a shell of nothingness, sealing off the rage bubbling inside. He looks from Josh to me. "*Sí, qué vergüenza,*" he mutters. Moch and Comba do synchronized head nods and walk away. I kind of wonder if they talk to each other or just grunt.

I scramble to my feet and push Josh to his car. "Let's

go. Now." My lip stings. My stomach aches. And I thought we could solve everything with ski trip sabotage. Sure. Let's have some airplane fly overhead with a cheesy message and everyone will be friends. It all seems so pointless now—like the joke's on us, on Babylonia.

We drive in silence to my house. When we get there, I say, "Please, Josh. Please don't fire Mrs. Mendez. She's a good woman. They're a good family. Please."

Josh leans his head against the steering wheel, exhaling. "What just happened?" he asks.

I swallow back the words but can't keep them down. "Ellison Industries. That's what."

Josh pales. I squeeze his arm.

Josh puts one hand over mine and runs his thumb over my split lip. I wince. "Are you hurt?" he asks.

"I'm okay. Are you?"

Josh shakes his head. "You know a sad thing?"

I could name about a thousand.

"I knew. I knew about my parents and the people who work for us. I've always known."

He stares ahead. I open the door and step outside; icy wind bites into my cheeks.

Burdened by our parents' sins. Hopeless.

18

SUNDAY SPREADS BEFORE me like a life-without-parole sentence. I'm tempted to mark the minutes on the wall with a pencil. I replay the scene at Mocho's over in my head. When did he start to hate so much? It's like there's no difference between him and Nim.

I look at my phone. No messages from Josh.

Nim's texted me another five times, all with the same message: please please please.

It's embarrassing how pathetic he can be. I stare at the message and write back: Place your bet.

He writes: $350 Broncos—Moneyline.

Me: Spread?

Nim: MONEYLINE.

I roll my eyes. The Broncos are seriously favored, so if they lose, Nim's gonna take a hit. Big-time. And if they win, he won't even make a hundred dollars. It's too easy to pick a sure thing. He will always be a total amateur puke. That's what he is. Regurgitated genetics. Anyone with two cents for brains wouldn't place that bet.

The TV is white noise in the background. The divisional playoffs are on. Today, watching twenty-two guys run up and down a field is about as interesting to me as watching grass grow. I look at my numbers. Leonard would take a halftime bet.

It was so easy. Then the rush, like having a cerebral implosion of happiness.

I push the thought away. It was a one-time deal. That's why I'm good at what I do, because I'm never emotionally invested. It doesn't matter who wins or loses. All I care about is the bottom line and making my money.

Steady income. No risks.

But yesterday.

Never mind.

Lillian is cleaning up the yard, bundled in a heavy coat three sizes too big—one she got at the secondhand shop. She snips off dead branches and tears away the spiderweb-rooted underbrush from below the mailbox.

I bring her hot chocolate.

It tastes good. We sit together, looking out at the yard, an old afghan wrapped around our legs. The yard is pretty—cared for. Something to be proud of. There's a peace about Lillian when she gardens and works in the yard, like all the political injustices of the world don't matter because she can pull weeds. She's not restless or angry or thinking about brochures and legislation.

Times like this, I feel like I matter.

"We need to plant something to go around the mailbox post this spring. The spirea took a turn for the worse." Lillian points to the mailbox.

I look at the pile of deadish-looking plants Lillian tore out of the half-frozen ground.

"We could change these, too." I point to the geranium bushes.

"Why change what's already so perfect?"

"They're just geraniums," I say, feeling that wall of thorns crawling between us.

"They're more than that. The spirea went. The geraniums stay. They've been there seventeen years now."

"All the more reason to change them. Wouldn't you like a makeover—change something so that you can feel different?"

Lillian wipes her hand across her mouth, glistening with powdered hot chocolate. A couple of freeze-dried marshmallows bob in the watery beverage. "Everybody'd like to change something." She's dangerously close to sounding like the high school counselor and beating me over the head with one of those Ten Step books.

"Or someone," I say, then bite the inside of my cheek, breaking through the skin. It tastes like I'm sucking on my car keys. I sometimes wish she'd just say it—say how much Mom and I screwed up her life plans. That would be easier than living with the constant sense of being a trespasser—unwanted.

Lillian takes another sip, cupping the mug in her hands. "What happened to your lip?"

"Nothing," I say.

Lillian stares at me—lines webbing around her eyes like spires. "I wouldn't change a thing, Mike," she says. "Especially those geraniums." She says it like those geraniums mean everything in the world.

Geraniums are *just* geraniums. But at least I have my six words for the day:

Purple geranium weeds. Black-eyed violet perfection? Whatever.

Lillian stretches. "Thanks for the hot chocolate. It's been a long afternoon."

"What do you want for dinner?" I ask.

"We have some pot pies in the freezer. That'll do for me."

"I'll go to the store and get salad. Just for a change."

"That'd be nice." She goes inside and gets out her purse, handing me five dollars.

"Lillian, I can afford salad."

"So can I," she says, and heads inside. "See you for dinner."

◆

I swing by Mocho's house on the way to the grocery store because I can't stop thinking about yesterday, about Mrs. Mendez.

Mr. Mendez answers the door, opening it just a crack. When he sees me, he smiles and opens the door wide. "Michal, how are you?"

I scuff my foot across the half-frozen metal porch. "I'm okay. Is Moch here?"

Mr. Mendez invites me in. The house is dark. Moch's cousins are playing checkers in the living room. It takes me a while to adjust to the dim light, compared to the bright winter afternoon outside.

"Is everything okay?"

"Laura is sick."

"Can I do something?"

"Is okay. Mr. Ellison called. He wants Laura to work in town now—not out in Genoa."

I exhale. "You could've told me. I could pick her up."

Mr. Mendez smiles. "You're a good girl. Lillian raised you right."

I feel like such a phony—like everything I do is for show. "Moch?" I ask.

He shakes his head.

"Can you tell him I came by?"

I don't want to go home. I drive out to the river, to the shantytown Moch talked about. I park a short distance down the access road and cut across the rusted iron bridge that has a BRIDGE CLOSED sign on it, keeping cars away. The entire center part has crumbled into the Carson River below. I walk on the skeletal structure, its iron bones flaking with my footsteps. It's easy walking, and the community is easy to find. I just follow the smell of burning sage tainted with the acrid smell of burning rubber.

A ghetto of families lives by the Carson River, tucked far enough away from the road that you don't have to see them if you don't want to. Their ramshackle homes are built with our garbage: discarded fiberglass sheeting, old box mattresses with coils of springs coming out, plastic lawn chairs and Coke-bottle walls encased in mud. I circle around and watch from a hill. They light small fires; kids are playing too close to the burning embers. *Why do they come?*

I recognize one kid from school—another from Moch's gang. None of these kids got ski passes. I feel like I'm drowning.

A botched ski trip. A few Commandments. I really thought that would make a difference. But it was just a show.

Back at home, Lillian and I eat our pot pies and salad. The games are over. I organize the bets, payoffs—a spreadsheet of wins and losses. Nim lost. Again.

I've done an extra-credit assignment for calculus and one for physics, and I was considering writing an essay on the Donner party for AP History. Somebody should rescue me from me.

Night falls. Messages have been sent—losers and winners notified.

Josh hasn't called.

I listen to the wind outside my window and stare out the black square of night. It feels like normal again. Like how things were just a couple of weeks ago.

A life of predictability. That's what I want, what I like. That's what makes sense to me, how I've survived.

Others' lives unfold. Great sideline view.

19

Commandment "Thou Shalt Not Covet Your Friend's Name-Brand Jeans or Boyfriend/Girlfriend" Broken by Sophomore Who Now Has New "Borrowed" Jeans and "Borrowed" Boyfriend

Garbage Disposal, la Cordillera, and . . . Babylonia? Modern-Day Vigilantes, Robin Hoods, or Thugs?

Cuccaro Runs Cardinals to Conference Finals in a Baffling Upset in Divisional Playoffs

SETH'S BUSINESS SECTION— *Wall Street Journal* style—dedicates the entire page to buying and selling popularity stocks. He created a barter/point system that could quantify someone's popularity based on random criteria: looks; style; extracurricular activities, including those not approved by the school board or parents; access to private transportation and illicit substances; and a few more things. In the end, according to Seth's Popularity Roulette, Bronek, the exchange student from the

Czech Republic, is the most popular.

Seth passed out his first-round copies of *PB & J*. Groups
of kids are huddled together, talking about the botched ski
trip. It feels like it was weeks ago. The collective conscious-
ness of Carson High is still stuck on Friday. I'm stuck on
Saturday at Moch's house. And the rest of the school is
asking who Bronek is. It's going to be one of those Where's
Waldo days at school. By lunch, Bronek will have a whole
lot of new friends.

Irony is lost on the masses.

But something's different. Kids aren't just talking about
the trip. They're talking about Babylonia. Babylonia is in
every breath taken, every word spoken.

Babylonia is everywhere.

I open my locker, bracing myself for the avalanche of
books. Sitting on top of a semi-organized pile is a little box.
I open it and find a braided leather bracelet with a silver
dice charm dangling from it.

"Do you like it?" Josh is leaning against the locker next
to mine. "I couldn't find anything else really bookie-ish."

I nod. "Thank you." I can't find any other words in my
brain, then blurt out, "How'd you get into my locker?"

Josh smiles his crinkly-eyed, half-moon smile. He leans
in, clasping the bracelet onto my wrist. "You're not the only
one with tricks up your sleeve." His lips brush against my
ear, and I'm afraid my entire body will go into some kind
of nuclear reactor shutdown, like my face will glow red and

my head will start spinning. He stands up. "Sorry I didn't call yesterday. Things were . . ."

"It's okay," I say, fighting to keep my composure. I lower my voice. "Mr. Mendez told me Mrs. Mendez will be working in Carson?"

He nods.

"Did you say—"

He shakes his head. "Dad's got a real skewed sense of morality, so I think bringing up the fact he illegally employs the mother of a gangster wouldn't be beneficial to anybody."

I nod. "So why the change?"

"The change of venue? I just asked him to. Since I never ask him for anything, I guess he decided that he could comply with my wishes." Josh shrugs. "We don't talk much. He's more of a memo leaver than a dad. Every morning I wake up to a nice sticky note of instructions." Josh pauses. "I can't remember *not* waking up to that. Weird, huh. He even sticky-notes my birthday."

"Thanks," I say. "For asking for that."

He skims through the paper while we walk to class. "Who's Bronek?"

"I think that's the point."

"Seth's good," Josh says. "Really good."

I can't help but wonder what Moch would write. Like maybe Seth could bring him on as a columnist—"La Cordillera Beat: News from the Front Line."

We pause at Mrs. B's door. I see Josh inhale, holding his breath while he peeks around the corner, then rushes to his chair as silently as possible. I follow. Moch is at his desk, head lying in his arms, sunglasses on, hood up, sleeping.

Exhale.

Trinity walks in with her entourage, huffing like a fairy-tale bad guy. She's wearing tired chic today—her hair swept up in a loose pony, matchy-matchy purple Adidas sweats and old-school Converse. She sits down, crossing her arms in front of her, ready for war.

Inhale.

Mrs. B comes in and slams her books on the desk. Moch jerks awake. "Good morning, class," she says. "Who's ready to share?" she asks.

The class, as usual, slips into the silence of dread.

Mrs. B claps loud—unnaturally loud for such small hands. "Wake up, kids! It's Monday. It's *your* time. Who's up?" I wonder what Mrs. B sees from her side of the class— a group of misfits she's trying to guide through the joys of literature; lost causes; America's future. Who knows? She smiles. "Miss Ross, I do look forward to hearing what you have to share." Mrs. B's eyes narrow just a touch.

Trinity's jaw tightens. "I have a memoir."

Mrs. B smiles. "Please. We'd love to hear it."

"Six words," someone says.

The class giggles.

"Let's have Mike keep track of my words. You know

all about counting, don't you?" Trinity flicks her tongue. If she's trying to pull off femme fatale, it's working. Every guy in the room is awake—incredibly awake.

"Better than Caleb, anyway," I say. Her boyfriend lost seventy bucks this weekend. If Trinity blew Sanctuary, Caleb and his friends would probably burn her at a stake à la Salem witch trials. Caleb's never missed Sanctuary. Ever.

"Miss Ross, we're waiting." Mrs. B doesn't know what's going on, but we're smart enough not to continue before she catches on.

Trinity smiles, and I'd swear I just saw some kind of light glimmer off her teeth.

Bling!

She says, "Free breakfast, free health. Culture of handouts."

"Seven words," I say under my breath.

Moch stands up. "Can't accept handouts with clenched fists."

Trinity fires back, "Drug dealers. Pimps. Tattooed lawn maintenance."

"Buyers. Hypocrites. Trust fund pampered elitists." Moch mutters, "Yeah. Like I'd really want to go on *your* ski trip. I can use your ten-dollar words, too, you prissy—"

Catalina Sandoval raises her hand. If anybody goes by unnoticed more than me, it's her. She doesn't belong to la Cordillera or any clubs. She just studies. All the time. Every lunchtime she goes to the library. Every afternoon she stays in Mrs. Hensler's class to get help with calculus. "My family—" She pauses and takes a deep breath. "We don't have papers. I used to bring home food on the weekends from Brain Food."

I blush. Everybody knows Brain Food is a program for low-income families. They give kids enough calories for the weekend. I used to take it home, too. Why am I ashamed?

Catalina's cheeks get redder as she talks. "My parents work hard. They can't afford doctors or new clothes or anything. I am grateful for free lunches, free health, Trinity. Last week my pa got hurt at work—a nail went all the way through his thumb. His boss sent him home, only paid him half day. We went to Clinica Olé. They took care of him. Gave him a tetanus shot, stitched his thumb up. For free.

"He went back to work the next day. He gets less money because he's less productive. So you say he got this medicine for free. It wasn't free, because my pa has built many of your homes here. Nothing's free. He'd already done his time. And there are lots of places that have made sure that people *get* that." She turns to Trinity. "I'm not a border bunny, spic, beaner, drywaller. I'm a four-oh student who is determined to get my papers, get legal, and prove you all wrong about who I am. I am Mexican American. I just don't have a little piece of paper to prove it. But it's *who I am*."

We wait for Mrs. B to say something—to bring this back to Creative Writing or memoirs or something. But all she does is sit on her desk, her red nails drumming on the desk, one leg wrapped around the other, her spastic beelike energy drained.

"I wasn't talking about you," Trinity says, staring at Moch.

"Yes you were," Catalina says.

Mrs. B's finger lands on my name. "Mike? We haven't heard from you in a while." Mrs. B is on a Creative Writing–teacher high. It's like six-word-memoir anger management in here.

I flip open my notebook and read. "Half Mexican. Half American. Not anyone."

The class is quiet.

"It's dumb," I say. "I don't know why I wrote that." I bury my face in my notebook, trying to hide from Moch and everyone else.

"Your grandmother is a great lady, Mike. She's someone to look up to," Catalina says in a hushed voice. But one everyone listens to. I'm ashamed I never think of my grandma as someone exceptional.

"And you, Mr. Ellison? What do you have to say?"

We turn around to see his hand dangling in the air, half committed. He pushes his bangs out of his eyes, a flush of color to his cheeks.

Josh clears his throat. "Reconciling parents' sins. Retracing. Backtracking. Sorry."

20

Rocky-Style Conference Championships This Weekend: Why We SHOULD Bet on Cardinals, Our Modern-Day David

Kudos to Cultural-Minded Prom Committee: Bronek Picks Theme Song: *"Hříšná těla, křídla motýlí"* **by Some Czech Chick We've Never Heard Of**

Sanctuary goal post 3:00 Thursday

"GOOD AFTERNOON. Conference championships are going to be big this weekend. Especially after last weekend's upset between the Cardinals and the Rams."

A few groan.

"I know," I say. "Tough break."

"Seventy bucks tough," says Caleb.

"Seventy? I lost fifty *plus* getting jacked off for the ski trip. Sixty bucks to stare at a stupid banner and get some lame-ass school Commandments. *Shit.* My entire pay-check. I've been bumming rides for the past week. I don't have cash for gas." Tim, body-shop guru and resident car mechanic extraordinaire grumbles.

Bet what you can lose. But I don't tell them that. They already know. They're here for the rush. I flip through the pages of *The Gambler*, thankful for the gambling-addict wisdom of Fyodor Dostoyevsky.

"Open your books, please." I read:

> *Sometimes it happens that the most insane thought, the most impossible conception, will become so fixed in one's head that at length one believes the thought or the conception to be reality. Moreover, if with the thought or the conception there is combined a strong, a passionate, desire, one will come to look upon the said thought or conception as something fated, inevitable, and foreordained—something bound to happen.*

The mood has changed. Conception, reality, fate, inevi-tability—ideas they needed to hear. That's probably what Moch should hear, though I don't really know how I'd pull off pep talks with gang members.

I let the words sink in, feel how everybody's waiting, calculating, ready to pay for a rush.

"Here are the weekend specials. I've got some exotics on the table. Bet on the first team to score, how they score, and if you lose the overall bet, you don't pay the juice."

The guys are quiet.

"It means it's a free bet, guys. I don't get anything. You win, great. You lose, you don't pay me my vig."

Some grumble.

"Never mind." It's hard to go beyond basic betting with this group.

Nim's hanging out in the background. He still owes me the three fifty he bet on the Broncos. He's a locust. A rash.

I rub my fingers and thumb together and glare at him. He holds his hands out, open palmed.

He's a gnat.

Dean Randolph comes by and *tsks*. He stops. "Any of you have anything to do with that Babylonia crap?"

Sure, Dean Randolph. Josh Ellison and I broke into Mrs. Martinez's office, stole the tickets, and distributed them. That, totally unnoticed by staff and administration, sabotaged the Pearly Gates Heavenly Ski Trip.

"Geez, Randolph," Tim says.

"Mister," Randolph growls.

"Mr. Randolph, a bunch of us here paid sixty bucks to go skiing. That money's gone. I'd like to kick Babylonia's . . . you know what." Last weekend put Caleb back a good hundred and thirty dollars in just ski passes and bets alone.

Randolph leaves, the bets are placed, and I head to the parking lot, wondering when the gray-slush days of winter will be gone. "You gonna place a bet?" Josh asks.

I shake my head. "I'm satisfied with being a one-hit wonder." I'm itching for the trip, the surge of adrenaline in my body. Just watching the game knowing that everything's on the line makes it different. Alive.

"It's worth it."

"Nah. I like a sure thing. No bet or plan is foolproof, right?" *Why am I lying?*

"Except for abs-tee-nance."

I laugh. He mimics our health teacher, Ms. Overland's, southern drawl, pinching her lips together in that prissy-virginal-nobody-touches-my-boobies kind of way.

"Want to go to the movies tonight? Javier and some others are going."

I automatically crawl back into that tiny safe place where I'm welcome. "That's okay. I don't want to be a tag-along."

"Why would you assume that?"

I pause. "I don't know."

"You said you'd go to the movies with me. Remember?"

With him, not half the student body. "Sure." *After almost getting killed while hot tubbing. I don't think I should be held responsible for anything I said that night.*

"C'mon. Movies. Pizza."

"That's pretty *normal*. I haven't ever really done normal. Where's the danger in it?"

"We could duck into a second film—do a double feature."

"Now you're talking. I was afraid we'd become TV teens there for a second."

"So, we're on? What time can I pick you up? Six o'clock?"

"Six is good."

"Six it is." He walks to his car in a lanky swagger that just makes me want to . . . I mentally splash water on my face. I've finally made an awesome friend who's not a gangster and I don't think I should blow it harboring lascivious thoughts about him.

On the way home, I swing by Moch's house. I knock several times. Nobody answers. I work my way around the house, hoping I can peek in, just to see if everything's okay, when I hear shouting.

Behind Moch's trailer park is a huge field we call no-man's-land. It's where all baseball games have been played since we lived here. It's the place where we used to build forts and play tag, hide-and-seek . . . whatever. And now that we're older, it's the place where kids go to party, drink, probably get stoned. I don't think they're doing poetry readings out there.

I follow the voices.

A crowd has already gathered. Kids are shouting. Caleb Masterson holds up a bat and lowers it, cracking down, making a sound like somebody walking on glass. Nim's there. Laughing. Kicking at the kid who's curled as tight as a snail shell in the center of the group, a sickening sound coming from his throat, like he's gurgling his tongue.

I see the flash of metal before I see Comba. Caleb falls to the ground. His varsity jacket turns black by his stomach, his hands a cartoonish red color.

Then everything goes in slow motion. Comba takes the knife, wiping the crimson blood from the blade on a patch of filthy snow. He scans the crowd that's now gone silent, his eyes lifeless—like two black marbles.

No soul.

A soft moan comes from the kid they were beating up.

The jocks grab Caleb and pick him up in their arms, dragging him through the field. I don't even realize I've dialed 911.

"Nine-one-one. What is the exact location of your emergency?"

"The field."

"What field, ma'am?"

"Um . . . It's the one behind Pine Cone Trailer Park."

"What is your emergency?"

"I think . . ." I shudder and try to keep my voice as even as possible. "I think somebody might be dead."

Just as I say it, I feel someone's hand on my phone, pulling it from me, hanging it up. It's Moch. A bunch of his friends rush to the guy on the ground. He's unconscious. Comba's there. I do everything to *not* look at him.

"Is the clinic open today?" Moch asks.

"Clinic?"

"Look at me, Mike. Is *la Clinica Olé* open?"

I nod.

Moch squeezes my arm. "Get out of here. Now." They pile the groaning kid into a car and drive away, leaving me alone in the field, staring at a puddle of blood. I pick up the bat, staring at red-black spatters on it. A field mouse darts in and out of dried tufts of long grass. A screen door bangs in the wind. Sirens wail in the distance, getting closer.

I watch as the half-frozen earth soaks up the blood; then I turn and throw up.

Gangs: tattoos, knives, lettermen jackets, bats.

21

THE BAT'S IN THE BACK OF
my closet. I don't know why I picked it up, why I took it. I
tell Josh about the fight. Not the bat. "Did they see you?"
he whispers. The movie previews are almost over.

"Not Nim and those guys. Just Moch."

"Lucky."

"Yeah. Never really thought about it. Comba scares
me. Really scares me. But now, so do they. It's like they're
all the same. So much hate."

"So what are you going to do?"

I shrug. "Nothing. I don't know."

Josh grabs my hand, lacing his fingers in mine. "Is this
okay?"

I nod. "Yes."

He turns to watch the movie. I try to focus on the screen

but only see the repeat of this afternoon. *What should I do?*

Seth calls me on Saturday, asking if I have a scoop. That guy knows *everything* that's going on. "No comment," I say.

By the time Monday comes, the fight in the field is legendary, with Caleb Masterson facing the evil gang bangers. Nobody mentions a bat, a kid being dropped off at the ER, or the fact that Caleb's injury was really superficial. Lots of blood for something so inconsequential. It sounds like I've had hangnails worse than that.

From the looks of *PB & J*, Seth didn't get the info he needed.

Babylonia Needed for Fabric Distribution: Cheerleaders Are Cold

Are YOU a Gang Member? Checklist

According to Seth's checklist, every person in Carson High is part of a gang, the most ubiquitous presence being that of band members. I'm kind of happy to be reading about the dangers of woodwind instruments and pleated belts, Seth's term for cheerleaders' skirts, as opposed to the real world, anyway.

It's like I'm always caught in the gray area between right and wrong.

Moch isn't at school. Classes are eternal. I can't even get into the heated debate in Government about the death of the American dream. When the final bell rings, I rush to my car. I just want to check in on Moch and Mrs. Mendez.

Josh texts me: My place? Homework.

I reply: OK. 4:00.

Mr. Mendez is pacing back and forth in the house when I arrive. Mrs. Mendez is lying on the couch.

"Are you still sick?" I ask.

She shakes her head. "I'm fine. Finefinefinefine. Just tired. That all."

"A flu. The doctor says it's a flu. But I don't think so." Mr. Mendez runs his fingers through thinning gray hair.

"Did you see Lillian?" I ask. I get my phone out to dial her number.

"We went to Urgent Care." Mr. Mendez scowls, deep creases above his nose. "It's closer, you know. Everybody there had the flu. But this is different. We don't go to Urgent Care for a flu. He hardly looked at her. She needs more tests."

"Tests. Heart tests. Blood tests. Pee tests. So we spend a thousand dollars to see my heart dance? Stupid," Mrs. Mendez says. "That is money for the restaurant."

"We'll get the money back." Mr. Mendez shakes his head. "I think it's more than a flu."

"What about heading to the ER? Can't you just check in there?"

Mr. Mendez bristles. "We pay for our doctors."

I nod. "I didn't mean—"

"I'm just tired. So he worry. Is normal. Work is hard."

I picture her bent over greasy Kettle chip carpet stains; my stomach aches.

"You're tired all the time," Mr. Mendez says. "You don't sleep. You don't eat. You're sick."

Mrs. Mendez smiles. "Efficient. You don't have to feed me no more."

"*No me parece chistoso . . . ni un poquito.*"

Moch peeks out of his bedroom, sees it's me, then hides away again. I hand Mr. Mendez some papers. "Homework. I picked it up for Moch."

"Thank you." Mr. Mendez goes to knock on Moch's bedroom door, pauses, drops his fist, and comes back to the living room. "I'll make sure he gets it."

I nod. "Are you sure I can't call Lillian? She can do something. Maybe we can get dinner for you?"

Mrs. Mendez laughs. "Her cooking put me in the tomb. *No, gracias.*"

I kneel beside her and kiss her forehead, salty with sweat. "Are you sure?"

"Go. Come back next week. With Liliana. We eat real food then."

I don't stand up.

"*¡Andale, Mija!*"

"Yee-haw!" I say.

She laughs. "Silly American girl." She cups her hands on my chin. "Don't give up on Mocho. You know why we call him Mocho?"

I shake my head, embarrassed, again, that I don't know my Spanish.

"In Mexico, *mocho* is for someone who is very, how do you say, a big fan of God."

"A fanatic." *My mom.*

"Yes. Fan. Anyway, Mocho give mass to us every Sunday when he is a boy. Every Sunday, he call himself Padre Emilio. So my mama see him and say, '*Qué muchacho tan mocho.*' Mocho stick to him. He's no more Emilio." She sits up and whispers in my ear. "He still wear Santo Pablo, patron *santo* of writers, on his chain."

"I didn't know that."

"Of course you don't. That's why I tell you. You're a good friend."

"Mrs. Mendez, please go to the clinic. Maybe Lillian can have a look at you. She can recommend doctors." I clear my throat. "That have payment plans. So you can just get a good checkup." I wait for Mr. Mendez to get upset, but he just sits in the recliner, rocking back and forth, hypnotic. Dazed.

She throws her arm up in the air. "Bah. I prefer my restaurant. *¡Andale!*"

"Okay. Okay." I leave and work my way around the house and knock on Moch's window.

He pulls the curtains to the side and opens the window. "*¿Qué?*"

"Is your friend okay?" I ask. "The one from the field."

I can't get the sound of the bat cracking on his head out of my mind. It's the only thing I hear.

Moch shakes his head, the curtain slipping back into place.

I drive away. The warmth of Mrs. Mendez's callused hand on my face has been replaced by an icy feeling in my stomach. They have spent so much time working and saving and working and saving. She's got to get better.

Where will she get the money for those tests? I hear Lillian ranting enough to know that a few tests translates to thousands of dollars.

Thousands of dollars.

Where?

The Super Bowl. No. No more bets.

What about Moch?

No. To ask him to get more money would mean more deals. . . .

And maybe there's hope for Mocho. Maybe he's not lost. Maybe Mrs. Mendez is just tired—pregnant. Whatever. Maybe she doesn't need those tests.

Maybe Mrs. Mendez and everybody's just fine.

Mrs. Mendez doesn't look fine.

Moch is fine. Maybe . . .

Maybe I should stop trying to figure out Mocho's life for him and worry about my own.

Lost: Hope. Looking to belong, survive.

22

"IT'S SUPER BOWL SUNDAY,"
Josh says. It's just hanging there—like a helium balloon we can bring down and hold on to. We've worked out a good bet. Almost a sure thing.

Ab-stee-nance. Mrs. Overland's southern drawl creeps into my brain.

But this is really, truly, almost a sure thing. It's like betting with a condom.

I need to keep Planned Parenthood out of my betting vocab.

The week was nuts. The Cardinals, who began the season as a hundred to one for winning the Super Bowl, have now become the popular underdog, which kind of messes up my spread. Sometimes hopeful bets turn out—but when an entire nation gets hopeful, it messes up the balance of things.

I don't have any cash to bet.

"Super Bowl Sunday." He lowers his voice. "You've gone back to bench warming. You're a totally different person when you're in the game, Michal."

"Are you really going to do a whole 'play the game' analogy?"

"Totally." I can hear the grin in his voice. "Ready? You now: ass splinters, bench warming, Pay-per-view spectator, living in the safety zone, perma-time-out. Shall I continue?"

"Here's the deal. A friend needs money for some tests. Medical stuff."

"Well, that's even better! We can call it a gamble-thon. Think about it, Michal. This is the essence of Babylonia—like a Robin Hood gambling enterprise. We'll take the winnings from our last bet and invest."

"I already invested those winnings. In my credit-card bills. I buy a lot of—" Why do I have to justify my clothes and my credit-card debts and all the crap I spend *my* money on?

"No problem. I've got mine—three hundred seventy plus. Okay. Less. Almost three hundred. Um. Two hundred and something." He clears his throat. "Can, um, we bet more than we have in hand? This Leonard guy—"

"Yes," I say. "We can."

"Perfect. Babylonia's a team. So we pool our money—"

"That we don't have."

"We'll win."

"We have to."

"And you give the winnings to your friend."

"Don't you even need to know who it's for? What it's for?"

"Would you? If I asked the same?"

I think about it. "No. I guess not."

"Okay. Super Bowl party. My place. I'll pick you up soon. Call Leo."

The chips taste stale. The Coke's gone flat. I watch as everybody analyzes the halftime show, all the guys waiting for a boob-reveal repeat. The last ten seconds of the game flash before my eyes in freeze-frame images. The fumble. The freak seventy-yard sprint to the end zone. The touchdown. The ball being spiked. The dance, gyrating hips, back flip, the same-team tackle. The Chiefs winning.

The Cardinals losing.

Josh and me. Losing.

The room feels closed in, suffocating. Sticky-syrupy Coke pools on the coffee table and has dripped onto what looks like an expensive Persian carpet. Confetti papers flit and float in the air, the pink, yellow, orange, and red dots scattered everywhere, drifting to the floor, sinking in the puddles of carbonated sugar, congealed orange cheese dip, and grease.

Mrs. Mendez's stooped figure, just a shadow in the shouts, picks up the half-empty plates of greasy food, passing between us almost invisible. But I see her.

Josh sees her.

Where am I going to get four hundred dollars between now and tomorrow?

She pauses; a cup slips through her hands. She falls to her knees. At first it looks like she's picking up the cup, but she's frozen in place, pale, face glistening with sweat. She stumbles to stand up, then sits down, leaning against a chair.

My legs feel heavy, like Beelzebub's gargoyles are pulling me to the center of the earth. I put my hand in front of my mouth to make sure I'm still breathing. "Mrs. Mendez," I whisper. "Mrs. Mendez?"

Josh pushes past everybody. I make my way to her, lamely putting a damp napkin on her mottled and blotchy face. She smiles at me and puts her hand in mine.

Josh has already called 911. "Moch. Call Moch," I say, tossing Josh my phone.

Josh blanches.

"Call. Moch. Now."

An ambulance arrives. Paramedics rush into the house. I hold tight to Mrs. Mendez's limp hand. The paramedics talk into radios.

"Nonresponsive."

"Cardiac arrest."

They move me out of the way. They shove needles into

Mrs. Mendez's arm and an oxygen mask on her face.

"We're losing her," one says, and rips open her uniform, rubs together paddles, and sticks them on her chest. "Clear!"

Her body hiccups.

"Clear!"

We stare at the monitor, waiting for the heart line to peak, listening for thumping instead of a steady beep.

They throw questions out into the evening: "Is she allergic to anything?" "What kind of prescription medication does she take?" "Has she been sick?"

"I don't know. I don't know. I don't know. Yes. Yes. She's sick."

"Sick? With what?"

"A stomachache. The flu. The doctor at Urgent Care said she had a flu. That's all." My lip quivers. Hot tears spill down my cheeks. Mrs. Mendez's body arches in response to the shock and goes limp. Josh's parents arrive—at least I think it's them. They stand back. Mr. Ellison's talking on the phone.

Making calls.

Josh's hands go limp at his sides.

"Let's move," the paramedics holler, lifting her on a gurney and out to the ambulence. They shut the doors, leaving me outside.

We caravan to the hospital, the ambulance horn screaming, lights flickering, dodging in and out of light traffic.

Halfway there, the sirens go silent. The ambulance slows down to speed limit. I choke back sobs, wiping tears off my cheeks.

Josh takes one hand off the wheel, pulling my head against his shoulder.

We follow the lights in silence.

Take me, God. Bring her back.

23

"COME OUTSIDE," Josh says when I answer the phone.

"It's after midnight."

"Get dressed. Wear dark colors. Come outside. I need your help."

Josh stumbles into the house when I open the door, almost knocking over a flimsy TV tray with one of Lillian's houseplants on it. A cactus, of all things. "Watch it!" I grasp the tottering tray and prick my finger on a needle. The soft petals flutter. "What are you doing here?"

"We need to get that money to Mr. Mendez. I need help."

"To go to the ATM?"

"That's one way of putting it," Josh says. He chews on his nail. "Listen, Michal. I don't have access to any accounts. But I know where we can get money. I just need help doing it."

I push away the little alarm in my head—like an exclamation point in my frontal cortex saying, *"NO! NO! NO!"*

Somebody oughta grab my upper-arm flab and pinch. Hard. I do a mental squeeze. I just want to erase Moch's and Mr. Mendez's expressions. They got there just after we did. Mr. Mendez saw me, my face, then rushed to the doctors. "I need to see her. Please."

He came back and sat across from me. "They said she had the flu. The flu."

I nod.

Then the bill.

Sorry about your loss. Yes. We do take credit cards.

I can't help but hate Josh's family now. It's not like they did anything. But maybe if Mrs. Mendez had had insurance. Maybe if she had gotten those tests. She'd still be here.

We were supposed to win.

Josh stands on the porch looking wilted. Ashamed. He holds out his hand. "I need to do this."

"What are we going to do?"

"Trust me," he says, "we won't get caught. It's a foolproof plan."

"And if we do get caught?"

"It's all me."

"That hardly seems fair," I say.

"Who can afford the lawyer?" he says. "My dad's an

asshole. This has been established. I will never, ever spend a single night in prison. Ever." He says it like a great truth—one of life's givens: the sun will rise; Cain killed Abel; and Josh Ellison will never spend a night in prison.

We stand together on the porch. He looks at his watch. "This money belongs to her and her family and then some. I *need* to do this." Absolution and penance—right the wrongs.

I close the door behind me. We walk a block to an old Pontiac. "I borrowed this from a friend," he explains.

I don't ask who. We drive past Dayton, where Ellison Industries' sprawling presence looks like something from Area 51, parking in the back of the buildings. I half expect to see some guys in white lab coats wheeling out sheet-covered body shapes on gurneys. A chain-link fence surrounds the premises. Guards drive around in golf carts patrolling the area.

He tosses me a ski mask and gloves. "Are we really gonna do this?" I ask.

He nods. "We don't have a choice."

I can't work out the probabilities of getting away with this in my head because I don't have all the information in front of me. The only source for creating odds is Josh's assurance versus years of criminal investigation TV series in which the bad guy always gets caught.

What are our odds?

Mrs. Mendez had a flu. Now she's dead.

What are the odds?

Josh grabs my hand and squeezes. "Ready?"

I nod.

I time the guards. There's approximately seven to nine minutes between passes. Josh points to a door in one of the big warehouses. He holds the keys up. "We need to climb this fence and get there. It's about a hundred and fifty yards."

"We need to do it in less than six minutes," I say. "Just to be safe."

"Okay."

We pull on our ski masks. As soon as the guard in the golf cart turns the corner, Josh gives me a boost so I can scramble up the fence. He follows close behind. I climb over and jump down, knives of pain radiating from my feet up my shins. My knee practically gives out on me. Stupid glass. Stupid knee.

"C'mon," he whispers.

"I can't see," I say, trying to pull my fogged up glasses from my mask.

"C'mon, c'mon. Trust me," he says, and grabs my hand. We sprint to the door. He manages to open it, and we throw ourselves into the small office, closing the door softly behind us just as the golf cart's lights hit the door's window.

I move to pull off my ski mask and glasses when Josh grabs my arm. "Lie facedown. Now," he whispers.

He spray-paints two cameras around the office.

"I think that's all of them," he says in a whisper. He taps his finger to his lips.

I nod and pull my glasses out, in a lame attempt at cleaning the lenses. My heart feels tight in my rib cage, like the pounding will shatter my bones. I can hear the blood rushing through my body and tap my ears. It's probably not a good thing to be able to hear your own blood.

We hear footsteps outside. Heavy boots. I lie on the floor, face pasted to the cool tiles. We wiggle to the door and sit against it. A flashlight sweeps across the room, pausing on the closet. The guard jiggles the doorknob.

Locked.

His radio beeps. The crackling sound of a voice coming through, asking about Warehouse Number Four.

"On my way." He rests his hand on the doorknob. We listen to the jingling of keys. The radio beeps again. He walks away, the sound of footsteps echoing in my brain. I can't tell if he's still out there or if it's just my brain on some freak-out repeat track.

Josh squeezes my elbow and motions toward a desk, opens a wooden panel. Behind the panel is a safe. Josh opens it on the third try. "He's so obvious," he mutters.

Josh takes out the bag of cash.

Five thousand dollars.

"Five?" I motion with my fingers.

He nods.

"All of it?"

He swallows. "Funerals are expensive."

A sick feeling sweeps over me. My glasses blur and I rest my head between my knees. Josh squeezes my hand. "I'm sorry."

The paper that was tightly wrapped around the bills is empty. I wipe my eyes and look around the office for paper. My hands feel clumsy in the heavy black gloves, and I have to keep reminding myself to keep them on.

I find paper and scissors and cut a pile into bill-sized pieces and am about to shove them into the band when I hold up my hand. "Pen?" I ask.

Josh hands me one.

I write on the top piece of paper: *From her beacon-hand glows worldwide welcome . . .*

Josh nods. He takes the paint and sprays *Babylonia* on the wall.

Struggling to find meaning in death.

24

AFTER JOSH AND I LEAVE
the money for Mr. Mendez, Josh takes me home. I can't
sleep. I can't think about anything but Moch and his face
at the hospital, so I return to his house and stay outside. He
doesn't come home that night.

I look for him on Monday and Tuesday, even drive up
to American Flats.

I finally see him outside the place his mom and dad
were thinking of renting for their restaurant. I think he's
trying to find a way to keep her close.

I follow him home Tuesday night and go to him. But
he's become the Moch with dead eyes—no poetry. He
forgets about the mango sunsets and coconut moons, the
flavor of family that oozed from his trailer house and onto
his English paper. He forgets his mom—her memory is a
pile of ashes, burned down by his anger.

◆

Winners start asking for their payoffs. "Sorry about Mrs. Mendez, Mike, but, um, how about that cash?"

Even Nim's pretty low-key about things. He only won a couple of hundred dollars, anyway.

Leonard called on Monday. When I told him I couldn't get up to Reno, he said, "People die, Mike. The game goes on. You've got until Wednesday to pay up. This is your only break."

It's Wednesday.

At school, everything remains the same—as if Mrs. Mendez never existed. I wonder if I'm the only one who can feel the void she left. How can anybody know she's the closest I ever had to what could've been?

If someone dies, and nobody notices, was she ever alive?

Moch hasn't come back to school this week. I kind of need him. I just need to feel like I'm not the only one that hurts like this. I've already done this trip alone—when my mom died.

Remember that time?

Mom went off on a springtime religious retreat and Lillian stuck me in this horrible day camp where we were corralled around all day long by pot-smoking college students who didn't have the money to go on spring break, so they spent their week watching us do crafts and play kickball.

Lillian came to pick me up right after camp and drove me to the A&W on the south end of town. I had a frosty mug of root beer, the icy water sweating and beading on the glass. I looked up at her over the foam. Lillian didn't do grandma stuff like baking cookies and buying sugared cereal. So something was up.

Mid-gulp of my first, and subsequently last, root beer, Lillian said, "Mike, Roe has died."

"Roe." I mouthed the word.

"Your mother."

Mother. Mama. Mami.

Dead.

The root beer congealed in my throat like iced syrup, stopping at the top of my esophagus, cutting off my air supply. I could feel the liquid sliding down into my chest cavity, then settling in the newly opened hole in my stomach like some kind of prehistoric tar pit.

Lillian talked, her burgundy lips surrounded by spires of pucker lines from tsk-tsking for so many years.

She kept talking. "Springtime, melting snow, avalanche season . . . didn't feel anything."

I looked into Lillian's eyes and could see the lie. How could Mom not feel panicked while they suffocated in a rickety bus painted with the words ᴡ s Mʏ r u ᴡ s pᴡ Y *in a rainbow of neon colors to celebrate the Lord?*

I cleared my throat. "And my dad?" I asked.

"Ray Hoyt."

I searched through the catalog of names we had called our Father: Elohim, Jehovah, Shepherd, Yeshua, Emmanuel, Jesus, Christ. Ray Hoyt wasn't on the list.

The name Ray Hoyt stuck in my brain like a tick.

"Where is he?"

"He died. In Korea."

"He was a soldier?" There was hope that my father was a great warrior for a cause. He might not be Yeshua, but maybe . . .

She shook her head. "No. He was an English teacher and suffocated while eating live squid."

Lillian and I sat across from each other, just a couple of feet away, separated by a tall mug of fizzless root beer and what felt like a million miles. The silence weighed down on us, only interrupted by the occasional jingle of bells when customers came in and out.

That night, she lit her candle—praying to her Virgin of Guadalupe.

A little too late.

Lillian reads the day-old papers that cover vandalism and escalating gang violence. Maybe being a day behind isn't such a big deal. She works double time at the clinic, dressing wounds kids say they got in accidents and falls. Same story, different day.

I ask her about Moch. She shakes her head. "He hasn't been in."

"Have you heard about a kid named Luis? Luis Sanchez?" I ask. I finally found out the name of the boy in the field. I just want to know if he's alive.

Lillian shakes her head. "Do you want me to ask around?"

"Can you?"

Lillian nods. "Yes."

I sigh, relieved she doesn't ask why. Time has become this thing we all have to do to survive—like some kind of measurement for endurance. It's Wednesday—a marker that tells me three days have passed even though it feels like an eternity.

Josh and I are sitting on the hood of my car, parked outside the cemetery. He's got a bag of ice on his eye. Moch and some other guys jumped him this afternoon. Josh just took it. He didn't fight back, instead let them pound him until they got bored.

Moch's heart wasn't even in it. Josh would be dead if Moch wanted that. It's unsettling how obvious it is—how Moch has become somebody who kills.

Josh was just anger management. Moch needed to pound the shit out of somebody, and Josh being there was a good start.

"Everything we own, every trip we've ever taken . . .

everything is a lie." Josh brushes some dirt off his designer-brand jeans. "These clothes, my car . . . everything."

I put my fingers to my nose. I can't get the stench of the hospital off me, even though I've washed my hands and face about a thousand times in the past week.

There's an article about the vandalism at Ellison Industries titled "Group Named Babylonia Sought in Ellison Industries Robbery."

It's tucked away on the third page of the newspaper. "No leads," Josh says, and hands me the paper. The words blur. It was all for nothing. His dad's short a few thousand dollars. We're short Mrs. Mendez.

"I have to get to Reno to pay Leonard," I say. My neck hurts, head hurts, back and arms hurt; my throat hurts, ears hurt; it even hurts when I blink.

"Will it always feel this bad?" Josh asks.

"The fist-in-stomach feeling never leaves. Except on those really special occasions."

"Like when?"

"Like . . ." I think about it. "Like with Babylonia. But that's gone now, too."

Josh nods. "Let's go to Reno."

My car sputters to a stop a block from Leonard's offices at Clandestine—a dive bar off East Second Street. I listen to the familiar whine and hack of the engine. "C'mon, Little Car." If there's anyplace on this planet the beast *might* be appealing, it's East Second Street. I tap the dashboard, waiting until the pinging sound stops, hoping that I don't have a hole in my radiator hose . . . again. Little Car coughs to life and we crawl into Leonard's parking lot. I exhale: "Are you coming in or waiting?"

"Waiting."

I walk across the gravelly parking lot and take a deep breath before entering Leonard's lair. In the back room, people play pool. Some guy breaks and the entire room explodes in a chorus of profanity. Another guy is sleeping at the bar, a string of drool hanging from the corner of his mouth to the counter. Women walk around the bar, out of place in their shimmery, barely-there cocktail dresses as if they were mechanical displays at a breast implant conference.

I go up to the bar. "Can you tell Leonard that Mike's here?"

The bartender raises an eyebrow. "A little young, aren't you, kid?"

"Please," I say.

He motions to the left.

I work my way to the back of the bar and tap on Leonard's office door.

"Come in."

I hand Leonard the envelope with the cash.

Leonard drums his fingers on the desk. "Last time I wait for money. Don't fuck with me." He's definitely not a condolence-card kind of guy.

I try to ignore the bruised and split knuckles of the guy standing behind him.

"Thanks, Leonard. Always a pleasure."

"You know why I help you out, Mike?"

Oh geez. Today it even comes with a Godfather speech. I wait, knowing I can't leave until I'm dismissed.

"You've got potential, kid." Leonard flicks ash from his cigarette. "But what the hell are you doing placing bets? What the hell are you doing in this scumball life?"

For a second I see Leonard—a flash of the real Leonard. Some picked-on, effeminate nerd who found a way to survive.

Flash forward—there's me, sitting behind a desk at a smoky bar. And there I am in designer jeans, a too-expensive T-shirt, and my Old Gringos, having my cronies beat the tar out of some guy who doesn't pay me.

Not likely.

I'm going to the University of Washington. *The* U-Dub. Huskies. Seattle-bound. I swallow back the sick feeling I have because it all feels like a dream. My *future*. Like that word means anything anymore.

Outside, Josh is leaning against the car, hands crossed in front of his chest. His eye looks puffy and bluish.

"Everything made sense last week," I say. "But now . . ."

He pulls me to him, tight against his chest, resting his chin on my head.

U-Dub seems a million miles away. I need something to

get me through now—like maybe I can download a map to the future. *Mrs. Mendez dies. Turn right. Walk straight. You should arrive in approximately ten minutes.*

But the only way to tomorrow is surviving today.

Which sucks when tomorrow doesn't look a whole lot better than today—a succession of emptiness, purposelessness.

WANTED: Directions to find tomorrow. Urgent!

25

Recession Affecting Brain Food's Outreach: A Program That Feeds 800 Low-Income Kids in the Community

Administration Still Hasn't Approved *"Hříšná těla, křídla motýlí"* for Prom Song

Babylonia Coincidence Not Likely

SETH'S *PB & J* DEDICATES AN entire page to the symbolism of Babylonia from ancient times through to today. It references the practically invisible article in the *Nevada Appeal*. He discusses a book called *The Richest Man in Babylon* and compares modern-day society to the greed and indulgence of the kingdom of Babylon. "Wealth is equivalent to security. So, wealthy ones, take heed."

In Mrs. B's class, half the kids are ready to tear into Seth. "Why?" he says. "I'm just saying . . ."

"What are you saying?" Mrs. B challenges him. She holds up *PB & J*. The class gasps. "What? You think I don't read it?" She taps her fingers on Seth's desk. "Do you think you get to pump this thing out every week without a little help from the staff?"

We do a collective jaw drop, and I mentally take back every awful thing I ever thought about the pointlessness of homogenized education.

"I don't know," Seth says. "But I feel like there's got to be a connection between the two robberies. And they were really . . . targeted." He blushes when he looks at Josh. "Sorry. It just seems too coincidental to dismiss."

Josh shrugs. "That's cool."

Moch's empty chair glares at me.

"My dad and mom bust their tails to put food on the table so some self-righteous group can steal it?" Trinity seethes. "*And* I'm the one out sixty bucks for ski trip tickets because somebody thought it was *cute* to rip us all off. That's just *wrong.*"

"Well, you guys could've kept a register, you know," Catalina says and rolls her eyes.

"Nobody's stealing from your mom and dad," Seth says. "Are they?" There's a challenge in his voice.

"So, you're all into Babylonia. Babylonia, who screwed a few hundred of us out of the ski trip *we paid for*, and now you're saying it's the same group that stole from Ellison. If they're so freaking amazing, what are they doing with the money?" Trinity asks.

The class erupts into a heated discussion. Mrs. Brooks tells everybody to sit down and settle down. She does it in a tone that makes us all listen.

"There are no easy answers," she says.

"I think Babylonia is wicked sexy," says a pom-pom. I wait for her to fan herself and place the back of her hand on her forehead, swooning to the nearest chair. *Sheesh.*

"Yeah, real sexy stealing from us. Real sexy getting Mrs. Martinez into hot water." Trinity is one head spin away from an exorcism.

"Big deal. A botched ski trip. And now Ellison. It's not like either are missing the money," Tim says. "So what's a few thousand dollars to some guy who drives around a Mercedes-Benz?"

"A Lexus RX400h, actually," Josh says. "Eco conscious. A SULEV—Super Ultra Low Emissions Vehicle. Mercedes doesn't have an eco line. Yet."

The class laughs. It's good the rich boy has a sense of humor about his wealth.

"It's not like there's even a proven connection between the two," Mrs. B interjects. "Except for an article filled with more supposition than facts."

"Okay. No *proven* connection. But what if?" Seth says. "It's a little perverse, but I admire them. We're worried about class rings, prom, graduation shit—um, stuff. Sorry. But they're beyond that."

"Because they're thieves?"

"They're not stealing from just *any* rich," Seth says. "The student council, who"—he looks at Trinity—"organized a pretty *exclusive* ski trip with the entire student body's money, *our* money, to cushion your trip."

"It's not like we're living in a Commie country. I have the right to be rich, as do you," Trinity says.

"It's not anybody's right to take and redistribute. That's total crap," Javier says, joining the conversation. "Stealing is wrong."

I'm surprised he's not on our side.

Seth says, "I just suppose . . . "

"Suppose what?" Mrs. B asks.

Seth shrugs.

"Welcome to the real world of journalism. Hunches are fine. But to be put in print, you've got to have more than a hunch—usually." She winks at him. "Keep that in mind for the next time you *read PB & J.*"

Supposition. Hunches. Right. Wrong. Blurry intentions.

26

AFTER MRS. MENDEZ'S OPEN-coffin rosary Thursday night, Clinica Olé was broken into in the middle of the night, and everything was stolen—medicine, gauze, even the toilet paper. GARBAGE DISPOSAL was painted all over the clinic. The surveillance cameras didn't get a good shot of the looters.

They stole the vaccinations, too.

It's now Friday.

Today we bury Mrs. Mendez and the dreams that died with her.

Don't give up on Moch.

I'm trying not to. Really trying.

A spray of wine-colored roses and green stuff that spires out covers the entire coffin. A few roses, actually. More spray. Lots of filler.

I leave a picture of Moch and me next to her coffin and find my way back to Lillian and Josh. Each time I inhale, I'm breathing in death—that sickly sweet smell of lilies mixed with body odor, fermented perfume, and candle wax. It feels stuffy, closed in. Weirdly hot for February.

People stand, then sit, then kneel, chant, and hum; my pounding heart drowns out the sound of the humming prayers. Josh wraps his hand around my wrist. "Are you okay?"

I shake his hand off and focus on the guy in a polyester suit who's giving a speech in Spanish. I've never seen this man before. I don't know who he is or his relationship to Mrs. Mendez. He didn't know her, I'm sure. He doesn't know about the rattle of mismatched pots and lids; the perfume of cinnamon and chili peppers; the love in her world. *He wears a polyester suit.* He has no poetry.

"Remember her life," Lillian whispers.

Instead of remembering Mrs. Mendez's life, I only see her glued-shut eyes, hands crossed in front of her chest. They even painted her nails.

I look around at the blur of faces. People are shaking hands now, saying "Peace be with you." They comfort each other. More prayers. More kneeling. Then people go forward to eat wafers, drink grape juice.

The mass ends with "I Shall See My God."

Four pallbearers heave the coffin onto their shoulders,

and some greenery shifts and falls off the polished wood when they walk past us. Mocho's wearing black glasses. The other pallbearers include Tío Martín and two other cousins—all but Tío Martín wear la Cordillera armbands. Their cheeks glisten with tears and sweat.

They walk through the heavy church doors, leaving us in silence.

The cars caravan to the cemetery. Lillian drives Josh and me. Kids play in their yards. A homeless man pushing a shopping cart piled high with everything from dingy blankets to shoe boxes stops and removes his hat, placing it over his heart as we pass. Nobody else on the streets seems to notice the funeral procession, or care.

We walk to the gravesite. The fresh earth piled next to the massive hole in the earth.

She was my family! I want to scream into the sky.

"Let us pray." The priest reads the Book of Isaiah, chapter 35: He talks about strength, divine compensation, a holy way only for those who are pure and wise—a place of happiness, void of sorrow and mourning.

He's describing Babylonia.

In the middle of the sermon, Moch rushes toward a man standing on the outskirts of the crowd—the doctor who treated Mrs. Mendez at Urgent Care. Moch pushes him. "The flu. You racist bastard. The fucking flu." The doctor doesn't even block the punches. Moch's hands get heavy, his fists leaden with grief until they drop to his sides. Useless.

Mr. Mendez wraps his arms around Moch, but Moch pushes him away. He points at the doctor, shoving his finger in his face. The doctor's tired, watery gray eyes meeting hate.

The doctor's shoulders slouch. He turns and leaves, making his way to the cemetery entrance, to mourn in his own way. I want to think he didn't dismiss Mrs. Mendez as a typical system abuser because of how she looked, how she dressed, how she talked. Everybody has the flu this week.

Everybody.

Josh's mom and dad stand in the back of the crowd, appropriately dressed, looking just-right sad. Josh's ears burn red and I understand his memoir:

Reconciling parents' sins. Retracing. Backtracking. Sorry.

27

OVER A TASTELESS DINNER,
Lillian brings up Luis. "I found out about your friend Luis.
He's in critical condition at Washoe Med. Up in Reno."
She looks me in the eyes. "He took a brutal beating. I'm
sorry."

I try to swallow down the cardboard pasta slathered
by what Molto Bene tries to pass off as "just like nonna's
chunky garden variety bolognaise sauce" . . . in a jar. Lillian
reaches her hand across the table, but I can't bring myself to
meet her halfway. It just lies there. Empty.

There's nothing to bet on this weekend. There won't
be anything for a couple of weeks. Between Super Bowl
and NCAA basketball games, there's a bettors' lag—like
a kind of black hole of nothingness in sportsbook. Kids at
school don't usually bet on golf, cricket, or horses. It's my

equivalent of a post-Christmas slump. And it sucks. I have too much time to think.

That night Josh calls. "Do you want me to pick you up?"

"No. I don't want to do anything," I say, feeling the ice creep into my body and throat.

"Why not?" Josh asks.

"I just need a break from this stuff. I'm tired. I need to focus, get my head back into classes, AP tests, and all that stuff."

Silence. I rub my temples, lying on my bed, putting the phone on speaker. Tears trickle and pool in my ears.

"So we'll hang out tomorrow," Josh says.

"Josh. The game's over. I can't do this."

"What's *this*?"

"Pretend it's okay. It's not. Nothing we do can makes any of this better. I can't play make-believe like you."

"I wasn't pretending," Josh says. "About anything."

I feel a tightening in my chest that swells and creeps up my throat. I wipe my arm across my eyes and click my phone shut.

A couple of weeks go by. Lagging. Purposeless.

PB & J reports about the toxicity of the *Olé* lunch specials and the probability of the health department shutting the school down. There are some really good articles about our fragmented student body, a Czech cuisine recipe section, and a series that compares University of Nevada's flailing basketball program with a woman going through rehab in *The Real Housewives of Washoe County*.

The freshmen stage a sit-in—parallel rows of kids singing "The Rivers of Babylon"—demanding the Coke machine get put back. We were something—*meant* something. They totally missed the point.

Babylonia is a distorted memory.

Moch comes to school, off and on. I always bring his homework to his home, leaving it on the porch. The house feels empty—lifeless.

One night, I find Mr. Mendez eating a chicken pot pie. It looks so out of place on his plate. The smells I so loved before are almost gone. Microwaved cardboard has replaced eye-burning chili powder, shredded beef, and the sweet smell of crushed corn to make tortillas.

"Mr. Mendez, what about the restaurant?" I ask. He was going to be head chef. Mrs. Mendez always said she would be his assistant. "You can still do that. For Mrs. Mendez."

Mr. Mendez shakes his head. I don't think, though, it's about the money anymore. It's like Mrs. Mendez was the only thing keeping the family together.

At school I avoid Josh. Thinking about him makes me anxious and lonely and angry and tired. I try to nudge the memories aside, to go back to the way things were; the way things should be. I twirl the silver dice on my bracelet, glad it's cold so I can hide it under the sleeves of my sweaters. I wear it every day.

Seth comes up to me one day and says, "Hey, Mike. What's up with you and Josh? He's the poster boy for dejection these days."

I shrug. "Nothing's up. Or ever was. We're friends. It's just I got behind on homework and stuff and need to keep focused on what's important." But I'm not sure what's important anymore. It should be U-Dub. Getting out of here. Never looking back. It's just hard to make sense out of anything.

Seth reads through my lies and nods. "Give the guy a call sometime, okay?"

It's dark. Lillian's at the clinic. I've done my homework, cleaned the house twice, and constructed a teepee in my room by hanging a blanket from a hook in my ceiling and attaching it to my bed posts with rubber bands.

I think I'm going crazy.

My phone beeps—my social phone. Josh's name flashes on the screen. I turn it off. Nobody else calls me on it anyway.

Then I hear tapping on my window. "I know you're in there!"

If I'm quiet, he'll think I'm asleep. I hold my breath. Then exhale. *Just breathe.* It's not like he can hear breathing through walls. My bookie phone rings—the ring tone about as subtle as our school fire drill. He bangs harder on the window. "Get up! Get dressed! Now!"

The banging has moved to the front door and I weigh my options. If I ignore him, I'm pretty sure he'll pound on the door all night. If he keeps it up, someone will call the police. The police means Lillian means explanations means . . . *What does he want?* "Fine," I mutter and go to the living room, opening the door a crack. "What do—"

Josh shoves the door open and pushes his way into the trailer house. "Get your coat on. Now."

He shoves my coat at me, grabs my hand, pulling me out of the house, pushing me into his car. "Josh," I say.

He holds up his hand. "Just . . . just pay attention." He doesn't put on any music. We drive in silence to Stewart Street to a burned-down homeless shelter, the ground scarred and blackened. He drives a little farther north until we're in a field near the softball fields. "I followed a couple of guys from La Clinica Olé one afternoon. They work construction." The makeshift homes are much like the ones I saw at the river. Soggy cardboard boxes sag at the top, plastic grocery sacks doing little to keep anybody dry. There's a small group: three men, two women, four kids, tucked in what little shelter the barren lot offers, their homes in a semicircle under the limbs of a giant elm tree.

We drive to a trailer park, so worn down and poor it makes Lillian's and my home look like the Ritz. Trailers totter on concrete blocks, aluminum siding bowing from the number of people who live in each place. I can't help but picture God with a giant can opener, pulling back on an aluminum ring, peeling open each home. I know some kids who live around here. I'd just never really paid attention.

Josh pulls into an abandoned gas station off Highway 50. "This place here, this is where the workers wait. They get here before six a.m. and wait for a day's work. Some stay all day—until four thirty, five. Too late for anything, but they stay until the day ends because leaving early would be like giving up, going home empty-handed."

I remember the days Mocho's dad had to do that, the days Mocho would eat dinner at our house. Lillian insisted on stuffing him until his stomach swelled, a funny sight next to his washboard ribcage.

We drive to back alleys and motels—like we're discovering an entire new world within the limits of the city, a world I've never seen. A world of scattered lives, piecemeal dreams. Josh hands me a list of organizations including FISH (Friends in Service Helping), Brain Food, Clinica Olé, the Boys and Girls Club, Planned Parenthood. The names blur on the page.

"You don't get to do this," Josh says, his voice steady, hushed. "You don't get to go back to your safe place and leave me here. Alone."

Tears burn my eyes and I blink them back. I bite down on my lower lip. "What does this matter?" I pass the list to him.

"You act as if sadness is a privilege. Just for you and

you alone. *Everything* matters. *They* matter. *We* matter. Babylonia."

We. Babylonia.

"Mrs. Mendez mattered," Josh whispers. I hate that he says it past tense. Josh turns my face to his and cups it in his hands. "Were you pretending?"

I can't catch my breath. I shake my head. He leans forward, lips touching my forehead, soft like raindrops. He tilts my head up, outlining my mouth with his thumb, never taking his eyes from mine.

I swallow. It's like my saliva ducts have totally turned off, and if what's going to happen is what I think is going to happen, my tongue has gone the way of the Sahara and feels like sandpaper. I swallow again.

He leans forward, pulling me toward him, and I feel his lips brushing mine, then pressing harder, sending a seismic jolt through my body. My teeth clack against his; I taste copper.

I jerk away, somehow managing to knock his nose with my forehead. "Oh. Oh crap. Crap. I bit you. Oh hell. And broke your nose. Did I break your nose?"

Josh holds his face in his hands, leaning back against the seat. A smudge of blood on the palm of his hand. He shakes his head. "No," he says, in a stuffy voice, like Beaker from the Muppets. "I'm just fine. Really. I'm fine. Just give me a sec, okay?"

God hasn't been particularly proactive in my life, so I'm

hoping this one time, *just this once*, he might answer my prayer to be struck by a bolt of lightning. I wait.

Nope. Still here.

My face burns with shame. My hands feel like hot fields of sticky tar. The butterfly dance in my stomach has turned into a solid knot. Tears brim in my eyes because *I blew my first kiss.* As soon as I can control my voice without totally going blubbery and stupid, I say, "Do you think we need to go to the ER?"

Josh's shoulders shake with laughter, which only makes me feel like more of a freak show. It looks *way* easier on TV and in the movies. "Can you hand me a Kleenex?" He waves to the glove compartment. "I'm sorry. I'm not laughing *at* you. It's just . . ."

I pull out the box and hand them to him. He shoves a clump against his nose. His lip is already swelling. "I'm sorry," I say. "I'm so so sorry. I'm just—"

He has one hand shoving piles of Kleenex against his nose. He puts the forefinger of his free hand against my lips. It's like he *wants* me to implode, frazzle all my nerve endings paperback-romance style. He cracks a lopsided smile. "Wow," he says.

"Wow," I echo, and force myself to smile, which turns into a real smile, then a chortle to full-on snorting laughter. Tears fall. It feels good to laugh and cry and *feel* something other than anger and hopelessness. Even if it is biblical embarrassment.

"I missed you," Josh says. He winks at me. "Maybe we'll have to try that again sometime." He taps his lip. "When the swelling goes down."

I shake my head. "That's okay. It was just one of those silly, heat-of-the-moment things. We're good."

"Heat of the moment?"

"More like beginner's bad luck. I guess."

I notice for the very first time he has a faint dimple on his left cheek—almost imperceptible. I really shouldn't be noticing things like that. It's just too distracting. "Babylonia," I say, looking at the list. "Any ideas on how we can create a more equitable distribution of funds? We're going to need a lot more than an airplane banner and ten Commandments."

"I have a few," Josh says, wincing when he moves his hand away from his nose, which is swelling as well. Josh squeezes my hand. "Can we go back to your place? Hang out for a while?"

"Lillian's at the clinic all night. We've got ice."

"Ice is good."

"Ice is good."

Josh drives me home and we go into my room. He doesn't even think it's weird that I have a teepee hanging from the ceiling. We lie down together in the teepee, his leg linked with mine. I pull my patchwork quilt over us and plug in my iPod, and we listen to Stevie Ray Vaughan's "The Sky Is Crying."

The sky's crying. Blanketed in sadness.

28

I LOOK AT THE TIME. SIX THIRTY-TWO.
My teepee smells like dryer sheets and pine. Like Josh. My
iPod is still playing. I don't remember falling asleep and
don't want to move. I wish I could be here, in this spot, forever. Josh's arm is draped over me, his long fingers resting
on my hip. He's lying on his side, and my head is resting in
the crook of his other arm. Outside the light is violet. No
sign of day.

I stare at the clock until it turns to 6:33. Okay. Time
didn't stop. Josh has to get out of here, because if Lillian were
to catch us like this, she'd make us sit through her eight-hour
sex-ed video series followed up by thorough examinations,
obligatory oral contraception prescriptions, and a shower of
condoms. She's always ranting about the fact that schools
dedicate only one semester to sex ed. It doesn't help to point

out that most of us graduate without even knowing how to balance a checkbook. I look at the time again.

Just one more minute.

6:34.

Okay. Two.

6:35.

The furnace clicks on. I exhale. "Hey. Josh. You have to go. Lillian will be here soon."

Josh mumbles. His lip is a purple-bluish color, but at least the swelling on his nose has gone down.

I'm not really sure how to move now, how to wake him up. I finally decide to tap him on the shoulder. Tap. Tap. Semipoke. "Hey. Josh. You really have to go. Really."

"Five more minutes," he mumbles.

"NOW," I say, slipping out from under his arm into the cold morning air.

He groans, pulling himself up to a sitting position, shoving his feet into his shoes. He shrugs on his coat, practically sleepwalking to the door. His hair sticks out all over the place, unruly curls flopping into his eyes. I follow him out onto the porch and flick on the dim yellow light. The quilt hangs over my shoulders. I dance on the aluminum floor in thin socks, wishing I'd pulled on a pair of boots. White puffs of breath hang in the air. I shiver and squint at the thermometer but can't see the numbers too well without my glasses.

Josh rubs his eyes. We stand under the faded light. I keep expecting Lillian's car to come up the drive. Josh leans down and kisses me on the cheek, leaving a burning imprint there. He crunches across frosted blades of grass to his car. He looks back at me over his shoulder when he gets to it, pulling the collar of his black coat high around his neck. I can't tell where he ends and the car begins—just shapeless shadows.

I go inside, the screen door clicking behind me, and stand there until the first rays of sunlight drip into the yard, melting away Josh's footprints in the frost.

Carson Tahoe Hospital Reports Rising Incidence of Injuries Caused by Violence

Carson Athletes to Keep Your Eye On This Spring

"Hříšná těla, křídla motýlí": What Does This Mean?

Seth's editorial is titled: "Remember Babylonia? Yeah. Me Neither." He investigates the one-hit-wonder phenomenon, comparing Babylonia's splash to musical groups like a-ha and Dexy's Midnight Runners.

My head is too busy to pay attention to class. Teachers are prepping us for advanced-placement tests this spring. *Let the monotony begin.* Josh has sent me a thousand text messages, back to his overdrive pace after he probably drank a gallon of espresso. It's an A-block day. No classes with him or Moch or Mrs. Brooks.

After school, Josh texts me: Breakfast for dinner? 6:00? IHOP?

OK.

He's waiting for me in the entry, dressed in gray pin-striped pants, a green sweater that looks like it was made to match his eyes, and a soft black leather jacket. "Hey," he says. "I'm starving."

"You look—"

"Like I'm on my way to Sunday school. My mom's governor's mansion tea-party deal."

"No. Good." I'm the female version of Tarzan grunting at Josh. *Me Michal. You Josh. Good.* "Like, really," I say, then blush. I feel frumpy in my jeans, boots, and faded T-shirt, and make an extra effort to stand straight.

"Hey. That's the first time you've ever complimented me. Thanks." His face lights up, and he smiles a crooked smile, absentmindedly rubbing his bruised lip.

We follow the waitress to a booth that faces Carson Street. She places a pot of coffee on the table, filling our thick cups first, and takes our order. I watch the stream of cars headed south. The headlights blur together like a glowing string of yellow yarn. "So," I say, tearing my eyes from the street, turning to Josh. "Do you know where to start?"

Josh has written a name on a piece of paper and passes it to me. I nod. It's not a big surprise.

"Are you ready for this?" Josh asks. "Because there's no going back."

I think about Mrs. Mendez and the communities of people who are treated like trash. I think about Garbage Disposal and la Cordillera and how they only hurt and steal and kill. No purpose. No poetry.

"Yes," I say.

"What else do we need? What are we missing?" Josh asks.

"To leave no doubt. So that people won't wonder why they were targeted. They have to *know*." I push gummy pieces of waffle around my plate, then settle on drinking the coffee.

Josh talks about his family, his clothes, the trips they've taken. "Look at this," he says pointing to his shoes. "Look at all of this."

"It's not like you have to feel guilty because you have stuff. That's not a crime."

"How I got it, though, is."

I take out the manifesto I wrote the night before. It's short. Simple. It leaves no room for interpretation.

People ask what is the nature of the struggle—who are Babylonia's targets and why?

The migrant family is an invisible force. Invisibility has kept them marginalized, living in subhuman conditions. Your employees cannot afford food, shelter, or health—basic human rights. The systematic denial of said rights creates a culture of racism, classism, and fear. It creates a culture of violence and shame, oppression and elitism. The masses remain silent.

We will not be silent. Babylonia is their voice, their movement.

Congratulations and welcome to the twenty-first century. Your enlightened stance on modern-day slavery has made you target number one.

Josh reads it. "This is good." He takes the last syrupy bite of his pancakes, shoving his plate away.

I laugh. Nervous. Forced. "Are we really doing this?" I'm getting that same feeling—like when we broke into Mrs. Martinez's office and Ellison Industries; when we bet on Cuccaro running an insane number of yards; when Josh was going to kiss me. My chest tightens, tummy flutters, the prickly inside feeling like every nerve ending is on fire.

"We'll do all the jobs when the people are gone. People have routines. We just need to know the routines and get in and out—twenty minutes. Easy."

"And if one of us wants to back out—for whatever reason—we back out. No questions asked."

"No questions asked. Whaddya say, Bonnie?" Josh says in the cheesiest Texas accent possible. We're sitting across from each other in the cramped booth, knees brushing. His hand rests on my arm.

All feeling in my body has washed away except for where our knees touch and Josh's hand rests on my arm.

Every cheesy love song crashes through my mind.

"Well? Bonnie?"

I snap back to reality. "You do realize B and C were ambushed in their hideout and shot to death by cops from Texas and Louisiana. Super romantic." I blush. "I didn't mean romantic. Ah, hell."

Josh kisses the inside of my wrist. *Melting melting melting.* "Ready to embark on a life of crime?"

"Haven't we already?"

A step ahead of dragon's fire.

We pay the bill and drive to the house, our first target. We park down the street. Josh has done his homework. He describes the family's routines, the doggie door, the access from the garage to the main house. The house is at the end of a cul-de-sac. It feels trapped in. No escape. I count two sliding-door entrances on the ground floor, another sliding door on the balcony on the second floor. The windows next to the balcony have shades drawn.

Josh drops me off just before midnight. "Tomorrow morning? She leaves for work a quarter to seven. We'd have twenty minutes to get in and out and to school on time."

Tomorrow morning.

Josh tucks my hair behind my ear. I turn to him. "Tomorrow morning. Okay."

We both look at my house. There's a light on in the living room—like a little yellow square has been pasted on our blackened neighborhood. "Will you get in trouble?"

he asks. "For being so late?"

I shake my head. "To get in trouble, you have to matter," I say.

Josh brushes my cheek with the backs of his fingers. He plays with the silver dice on my bracelet. "I can't wait until you can see you with my eyes."

I blush, the warmth filling me, relieved that with Josh I don't feel like a leftover. I feel like now is everything, like I'm ready to toss the dice to determine my fate. Not worried about the odds.

I clear my throat. "See you in the morning."

Holding infinity impossible. It slips away.

29

IT'S 6:45. I PARK A FEW BLOCKS away. Josh meets me at the corner, and now we're here.

My glasses fog. I take them off, wipe them, put them back on. The rumble of the garage door jerks me back to the moment. I fumble with my glasses, push them on. Maybe I should get contact lenses.

Josh and I pull on the masks. "Babylonia," he whispers. "Babylonia."

When the car reaches the bottom of the curved driveway, we roll under the door just before it's about to close. The door stops midway down, hovers, then begins to go up. Josh quickly pushes a trash-can lid in the way, and we rush to the back of the garage behind a pile of bicycles and ski equipment, crouching under a heavy wooden table with a buzz saw on top.

The car returns. I listen to the click of heels. She mutters to herself, rolls the lid inside, standing for a moment before pushing a code and shutting the door all the way. We go into the house. Josh is ready with a box of dog treats. The professionally groomed shih tzu attack dog comes running at us, its piercing bark enough to shatter glass, tiny claws pattering across stone floors, long hair like a boutique mop. "Hello, Bijoux," Josh whispers. He holds out a handful of gourmet dog biscuits. Bijoux's tail goes into overtime happy mode and forgets we're not supposed to be there. We work our way through the rooms, the first light of day seeping in the windows. My black outfit feels too black in the purple predawn light.

There's better nighttime thief attire.

But at night, people are at home. During the day, people work.

Our rules: No one gets hurt. No one gets caught.

I'm pretty sure we can handle the first one. The second one, however, is the one that kept me awake all night.

Josh points to his watch, holds up ten fingers, then five.

Fifteen minutes before the maid arrives. Fifteen minutes.

Josh leads the way to the office. Every footstep we take sounds thunderous. Even my breathing feels loud, invasive. The house is creepy quiet. Lifeless. Just as I'm sure I've registered all the sounds, I notice the soft sound of music coming from a room down the hall. I point to my ear and shrug.

Josh nods.

We creep down the hallway, following the sounds of music until we're outside the room that has the music. I press my ear to the door, listening for anything other than the sound of music when I hear a click and a soft moan. The music is turned off.

"Snooze alarm," I mouth. "Who?" I point to the door.

Josh shakes his head and I follow him down the hall, back into the study. "Let's move. Fast." He pulls out a key from the desk drawer and motions to the closet. I close the office door with a soft click and sit against it, ear pressed to the door.

But all I can hear is the thrumming of my blood pumping through my body—a crashlike sounding in my ears. *Just calm down.*

Josh finds the safe.

No keyhole.

He stares at the key, squinting. He shrugs, takes out his backpack, and says, "Stand back." He lights his blowtorch and melts the safe around the lock, popping the melted piece of metal inside the safe. It makes a heavy *thud-clang* sound.

He turns off the blowtorch. We listen to the house, the sound of metal cooling, Bijoux's paws scratching at the door. Stupid dog.

I wait for someone to come running down the hallway. It's silent.

The house doesn't even breathe.

"A blowtorch?" I ask.

"I read it on eHow."

"Where'd you *get* it?"

"The school shop. From Auto Body class."

I stare at him and shake my head. "Unbelievable."

Josh opens the cooled-down metal door. "What are the odds?" Josh asks, pulling out a wad of cash. He leaves the jewelry.

"What are the odds?" I echo. I could probably tell him, given the time to work them out, but I don't work them out because of the niggling feeling everything we're doing is like shooting for a Hail Mary.

We take all of it—almost four thousand dollars.

He shoves the money into his pocket. We listen at the door before opening it. We creep down the hallway. I stand behind a door and keep watch while Josh spray-paints BABYLONIA in big letters on the back of the door, underneath AND HER NAME MOTHER OF EXILES.

We tape the manifesto to the door.

Josh looks at his watch and holds up three fingers. "We're fast. We're good."

We are.

We find Bijoux's doggie door. Josh points to it. "You first," he says.

I stare at the door, mentally measure my hips and butt, and shake my head. Josh's escape plan didn't factor in the size of my ass.

He nods toward the door and holds up his watch.

All I can do is picture the police showing up with me half in, half out. I can just imagine the calls across their radios, the stifled laughs, the *"remember that time?"* If I'm going to get caught, it'll be with a little dignity.

Josh squeezes my arm. "Go," he urges.

The muffled sound of clock-radio music reaches us through the door. I stare at the doggie door, shrug, and open the back door, stepping outside. I listen for the blare of sirens, some obnoxious house alarm. Nothing.

Josh pushes me forward, turns the lock from the inside, and pulls the door shut, the pitter-patter of Bijoux's claws close behind us.

We work our way to the side of the house, peel off our masks and the black clothes that cover our school clothes. I undo the plastic bags that I've tied around my feet, stuff my clothes into the bags, and remove everything but my gloves. Josh does the same. He holds his hand up, jumps the fence, and stands on the other side. "Clear," he whispers.

I toss our bags over, take a quick look around to make sure we don't leave anything behind, and scramble over the fence.

We take off the surgical gloves and shove them into the bags, too, working our way to the sidewalk toward our cars. The neighborhood is waking up: People are jogging; a man drinks coffee on the porch in his bathrobe, holding the newspaper in his hands.

They're going to know. They'll know we were there.

I feel like my fear will bubble up and spill out, like I'll be the missing piece when the police question witnesses, canvass the area, the blotch on their custom-designed American perfection.

Nobody sees us.

We're invisible.

My entire body tingles on a total epi high, like I've taken a bottle of adrenergics. This is walking on water, the calming of the sea, the blind man healed.

This. Is. Power.

"Hallelujah," I mutter.

Josh winks at me, his hair curling at the back from sweat, cheeks flushed. He feels the thrill, too. "Amen," he says, and pats the money he's shoved into his pocket.

We walk to our separate cars and drive to school, making it just in time for first bell. Kids are hollering, laughing, fighting. Some girl's crying. Two guys from band are playing "My Wish" by Rascal Flatts on their clarinets, passing around a baseball hat to collect some cash. I put in a dollar.

Everything sounds muffled. It's hard to hear anything over the boom of my heart. I wonder if I'll go blind and deaf from the adrenaline.

Josh catches up to me in the hallway, on the way to Mrs. B's. "Good morning," he says, handing me an ice-cold Starbucks latte. "Drink it," he says, "as if it's the hottest, freshest coffee you've ever tasted."

I nod, taking a sip of the bitter sludge and choke down a few sips. I suck on a mint because there's no way I'll make it through the morning without some kind of intestinal rebellion. My whole body is on overdrive.

Then I see Moch—walking down the hall—sunglasses hardly disguising a bruised face and swollen cheek. It's like watching a digital picture—the dots of color of who he is form on my retina. He's wearing a crooked smile, one I know doesn't reach his eyes.

I search for his chain, relieved to see the saint hanging from it.

"Moch!" I wave.

He brushes by me. The morning high is gone. All I feel is her absence.

I swallow back the anxiety and hold my cup up to Josh. "Babylonia," I say, trying to hold on to the buzz from the morning, trying to make my life mean something.

"Babylonia."

The tardy bell rings just as we slip in the door. Mrs. Brooks gives Moch one of those oh-so-sorry smiles. And the day proceeds as normal.

Time stops only for the dead.

30

Babylonia Manifesto Leaves No Room for Interpretation

NCAA Finals Around the Corner: Who Are You "Betting" On?

Czech Line Dancing: The New Craze at Carson High

Sanctuary 7:15 courtyard

"I'VE MISSED SANCTUARY, Mike," Javier says, shoulder bumping me. "What's to bet on this week?"

A few more come in. Curiosity, mostly. By the time it's seven fifteen, there are about ten bettors. Small crowd. But reliable. I've missed them. This is my comfort zone, what I know.

"This is unprecedented, gentlemen. Well, unprecedented, no. It's only happened three times since 1955, and none have been repeat offenders. The Tech is just one game away from having its second winless season. Let's keep it basic. It's just for fun."

"Fun with money, though," Javier says.

"Always with money," I say.

"Aren't you forgetting something?" Justin flashes *The Gambler.*

It's the routine, the way things have to be. I randomly open a page and read:

> *I find myself taking no thought for the future, but living under the influence of passing moods, and of my recollections of the tempest which recently drew me into its vortex, and then cast me out again.*

The words settle in. The guys laugh. I feel better, like I'm in control after taking the bets, writing them down in my notebook. The day feels *normal.*

I stop by Moch's after school. Just to be there, to try to keep some of Mrs. Mendez with me. *Babylonia is for her. For them.*

The house feels different, shabby. It looks like the house Moch is used to seeing—rundown. Ugly.

Lifeless.

My phone beeps.

Josh: Homework. Your place.

I look at the time. It's almost three thirty. I text Josh back: 4:00.

I sit on the porch, crooked aluminum steps. Winter slush has melted and now there's a patchwork of ugly brown clumps. I close my eyes and try to find that place where things were easier. My phone beeps again.

Josh: @?

I look at my watch. 4:10. Oops.

Me: 10 minutes. Sorry.

Josh never asks where I go. Never wants me to explain why there are days I just don't want to talk. After Mrs. Mendez's funeral, Lillian went into Clinica Olé overdrive. She's brought out the Virgen de Guadalupe, lighting the candle in the mornings, mumbling a quiet prayer in Spanish. I wish she'd talk to me instead of a statue. The only thing she says to me lately is "Let go, let God."

God hasn't really stepped up to the plate in my life, so I think I'll just do my own batting from now on.

When I get home, Josh is waiting with a pizza in hand. "Thanks," I say.

"You're welcome."

"Did you make the deposit?" I ask.

"Yesterday." He shows me the slip. A twenty-eight-hundred-dollar donation right into the account of Clinica Olé. It was easy to get the account information from Lillian's desk. I don't know what that will buy the clinic, but it's something.

Lillian won't be home this afternoon, so we go into my room and shut the door. I'm supposed to whittle back the twenty-six amendments to ten for Government. "Did you know that involuntary servitude is unconstitutional?"

"Define involuntary," Josh says.

I shrug.

Josh lays his head in my lap. "Hey," he says.

"We're supposed to be doing homework," I say.

"I didn't mean *school* homework. I meant Babylonia homework." He pulls out a list of names from his pocket and hands it to me. "Did you do yours?"

I nod and hand him my list.

Josh points to one of the names on my list. "No way. It's like proving the existence of, I dunno, a Ziz . . . unreal."

"Ziz?" I ask.

"Some biblical creature."

Josh is always surprising me. "You've read the Bible?"

"I am a product of Saint Luke's Christian Academy, Saint Theresa's, Saint Michael's, Saint Sebastian's, ending with Saint Barnaby's. After fourteen years of mind-numbing martyrdom and intellectual flogging, my parents decided it was best to unleash me on public schools; three years, five schools later, here I am."

I stare at him. "Wow."

"You?"

"Seven years of being immersed in the way of the Bible and its teachings sometimes creeps into my psyche. I lived with a church group in Nevada City until . . . until I moved in with Lillian."

"What happened to your mom?"

"Oh," I say. I forget that he's not part of my entire

history in Carson City—that it's possible *somebody* doesn't know my mom was a religious freak teenager who was buried in an avalanche in Great Basin National Park on a religious retreat. Even though it feels like I've known him forever, I realize he doesn't know me at all.

And that's okay. Because nothing from yesterday has defined how he sees me today—like when he started new at Carson High School, I got a chance to start fresh, too.

I could tell him *anything*. Mom could be *anyone*. But I just want her to be here. Alive. A mom. "She died when I was little. So I've lived with Lillian since I was eight."

"Sorry." This is when most people would stop talking and we'd slip into awkward silence mode. But Josh is like one of those windup toys that chatter until their cord runs out.

"What about your dad?"

"Dead."

"Geez. You're like a Disney movie."

"Without the wardrobe and fairy godmother." I poke him. "Are you a fairy godmother?"

He laughs. When he does, it's hard not to smile, like he has a way of making everything feel okay. "I'm sorry. I don't mean to laugh about it. That's rotten."

"It is what it is," I say. "It was a long time ago."

"So do you miss them? Your parents?"

Every day. Missing never ends. "I never knew my dad. And my mom—it was a long time ago. It's okay," I finally say.

"And Mrs. Mendez?" Josh says, looking away.

"She was as close as I've had."

Josh nods. "So"—he points to the Ziz name—"are you sure?"

I nod. "Positive."

"Sources?"

"If you haven't noticed, I've grown up with a lot of these guys. I know I'm right. What about yours?"

His list is short. It has two names on it. Big ones. Like mega-ultra-big ones. "Her?" I point to the name. "I mean, she's like eighty, right?"

"I've got my sources, too. And pretty close to home."

I swallow. "Yeah."

"You ready for the next one?"

"We need to be more prepared," I say.

"As in?"

"No more shih tzu doggie doors, for instance."

He cracks up.

"Yeah. Real funny."

"I've been studying. Watching—" Josh clears his throat. "*Crmnl mds*," Josh mumbles.

"Who?"

"*Criminal Minds.*"

"As in the TV show?"

He nods.

"So basically you're doing our home-invasion tactical research based on eHow and a TV show?"

"Well, I kind of figure they have more researchers

working on it. I've watched all the seasons to date. It's like a blueprint on how to commit a perfect crime."

"Apparently you've missed the end, when *they catch the bad guys*. Or didn't you pay attention to that part of each show?"

"But we're *not* bad guys."

"So there'll be some kind of karmic *CSI* slipup because, hey, we've got a purpose? We're doing this to benefit the community, to make death mean something, to get back at the bullies?"

"Do you have any better ideas?" Josh's cheeks get flushed when he talks about this. I get it. He thinks his dad killed Mrs. Mendez.

I scan the *Nevada Appeal* Josh brought over.

Has Carson City Become the Land of Vigilante Justice?
Anonymous Donation to Clinica Olé Covers Costs of Lost Vaccinations

"Hey. That's nice." I point to the Clinica Olé article and skim the rest of the paper. "Do you think somebody saw us?" I show it to Josh.

"We've done three robberies and used Babylonia each time, right? How come the *Nevada Appeal* doesn't write about the manifesto?" Josh asks, raising his eyebrow.

I shrug. "I dunno."

Josh smiles. "Think about it. Because the people know *why* they were robbed, those aristocratic assholes. They *know*. They're not going to report all the details. It's the perfect crime, Michal."

"How so?"

"They're cleaning up *after* us. But how did Seth know we left a manifesto?" He taps *PB & J*.

"I, um, sent it to him."

"You sent it to him?"

I nod.

"Don't you think we should talk about this stuff?" Josh asks.

"I know. I just got all excited about it when I couldn't sleep at three in the morning or something and wanted to make sure *somebody* read it, so that there wouldn't be any doubt."

"We can't stop now." Josh taps the list. "All these people are total hypocrites. This guy"—Josh points to our next target—"is easy. He does work for half the homes around here—cash jobs. He's the type to have his cash strewn all over the house before his Friday payday."

"And if there's no cash all over the house?"

"There's always gonna be cash—something worth our time." He pulls himself up from my lap and faces me. "Look at what we're doing. We're becoming something big. Magnificent."

I feel blood rushing through my veins, feeling the prickle

of immortality. Forever. It scares me because what comes after is emptiness and doubt. "I need to work out the odds. It's what I do. I need to know that we won't get caught."

"The payoff is worth the risk," Josh says. "Calculated risks. Like placing bets. We've studied the targets. We won't lose."

How can anybody be so sure?

31

I COULDN'T WAIT FOR TODAY, and now my hands feel sticky-hot in the surgical gloves. We crouch around the corner of the house and listen to round seven.

"I'm not going to go. Like, why should I go to some stuffy, horrible cocktail party with you?" The daughter's voice is screechy, whiny.

"I'm not going to say it again. *Get in the car!*"

"I *hate* you!"

The front door swings open and slams shut. I count four bodies going to the car, one sobbing. I hold up four fingers. Josh nods and we push ourselves against the cool brick of the house. I keep telling myself we're invisible. Nobody can see us.

The car pulls out of the driveway, its red brake lights

blinking at the end of the street.

"Okay," I mouth.

Josh nods and throws the raw steak over the fence. We listen for the dog, a deep growl lodged in its throat until it sees the meat. He downs the meat, whimpers a little, then is silent. We peek over the fence. The dog's tongue lolls out the side of his mouth.

"You didn't kill it, did you?" Josh asks.

I shake my head. "I hope not. Benadryl. Half a bottle."

We climb into the yard. This place is a dump, a breeding ground for crabgrass and tumbleweeds on steroids. I stop and stand over the dog for a second, just to watch his chest move up and down, up and down. "He's alive," I say.

"Half a bottle? A little heavy-handed."

"How am I supposed to know?"

The kitchen window above the sink, like always, is open. Josh punches open the screen and climbs in. I grab his hand, and he yanks me in; the sill wedges in my gut. I muffle a moan.

We replace the screen—a small tear in the corner the only trace of how we got in.

We search through desk drawers, kitchen drawers, cabinets, and closets. We creep upstairs. I tap my watch and hold up ten fingers.

Josh shakes his head. Fifteen.

"Hurry," I say.

I look in every single drawer upstairs. Josh goes for the closets. I join him, holding shoes upside down, looking for money, sweeping away at some cobwebs in the very back corner of the master closet.

"Good idea," Josh says, rummaging around the piles of shoes on the bottom of the closet floor. "Payday." Josh holds up a wad of bills that were shoved into the toe of the rankest-smelling cowboy boots I've ever encountered.

A door downstairs closes so hard the windows rattle. A girl is yelling, "I told you I didn't want to go! I'm not *ever* coming out of my room."

We listen as she runs upstairs, slamming her bedroom door, cranking up music on her stereo. Prepubescent teens with overgelled hair fill the air singing "Vampire Kiss and Tell." Doesn't anybody listen to Johnny Cash anymore?

I think I hear a car drive away.

My back is pressed against the closet wall behind a sea of flannel shirts. Over the music, the only thing I can hear is the thrum of my heart. My rib cage feels like it's pushing against my heart, squeezing it between pulses and throbs. We pull our masks on over our faces.

We're going to get caught.

They'll call in snipers and SWAT and shoot us down because of some adolescent kid and a tantrum.

I try to sift through my thoughts—other than the ones of my impending incarceration—to get hold of the situation. What's the best way to work the odds to get out of this mess that doesn't include taking a hostage and getting on Interpol?

Run like bloody hell.

Note to self: work out.

Sweat stings my eyes. I wipe my brow and blow upward, trying to de-steam. Josh puts his finger to his lips and peeks his head out. Light spills from under her bedroom door. The rest of the house is dark, except for a dim light coming from downstairs. Josh points to his eyes and points downstairs.

Stay in your room. Stay in your room. Stay in your room.

No one else is home.

Josh spray-paints BABYLONIA on the wall. I tape the manifesto on the door.

I listen for the girl upstairs, trying to detect any movement, but can only hear the refrain "Vampire kiss and forever love, bite and oooo-oooo." The music is muted behind closed doors, then floods the entire house in a screechy, high-pitched frenzy. I realize she's opened her door.

I hear the creak of hinges and hiccupy sob-talk. "She's ju-ju-just a giant premenstrual u-u-u-unit. And he's a swollen pros-sta-a-ate with a ne-ne-necktie." *Hiccup.*

I grab Josh's hand and tug at it. We rush from the house to the garage. There's a tiny broken window above the tool bench.

Does Josh have absolutely no dimensional perspective?

I point to my ass, then the window, and throw my hands in the air.

Josh shakes his head, nodding toward the door.

"Oh."

"After you," he mouths, and we step into the night. We close the door behind us, making sure it's locked just as we hear the screaming.

Hiding their shame. Our greatest ally.

32

Sanctuary 6:30 Schat's

                              I CHECK MY COMPUTER.
Nice. Text sent. Same with preprogrammed tweets.

Alibi in place.

I'm seventeen years old and worried about having a solid alibi. Breaking curfew doesn't seem like a big deal anymore.

There's something powerful about being the person nobody expects me to be. Most Likely to Stage a Heist isn't a yearbook category. Should be. Though I'd never qualify. And it makes me wonder if everybody's just a shell hiding the real deal. If that's the case, maybe Nim has a shot at becoming a decent human being one day.

Maybe Moch, too.

Lillian left me a note: *At clinic. Dinner in fridge.*

I can't stomach the cementlike mac 'n' cheese. I want

to go to Moch's house and eat an enchilada, a tamale—
something with color and flavor. But seeing a frozen dinner
at Moch's house again would depress me too much. I eat
an apple and lie in bed, listening to the *drip drip drip* of
the bathroom faucet. I finally put the margarine tub in the
sink. The sound is different—less *pingy*. Familiar. At first
the water *splats* against the plastic, but then as the tub fills,
the sound becomes muted and soft.

I replay everything about the past night—the sounds
and smells, reliving the feeling, a sense of euphoria, like my
brain is screaming. Like I'm really alive.

I look at the time.

Three o'clock.

I download "Vampire Kiss and Tell" from iTunes.

I think I'm going crazy.

Lillian knocks on my bedroom door. "Mike. It's getting
late."

Six fifteen.

Crap.

My curtains have that pinkish, almost daytime, light to
them. I can't remember the last time I wasn't up before the
sun. I pull on the cleanest-looking shirt I've got and some
crumply-soft blue jeans.

Need to do laundry.

I get to Schat's just after six thirty and buy a pint-size
cup of coffee, thinking I probably should switch to decaf.

But that would defeat the purpose.

Caffeine: legalized speed.

More come than I expect. A couple take out *The Gambler*. At first I think they're morons since we don't need the ruse, but then I realize it's part of their ritual. Superstition is as grounded as God—hearsay, but enough to keep you walking the line in case hell is real.

I open my book and read:

> *It was as in a fever that I moved the pile, en bloc, on to the red. Then suddenly I came to myself (though that was the only time during the evening's play when fear cast its cold spell over me, and showed itself in a trembling of the hands and knees). For with horror I had realised that I MUST win, and that upon that stake there depended all my life.*
>
> *"Rouge!" called the croupier. I drew a long breath, and hot shivers went coursing over my body.*

That wakes them up.

"Okay, guys, March Madness has begun. And this weekend, we're going to see who fills out the bubble spots. The thirty conference winners are automatically in, as is the season champ for Ivy League. Here's the list." I hand them the list of teams. "So we've got thirty-four spots up for grabs. Really, though, many of these bubble spots are pretty obvious. I've narrowed it down to fifty-three filled spots, leaving eleven teams."

I hand out the list of the remaining teams that might make one of the thirty-four bubble spots. "Low payoffs for the twenty-five teams that I see as sure bets. Higher payoffs for the remaining eleven spots. Not too high. Too many variables, especially considering it's up to a random group of ten people. But it's something to whet your palates."

My team's there. U-Dub. It's kind of a long shot, considering their record. But their best player, Alex Gutzman, was out for an injury during their four biggest losses, plus they have seven top-fifty wins away. The Huskies could just pull this off and sneak in.

And Gutzman's in his prime.

I feel the charge of blood rushing to my brain. *Zing!* It's not like I'm placing a real bet—one that matters. I could just bet on the Huskies to support my future alma mater, get a solid connection to my future. I calculate how much I should bet.

"Hey, Mike. You here?" Javier's handing me his bet and ten bucks. "That's all I've got."

"It works," I say. I take zero-period kids' bets first, then everybody else's. The crowd trickles to a few. I buy a pecan roll and sit down to eat. My hands tremble.

"May I?" Marilyn asks, and pulls out a stool next to mine. We haven't talked much since divisional playoffs, but just sharing that Saturday made things different between us, like saying "hi" in the hallways was normal.

She's nice.

"Would you like some?" I offer her a bite of my pecan roll.

She covers her mouth. "I'm doing the Keep My Mouth Closed diet."

"So that's why you're quiet in class, huh?"

She laughs. "Saturday Sadie, Karen, and I are going shopping. Just hanging out. If you'd like to join us."

I wait for the catch—the trade-off. She picks at black nail polish.

"Um. Yeah. Sure." I feel lame. *So this is how normal friendships begin? Shopping?* I laugh.

"What?" she asks. "Is shopping too normal?"

"Normal?"

"Well." Marilyn lowers her voice. "You're a bookie. Maybe being normal is boring?"

"It's just different." I turn red. "It's okay. I mean, that's not a big deal. I just . . . Never mind."

Marilyn smiles. "I'll call you tomorrow," she says.

"Sure," I say. *What are the odds?*

"What are we doing tomorrow?" Josh asks, pulling some books from his locker. "I can't *believe* how much homework I've got this weekend." He comes in closer. "I totally slept through first block." He flashes me a tardy slip. "Number four. So? Tomorrow—what are we going to do with . . . ?"

"I don't know. Let's have a homework day next week."

We haven't decided what to do with our last robbery funds. I've been doing a spreadsheet to work out the investment analyses of each place of interest and have narrowed the organizations down to Brain Food, Advocates to End Domestic Violence, and Planned Parenthood. All serve the population we're hoping to help.

"So, tomorrow?"

"I'm going shopping. Girls' day." It feels foreign coming out of my mouth. It's something in my magazines and in every teen movie on the planet. Girls' day. Like an institution.

"Can't you cancel?"

"Can't cancel. Shopping calls," I say.

"But tonight I'm stuck with some kind of community cocktail thing. We won't get to hang out."

I try not to be dazed by this—this newfound social life. This is what teens do: socialize, make plans, make backup plans, have boyfriends. I hope my cheeks don't turn crimson—hope Josh doesn't realize I kind of think of him as a very platonic boyfriend.

This is lame. A bracelet and larceny don't constitute a relationship.

Do they?

I come back to Josh midsentence. "—schmoozing with some guy who's running for Congress next term, blah blah blah. It's a perfect place to spy on our next hit. I bet he'll be there. You in for tonight, then?"

"I really *really* don't want to go to a party. Plus I have Mrs. Hensler, too. Calculus, Creative Writing, AP Government—Friday-night fun. I'm sorry."

"So when can we—" He raises his eyebrows up and looks a lot like the guy from *American Psycho*.

I shake my head. "Not for a while. We've got to let things cool down."

"That's what they'll expect. The sooner we hit, the more off guard they'll be."

"It's just—"

"We're *doing* something. You know how hard it is to get people talking about anything other than themselves?"

Josh is right.

It's a weird itch. I feel like we can be doing more. Making more. Lillian came home the other night gushing about another anonymous donation—enough to cover the stolen vaccinations. And it's a ripple effect of giving, because after the *Nevada Appeal* reported about anonymous donations to Lillian's clinic, it seems all of Carson City now wants to donate. Everybody's getting the spirit—wanting to be center stage. But "Anonymous" is getting all the press. "Anonymous" is the one who threw the pebble—more like a boulder, actually.

Anonymous is Babylonia.

"Next week," I say.

"Talk Sunday?" Josh asks.

"Yes."

"Betting this weekend?" Josh asks.

"On that I'll find something trendy, my size? Nope. Not betting on that."

"Why do you do that?" Josh asks.

"What?" I say.

"Always put yourself down."

I shrug and can feel heat rise to my cheeks. "I don't always put myself down. It's just a joke."

Josh scowls. "Anyway, I'll call you Sunday. Maybe I can invite you to breakfast? The Cracker Box?"

"I can do the Cracker Box. I've actually always wanted to go. Just never have."

The bell for last block is dangerously close to ringing. No classes with Josh today. We'll have Mrs. B first block on Monday.

"I have a tuxedo fitting after school." He pretend-hangs himself from a tie. "Have fun tomorrow," Josh says, squeezing my hand in his. "I'll call you!"

After school, I go to the grocery store and buy some plants, then drive to Moch's, leaving them on the porch. I bring Sonic Burgers to Lillian. I can't stomach another just-add-boiling-water meal at home.

She's not home, so I leave her burger on a plate in the kitchen and call Leonard.

"It's been a while," he says. I *hate* how sleazy-dweeb he is. It's an unsettling combo of traits. "Who do you have your eye on?"

"Three hundred on U-Dub."

"Go Huskies."

"Yeah. Go Huskies."

That night my heart bursts through my chest watching Gutzman make a miracle jump shot at the final buzzer. I collapse on the couch, letting the relief wash over me. My phone beeps:

Josh: Dying here at this cocktail party.

Me: Drama Queen. You're eating foie gras and drinking bubbly bevs.

Josh: Foie gras? The most expensive cat food on earth. Pass.

I laugh. Hope you survive. Bye.

I don't know why I don't tell Josh that I just won three hundred seventy dollars. Maybe that bet's just for me.

Power of anonymous. Purpose. Difference making.

33

The Tech Finishes Season 1–28: School Looted after Win

Underground Essay-Writing Ring Exposed

The Philanthropic Society of Babylonia: Thousands Donated

"YOU SEE THAT? ROBIN Hood," Josh says. He's added a few things to his ceiling—including the sign of Babylonia.

"Nice." I wonder if that's wise. *Wouldn't that constitute probable cause?*

"Yeah. I thought you'd like that. And we've only just begun."

"When your head shrinks from the size of the Goodyear blimp, let me know." I'm lying on the bed beside him, watching how I'm part of his collage now.

He plays with my bracelet, tugging on the dice. "Why can't you just enjoy this?"

"I can. I do. We've just got to stay focused."

Josh squints his eyes. "Focused." He widens his eyes

and squints again, then says, "Focused on what?"

"I don't know."

Josh tucks a pillow under his head. "I need a nap. Join me?"

"You're really cutting into those nine extra years."

"Ah, Michal, it's not quantity, it's quality. What we're doing—how I feel—it's as if we've captured infinity."

Before my face turns thirty shades of crimson, I leave Josh to his nap. I've got to organize Sanctuary, study for calculus. I've got to return Marilyn's calls. This new friendship thing weighs on me.

I've got to stop by Moch's and visit.

I've got to take a long cold shower.

I've got to stop loving Josh because he doesn't realize that to be infinite, there's no beginning, no end, and I feel like he's my beginning and ending and everything that counts in between.

Josh rushes up to me at the courtyard. "We're headlining five newspapers." He recites the headlines to me:

"'Babylonia Watch: Are You on Their Radar?' 'Babylonia Serial Burglars: What's Their Agenda?' 'Rise in Anonymous Donations Raises Eyebrows: Should Charities Accept Anonymous Contributions?' 'Babylonia Makes Vigilantism "Cool"' 'Babylonia Chess: Predicting Their Next Move.'"

"One Warhol portrait short of immortality." I count the words. "Six. I'd better write that down," I say.

"My memoir homework has suffered of late. Speaking of . . . good memory."

"I didn't want to bring the papers in. You know. It would look—"

"Too interested?"

He looks at my 7Up. "No coffee?"

I shake my head. "Going decaf." The only things I can stomach are saltines and 7Up. There's gotta be a Hollywood diet based on those two food ingredients alone.

"That's a serious step."

I nod.

Seth comes by and hands us *PB & J*. Babylonia doesn't headline it but Luis Sanchez does.

Freshman Luis Sanchez Dies at Washoe Med

Last January 24, our classmate Luis Sanchez was beaten, evidently by a bat, and brought into the Carson Tahoe Hospital ER by two adolescents who refused to give their names. While in surgery, he suffered a series of ministrokes and cerebral hemorrhaging, slipping into a coma.

He lost his battle yesterday afternoon, surrounded by his three younger sisters, mom, and dad.

Luis was a member of the school band. He played trumpet. His favorite song was "When the Saints Go Marching In."

His birthday is next week.

He would've been fifteen years old.

And it's like watching a disaster unravel in slow motion. Over Josh's shoulder I see Comba.

He is alone.

"No!" I shout. But I don't know if he can hear me, because Trinity is screaming. Caleb Masterson, Nim Binder, and three other friends push Trinity out of the way, stepping in front of her. The courtyard clears, kids running.

Dean Randolph pushes his way against the tide of panic—too slow, too slow.

Comba draws his knife, shoving the blade into Caleb, pulling it out, the slow-motion movement of Comba pulling the blade out. He makes another jab just as someone pulls him away, the crimson blade falling to the tiles. Moch has shoved Comba facedown onto the floor, knee on his back, screaming for help. "Call nine-one-one!" Teachers push the rest of us toward the gym.

Students sob.

We hear sirens come toward us. I hear some kid say, "Everything's okay. The cops and ambulance are here."

That's what I used to think.

And the thing is, I'm just as guilty. I watched them kick him. I watched them run away. I know who was there.

I did nothing.

I did nothing. And he died.

34

AFTER SCHOOL, I BRING A bouquet of minisunflowers to leave at Luis's parents' house. Their porch is covered with notes and flowers and pictures. I don't even ring the bell. Moch walks up with a group just as I'm leaving. I stop and wait. I just want to say I'm sorry.

When Moch and his friends get to the porch, a young girl runs out of the house. She can't be twelve. *"¡Hijo de puta! Es culpa tuya, ¡pedazo de mierda! Mi hermano se murió por ustedes. Ustedes."*

Moch drops his head and retreats like he's trying to reverse the scene. He doesn't look me in the eye. He turns on his heel at the curb and walks away, jumping into the car that's idling at the end of the road. His friends follow.

◆

"Can't sleep?"

"Sorry. Did I wake you up?"

"I don't sleep. That's been established."

Josh says this through a very ill-disguised yawn.

"Yeah. During the night. I bet you haven't made it through an entire block of class to date."

"You okay?"

"Just a little sad, I guess."

"I know."

"You do?" Why does my sadness feel like a train, and Josh is only on for the ride? Why doesn't he blame me for Luis Sanchez's death? Why doesn't he say anything about it, about what a coward I am?

"I do."

He sounds so sincere. Does he feel the loss like I do? Does he know how important Babylonia is?

"You know, if I didn't know better, I'd bet you're trying to catch up to those years of sleeplessness I've already banked. You're just jealous."

"Okay, Rip Van," I say.

"I'm glad you called."

"Thanks. I didn't know if I should."

"You always should. Wanna come over for pre-infernal coffee?"

"Pre-infernal?"

"Referring to the educational institution to which we belong."

"I don't do caffeine anymore."

"We've got decaf. Rosa makes a mean pot."

Mrs. Mendez is in the air. Rosa came the week after she died. And filled the place that can't be filled.

Maybe we both hear her—feel her.

"That wouldn't be weird—me coming over?"

"Weird . . . because?"

"Because. I dunno."

"I'm putting the coffee on. Decaf."

"I don't do just black."

"We've got Irish cream creamer, Italian cream, peppermint, French vanilla, and pretty much any kind of sugary guck you want in your coffee."

"I'm out the door."

The sugar has kicked in, and I feel alive, anyway. I check my pulse.

Yep.

Alive.

Josh is on major caffeine buzz—he made a separate pot—five cups, two hours.

I finally ask. "Have you heard? About Caleb?"

Josh nods. "Pretty bad. It looks like he'll be peeing in a bag for a long time. He's on a kidney transplant list."

I lay my head on the granite countertop, the smooth stone cooling my face. "I think I should probably come forward, say something. What do you think?"

"I don't know. Will you get in trouble for not saying anything before?"

He sits next to me, laying his head on the counter so we're nose to nose. "It's not your fault."

But it is. "Isn't there something about the guilt of silence of the masses or something? I did *nothing.*" I think about the bat tucked in the corner of my closet and get that same sick feeling, like I did at the field.

"You're doing something now."

"I have bad dreams, like I'm being buried in an avalanche of snow. I wake up suffocating."

"Disturbing."

I pause, then say, "That's how my mom died. Maybe she's haunting my conscience, telling me that I need to—"

"They're bad dreams. Nothing more."

"I want to go to the Great Basin National Park. Just see where she died. Say good-bye. Just . . . is that stupid?"

"We can go." Josh is so close, the tips of our noses almost touch. We have cyclops eyes.

"I can't breathe," I say. "My chest hurts all the time."

He rubs my cheek. "You're not suffocating. You're here."

"How much money do we have?" I ask, even though I know. I like to listen to the sound of the word: *thousand.*

"We got almost three thousand from our last job," he says. "That can help the Sanchez family."

"Can you pay off guilt? Is it working for you? About Mrs. Mendez?"

Josh cringes. I know that's what he's been trying. It doesn't work. I can tell by his face every time Rosa comes into the room—every time he sees Moch. "Others will come forward," Josh says. "They'll find out who did it."

"It just doesn't seem like enough," I say. "It never does."

"How can we make our money grow?"

"Open a CD? Invest in the stock markets? We've got limited options."

Josh raises his eyebrows. "But think about it. We could really make some cash. You *know* how to place the bets—smart betting. Not emotional betting."

I shake my head. I think about the bet I made, the one I didn't tell Josh I was placing. The Huskies made the bubble—they're going to compete, playing tonight in the first round. Major underdogs now on people's radar. My radar.

I won three hundred seventy dollars, and it felt like I'd won the world. But U-Dub isn't smart betting. I think of my list of imaginary bets—the ongoing list. I've won.

A lot.

"I don't know," I say.

"We're not making enough," Josh says. "We've gotten nearly ten thousand dollars in three robberies. We've given away over seven, leaving us with three. But that's just a drop in the bucket."

"It's too big a risk. What if—" We can't afford to lose this money. People actually *need* it. It's going somewhere, to Moch's family, Luis's family, charities. This money actually has a reason.

"The big question is this: What games are on this weekend?" Josh says.

"Some games tonight and tomorrow. Saturday starts second round—down to thirty-two teams. Bigger betting." Tonight the Huskies play. I want to place a bet on them— take my initial investment and earnings and see how far this will take me. I feel guilty keeping this from Josh, like I'm lying to him.

"So how much have we got to win?" Josh says, forever the optimist.

I open up my notebook. I've been thinking about this for a while—a long while. I already texted everyone last night and send out a reminder an hour before: Sanctuary 7:00 Library.

Josh's phone beeps. He looks at the text. "I'll be there."

I nod.

Drowning. Moments of panic, then peace.

35

"BIG CROWD," MISS CAMPBELL, the librarian, says, opening the doors for us. "Finals?"

"Senior projects, calculus, AP History, and French. We're studying zombie hour." I hold my decaf in hand, pretending it'll give me the zing I need. At least it tastes like coffee. *Mind over matter.*

We take out various textbooks. Miss Campbell would know we're full of it if we started reading *The Gambler.* There are only so many years the same group of kids can read from the same book. I've memorized something for the group, though, to set the mood:

> *No, it was not the money that I valued—what I wanted was to make all this mob of Heintzes, hotel proprietors, and fine ladies of Baden talk about me,*

recount my story, wonder at me, extol my doings, and worship my winnings.

It works. I've made Thursday and Friday worth something, given it meaning. Kids will go to Nim's annual party at Clear Creek but will only be thinking about the games. A few of us even place a few side bets on how long it'll take for Nim's party to get busted.

Bets are placed.

Saturday, third round begins and I'll take bets until noon, giving out a fair dose of hope for Saturday and Sunday bettors.

And Monday, Seth will have another headline for *PB & J*. A scoop only he'll get.

The house is practically invisible from the road; the cobbled stone driveway curves around leading to the cabin—more like mansion cabin, the giant home hidden behind a screen of old-growth pine trees. The automated radio goes on—four o'clock sharp. It's overcast—outside, the light is gray-bright.

We got a smattering of rain—a cloudburst that graced the dry foothills with drops of water, flooding the air with the spicy sage smell.

I inhale, grateful for the perfume of the mountains.

The bad thing—leaving footprints. We're careful to walk on beds of pine needles and avoid stepping in mud.

Josh points to his watch.

I hold up ten fingers times two.

He nods.

After Thursday dance classes, they go to Java Jungle and get smoothies before coming home. It leaves us about forty-five minutes, but we need to be in and out in twenty—just to be on the safe side.

We walk around the side of the house, ignoring the BEWARE OF DOG sign. The dog is an arthritic, incontinent bassett hound that can barely move. They leave the back sliding glass door ajar and him lying right next to it every afternoon in the hope he'll get the energy to relieve himself outside.

We drop a T-bone by his snout. He half wakes up, sniffs the air, attempts a growl, then rests his nose back on the bone, hanging his tongue out to get some of the juices.

"Poor dog."

"No kidding," Josh says.

Every house has its sound—like the way it breathes. Some homes whistle, like when windows are left barely open and the wind blows. Some homes creak. Some homes sigh. It all depends on which way the house faces, how thick the windows are, what the house is made of. I listen. This is a creaker—cracked-open windows facing east. A wooden cabinlike home next to the mountains, the hush of pine needles brushing against the windows, occasional pelts of sap making soft thudding sounds like thick patters of rain. The rumble-snore of the dog adds to the sounds.

It's a quiet kind of noisy—the kind of place too easy to get spooked, panicked. But when I take a minute to listen, it's like getting to know the house and its secrets. And I know how to filter the sounds.

I scan the room—a typical mess of Barbies and stray puzzle pieces, half-peeled crayons and Disney DVDs. I sift through the DVDs—in the pile there's a *Cinderella* repeat with a cheaply photocopied *Cinderella* cover.

Rookies.

I pop open the DVD case.

Bingo!

We work our way through the rooms, rifling through the medicine cabinet, another five hundred dollars in an expired prescription bottle of Amoxil. We search through the spice rack and junk drawer—finding bits and pieces to add to the take.

Josh points to his watch.

I hold up ten fingers.

We hurry upstairs and start with the master bedroom— getting some petty cash from blue jeans lying on the floor, an envelope taped under the office desk drawer, and the typical countertop small change.

We both head to the master closet to search through jewelry boxes and shoes. I stop. Something isn't right. Something feels different. The sounds of the house have changed. The automated radio has clicked off. The windows groan.

Clouds have opened up to spatter rain—uneven pelts on windows.

The closet door opens.

She coughs. Josh and I lock eyes and turn around to see a little girl in pink pajamas, a rat's nest of curls tied back in a ponytail. I'm not good with ages, but she can't be more than seven years old. She wipes her nose, a tear dripping down her cheek. She's holding a cell phone in her trembling hand. As soon as she gets a good look at us, she opens her mouth and wails.

It feels like somebody is pumping ice water through my veins, and my heart rate surges to try to push the half-frozen blood through my system. I'm quite certain my veins are spasming from the freakish hyper blood pump.

Josh grabs her phone and I wrap my arms around her, putting my hand over her mouth. I hold her tight. Too tight. "Shhhh," I say. "Shhhh shhh shh."

She bites my hand and kicks her leg high, her heel landing on my bad knee, grinding into it. I yelp and fall to the ground, the little girl on top of me. She makes a run for it and Josh nabs her, passing her back to me. I lock my legs around her, my arm around her neck.

"Just stop it," I say. "Just. Shut. Up." I glare at Josh. She's not supposed to be here.

Fat tears stream down her cheeks mixed with nose slime and that eucalyptus vapor rub smell. She's one snotty kid. "You're hurting me," she whimpers.

"I'm so sorry. I really am. I'm just really nervous right now, you know." I loosen my grip a little, just a little, and try to still the trembling in my hands, in my voice. "We won't hurt you. But you can't scream. Okay?"

The little girl nods. I loosen my grip more and feel bad because she's peed herself. Josh yanks a shirt from a hanger and hands it to her. She cries so hard, she hiccups. I pass her the shirt. "What's your name?"

"I'm not s'posed to talk to strangers."

"Smart," I say. "Smart. Um. How old are you?"

"Seven and four months."

"Okay. We're going to go now. We have to leave you in here, but someone will find you as soon as they get home, okay?"

"Can I call my mom?"

Josh and I exchange a glance. "We have to take your cell phone right now. But how about this, why don't I call her when we get out of the house?"

The little girl nods and coughs, sounding like she's been a smoker for fifty years.

"Do you, um, need any medicine in here? Water?"

She nods. "My inhaler is in my bedroom."

Josh brings her an inhaler, a clean set of clothes, and a couple of stuffed animals. "To keep you company," he says.

I look at my watch and flash Josh a zero.

He nods.

"Now, can you sit down over there?" I point to a little chair at the end of the closet and flick on the lights. "See.

It's nice in here with the lights on. You'll be okay. Someone will be home soon. Real soon."

Her bottom lip quivers.

We pull the closet door behind us. I expect a scream but only hear quiet crying behind the door. I pause. Josh shakes his head. "We've gotta go."

We run down the stairs, out the back sliding door, jumping over the half-dead dog. In the yard, Josh hesitates, then spray-paints BABYLONIA on the fence, and we stick the manifesto between boards. At the bottom of the manifesto, I write a little note to the mom.

We cut back through the woods behind the house, running up the mountain a little until we've circled around, ending up at least a half mile or so from the house. Then we make our way down to one of the side streets. Lakeview is nothing but curvy roads, homes tucked next to the mountains, and thick pines. It takes us another twenty minutes of walking to get to Josh's car. Sirens roar. I can see the blinking lights between the trees.

My head burns like someone's poking it with a cattle prod—inside out. I touch my smooth skin, expecting to feel an upraised scar: Babylonia.

How can everybody *not* see who I am?

When we get to the car, I slouch to the ground and cradle my head between my knees, counting until I can breathe steadily.

Scared of could've beens, might bes.

36

JOSH DRIVES US OUT TO Clear Creek. We sit on his hood, covered in a blanket, watching the stars, sipping on beer. At first, I felt like everything was mine. But then the little girl came and I can't shake the chill, this feeling of emptiness. Mrs. Mendez and Luis Sanchez are still dead. Caleb Masterson still needs a kidney transplant. He lost his football scholarship to some college in Texas. I almost hurt a little girl. I can still smell that eucalyptus scent she had in her hair, on her cheeks. *I almost hurt her.*

And Josh still hasn't kissed me. There's got to be some kind of posttraumatic bad kiss disorder. I've ruined him for life.

"The little girl," I say.

"She's okay."

"I could've hurt her."

"You didn't."

"What if she hadn't stopped screaming?"

"She did."

Silence. Then I say what both of us probably have wondered but never have had the nerve to say, afraid to say. Because who will I be when this is over? Who will *we* be? "How many more?" The cold just won't leave. *What if I never get that high again?* I take a long drink and fight to keep from spitting it out. *Beer is gross.* "It'll never be enough."

"It's not only about the money." Josh looks up at the sky. "Our lives mean something because we're *doing* something. We're helping."

Josh leans back on his windshield and pulls me to him, my head settled on his chest, feeling the steady beat of his heart against my cheek. We stay there, watching the stars in the indigo March sky for what feels like forever.

"Ready to go?" Josh says. "Did you finish your beer?"

I put down my almost-full beer can. "Liquid aluminum with a bitter aftertaste."

"You kidding? You don't like beer?"

I hand him my can. "No."

"It's an acquired taste," Josh says, drinking down his can, then mine. His breath smells yeasty. "Crazy Thursday night, huh?"

I try to keep the feeling of just a couple of hours ago—the feeling of right. It's so clear when we're doing it—like we're doing the right thing. But out here . . . I don't know.

I slip off the hood and stare up at the blue-black sky one more time, trying to push away the weight of insignificance.

I can't sleep. It's not late. Lillian's at the clinic. So I drive up to Saint Mary's in Reno and slip past the nurses' station, finding Caleb's room. The place has that sickening rose/carnation-that-masks-urine smell to it. Flowers, Mylar balloons, and teddy bears explode from every corner. There's a poster-size picture of him with his best friends in tuxedos hanging up. The place looks like a shrine. Store wrapped and neat.

"Are you a friend?" a woman asks. I didn't see her tucked in the 1-800-FLOWERS décor. She's sitting in an uncomfortable-looking chair near the foot of Caleb's bed. "It's late." She sounds defensive. "He's sleeping."

"Is he okay?" Stupid question. Stupid stupid stupid.

She doesn't try to wipe the tired look from her eyes. "No."

The answer hangs in the air. No.

"He will be, though," she says.

I nod.

"Can I tell him who stopped by?" she asks, but I'm already out the door, rushing to the parking lot. I never stopped by Luis's hospital room—never even bothered to ask Moch if he was okay. I drive home on autopilot, don't even remember going through Washoe Valley, ending up at Moch's house.

I tap on his window. "Moch? Moch, are you there?"

After what feels like forever, the curtains part. He looks at me. "What are you doing here?"

"I don't know," I say.

Moch comes outside. "*¡Qué frío tan hijo de puta!* Come inside. I'm not going to hang out in this cold."

Moch's house is unusually quiet. When I walk in the door, the familiar smells almost bowl me over. Tears prick my eyes.

I follow him in the trailer house, though it doesn't feel much warmer. He plugs in a space heater in the living room and throws me a blanket. "Your lips are purple." We huddle around it, holding our hands as close to the grill as possible. I listen to the *tick tick tick* as it heats up, and orange warmth glows on Moch's face. His silver Saint Pablo hangs from a dog tag–like chain, resting against his sternum. After a while he flips it around—the heated metal burning his bare skin.

"Lots of bets?" he asks.

"March Madness. You haven't been back at school," I say.

"Busy."

"Are you going to graduate?"

Moch shrugs. "Does it matter?"

We both know it does. We sit in silence, listening to the neighbors fight, dogs snarl and bark. A car backfires. A stillness settles in me, one I haven't felt in a long time.

Sitting here, warming up—this fits. Like this home is who I am, my history.

I lean my head against the couch, smelling her—the cinnamon, baked-crust smell mixed with bleach. Way different from the microwaved cardboard smell from my house. This is warmth. This is what I want back.

"It was an initiation," Moch says. "Pick a fight with Garbage Disposal and you can be in la Cordillera."

It takes me a second to realize he's talking about Luis.

"He died because of me." Moch twirls his chain around his fingers, not taking his eyes off the space heater.

His words settle in me like frost. No matter how close I get to the space heater, I can't get warm. I shiver. Moch looks at me through thick black lashes, like I'm worthy of his confession; like I can make any of it right.

The house is a decaying limb—a dingy gray place where people barely exist. I try not to breathe in the fading cinnamon smells because it makes her not being here so much harder. We're all slipping, falling, and just trying to hold on.

I stand to go. Moch turns to me. "I'm not sure where to go."

I bite my lip before saying, "Babylonia." I lean over and give Moch an awkward hug. "I miss her. It's hard to miss someone alone."

Moch nods. "I know."

Making sense out of senselessness. Futile.

37

Babylonia Leaves Parent a Report Card: "U"nsatisfactory on All Counts

NCAA Games Heating Up

Babylonia and Dental Hygiene

SETH HAS AN ENTIRE SECTION dedicated to what he believes is Babylonia's dental hygiene routine. In the Sunday *Appeal*, they reported the little girl mentioned that Babylonia had cinnamon breath and wore ugly ski masks. Seth goes on saying such damning evidence will surely trap the thieves. "Who, I mean, *who* chews cinnamon gum?" he asks.

I laugh, glossing over the article about Caleb because the whole thing gives me a sick-stomach feeling. My head hurts. I'm now downing as much Mylanta as 7Up.

Saturday morning, we convened an emergency Sanctuary for round three of March Madness bets—last round before Sweet Sixteen. I had over twenty guys come to place bets and moan about the upsets all around. Duke lost to Tennessee, PSU destroyed Northwestern, and U-Dub came out from under Gonzaga's shadow, *my Huskies*, who barely made the bubble, and won in a miracle shot.

Maybe miracles *do* happen.

I won another five hundred dollars. *Five hundred dollars.* Josh and I won almost seven hundred dollars. Everything was right—just right. We left money at Luis Sanchez's house in an envelope and donated to the foundation Brain Food.

I've had to make ridiculous excuses not to hang out with Marilyn. Finally, on Sunday, I told her I had to pay attention to the games. "After March Madness, I can shop till I drop."

"When does this end?" She sounded bored with the whole madness thing.

"Two more weeks," I said. "Then it's all over."

That seemed to appease her.

I close my eyes and replay the Huskies' final basket—miracle three-pointer, corner shot over Gonzaga's defense. I have a moment of invincibility—the "forever" Josh talks about. Peace.

Still.

That's all I want. To be still.

I watch the rise of Babylonia—how betting and Babylonia have overshadowed normal high school stuff. We're all kids can talk about. In Mrs. B's class, Sumi and Dawn did an entire six-word memoir, "Ode to Babylonia."

It was freakish.

Nobody's talking about next week's Aloha Dance—a lame attempt by the student council to make up for the ski trip debacle. They can't afford anything big, so they're having it in the gym.

March 22.

Tickets. Ten dollars for those who don't have their original ski passes. I think that's supposed to be some kind of compensation for the sixty dollars the other kids blew. Trinity, Callie, and the other student-council members rotate ticket sales, but their stack of tickets doesn't look like it's going down at all. The dance isn't going to be too big a hit.

Maybe kids just don't want to hang out together. Maybe they feel more comfortable in their little social circles that intersect like one of those Venn diagrams, only when they're instructed to do a group assignment together.

Nim walks by with a group of friends, his arm wrapped around Trinity's shuddering shoulders. Medusa wears a painted smile, like she's totally okay with her boyfriend hugging another girl.

The pit returns. The hole in my stomach can't seem to be filled anymore—I get just momentary bursts of release, then the familiar burn.

In Mrs. B's class, Moch shows up late, handing her a tardy slip. "Good to see you, Mocho," Mrs. B says.

Trinity stands to leave. "I won't be in the same room as *him*."

Moch's face turns ashen gray.

"Sit down, Miss Ross, and cut the drama." Mrs. B clears her throat. "Listen . . ." Her tone of voice softens. "We've talked about violence and what's going on with Caleb and I know he's hurting right now. But these kinds of outbursts and accusations really don't do anything but exacerbate the problems."

"Exacerbate the problem? That my boyfriend was *stabbed at school* by *his* best friend—" She points at Moch, ugly, angry fingers ready to place blame. "You call that, quote-unquote, exacerbate the problem?"

Mrs. B sighs.

"Distorted mirrors. Filtered memories. Everyone's guilty," I say, interrupting the debate.

"What's that supposed to mean?" Trinity says, and glares. Her eyes are puffy and red. Is it possible she doesn't know who Caleb is?

Or maybe I don't know him, either. She certainly doesn't know Moch. How could she know he spent an entire summer interviewing every person in our neighborhood to put together his first newspaper? He called it *Twenty Minutes*. The idea was that after twenty minutes, you could pretty much *know* someone.

Trinity, Caleb, Mocho, and I have gone to school together for ten years. We *still* don't know each other.

Trinity glares. "Well?"

"It's just a memoir," I say.

"I have one," says Moch. He pulls out a crumpled page and says, "Bloodied bats. Bloodied knives. Same. Same."

Trinity's face does this really unattractive pinchy, raisin thing. She turns a reddish color and collapses to her chair, sobs coming out.

Yeah. She knows Caleb.

I know Moch.

But I can't believe they're the same guy. Moch *stopped* Comba. Caleb, though, held the bat.

For the first time it occurs to me that Mrs. B could collect all our memoirs, give them to a court of law, and they'd have a pretty solid case against anyone in this classroom.

The loudspeakers interrupt the weird silence—spitting news and information at us. We're all called out for an emergency assembly.

I can't help but notice the hallways smell like cinnamon Trident. Some kids wear Babylonia T-shirts—the symbol we used on the ski trip invitation.

Josh catches up to me as we walk through the gymnasium doors. "Un-freaking-believable."

"No kidding."

"I'd never thought of the merchandising aspect of the whole thing," I say, half smiling.

Josh squeezes my arm.

We. Are. Babylonia.

Josh and I shuffle into the gym, working our way up to an empty area in the bleachers. I hear somebody *moo* and look around to see Nim laughing. He winks at me.

I can't believe it. I'm still a joke to him. The sound of Principal Holohan picking up the mic, its screechy feedback, thunders in my ears.

"Sit down!" some junior ROTC kid says, motioning me to sit. "Yeah. You!"

Josh tugs on my hand. It's like everything I've done doesn't matter because nobody knows. They're all looking at me as if I were yesterday.

I. Am. Babylonia.

Principal Holohan stands in the middle of the gym with Police Chief Dominguez. He takes the mic and says, "I'm here to talk to you about Babylonia."

Cheers and whistles fill the gym; then kids begin to whisper, "Babylonia, Babylonia, Babylonia." Hundred of voices whispering. The words, first like scattered raindrops, connect together, floating over our heads, filling the gym, growing like a tidal wave crashing on a shoreline. They get softer again and recede back out to sea. "Babylonia."

The gym goes silent, leaving Police Chief Dominguez drenched in sweat—the unforgiving fluorescent bulbs burning overhead. "There are two very confused individuals who believe taking the law into their own hands causes a lot of good."

"It does!" somebody shouts.

"Do not interrupt. I will *not* ask you again."

The gym settles into uncomfortable silence. It feels like Dominguez is looking right at me. Josh slips his hand into mine and I squeeze it. Hard. Not even worried about the fact it's way past clammy-gross and moving toward corpse-like waxy.

"These burglars are dangerous. They've already shown they're fearless. And every single Tweet, status update—every time they're mentioned—we are tracking you. Don't think Anonymous is all that anonymous. I'm here to tell you that this is not a game. This is not a fad, like some rubbery animal-shaped things you put on your wrist. These individuals are *breaking the law*, and they will be prosecuted. Nevada burglary, as defined in NRS 205.060, is one of the toughest laws in the country. If you want to be a burglar, Nevada's not the place to do it. It'll get you ten years in the pen.

"We will bring them to justice. And they will do time."

"Yeah, just like la Cordillera!" somebody shouts. I look around to see who shouted, but everybody's looking around at everybody, so it's hard to tell. I turn back to see Moch. He and everybody else sitting around him are wearing sunglasses. But if they know who shouted it, that kid's dead.

"We are well aware of the problems of gang violence in Carson City. As well as a new wave of militia groups targeting certain members of our community. I'm here to talk about Babylonia, the trickle-down effect of vigilantism, and how it affects our community, our safety. It is *not a game*.

"That said, we are offering substantial reward money to anybody who can lead us to the perpetrators of these crimes. Because we have reason to believe these felons are young, possibly even members of this school community, I wanted to address the high school personally. I want you all to know that whoever is behind these burglaries will not be doing them for much longer. Mark my word. Any questions?"

At least half the study body raises their hands.

"Why do you think they're dangerous?"

"They already left a seven-year-old bruised and incredibly shaken up," Dominguez says. "To keep her from screaming."

I think about how hard I held her, squeezing her in my hands.

"It's larceny. It's dangerous. And these burglars have no social agenda except to themselves. They're a couple of punks on a joyride—one that's going to end badly." Dominguez wipes his forehead down with a white handkerchief. "Let me be clear about this. Burglars aren't like you see in the movies. Hollywood has a beautiful way of romanticizing the most dangerous of things. These two could be drug addicts, part of a local gang—they're only thinking about themselves."

Josh's hand is slick with sweat. He pulls it away and

wipes it on his jeans, then grabs the tips of my fingers with his. It feels like my stomach has become Lucifer's dwelling place. The sense of bigness and wonder that once filled the gym when they chanted our name feels silly, like we're just going to become an afterthought. *Punks on a joyride.*

They've missed the point.

We're dismissed.

Somebody jams into me. Nim grins. "*Mooo*," he says, shooting me a look over his shoulder.

Can't find yesterday's me in today.

38

CASH REWARD OFFERED FOR BABYLONIA: 2K

THE POSTERS WENT UP overnight—like some kind of Christo building wraps, inside out.

TAKE THE COMMUNITY BACK!
BABYLONIA = ANTI-AMERICAN
GARBAGE DISPOSAL DOING WHAT LAW ENFORCEMENT CAN'T
WHO'S NEXT? ARE YOU? ARE YOU PREPARED?

By the end of first block most posters have been taken down. But the hate lingers.

Nim comes up to me at lunchtime. "Sanctuary today?"

"No," I say, sipping on my staple beverage, 7Up.

He raises his eyebrows.

"I'm going to a funeral." I stare at him. He wasn't holding

the bat but he was cheering Caleb on.

I didn't do anything.

I'm doing it now. Luis's family doesn't have to pay for that funeral. I can't begin to fathom what that medical bill looks like. He was hospitalized for weeks.

"So?" Nim's stupid, thug-head, unevolved self asks. "When?"

"For you? Never."

"Christ, Mike, what's this all about? That Babylonia shit? Those guys are total losers. You're a bookie. Since when do you give a shit about . . . about anything but the bet?"

"Take your business somewhere else." Now even 7Up burns going down.

"And half my guys."

"Be my guest."

"Fuck you, you dumb cow."

The only saving grace of Tuesday is when Josh texts me: You're worth WAY more than 2K.

I read it three times, then erase it.

It's been too long. I have the itch. The nights are the worst. I'm too tired to do anything but lie down on the bed and think. I think about Mrs. Mendez and Moch; Luis Sanchez and Caleb. I wish I could be thinking about proms and dances and graduation and U-Dub.

But all I can think about is the next hit, the next bet, the next win.

It's hard to balance a life of burglary and guilt with midterms. It's no wonder this stuff never gets into the yearbook.

My phone beeps: Ready?

Exhale.

I listen for Lillian. She's been asleep a long time. At dinner she decided to do the "involved" thing and ask about Josh and friends and when was I going shopping again. Finally, after dancing around the subject for what seemed like eternity, she blurted, "Are you using protection?"

I felt a great relief. She's worried about me getting pregnant. Something so basic, so normal.

After nearly choking on my Tuna Helper, I assured her that I wasn't having sex but would definitely use protection. She seemed happy—like we'd had a moment, we'd overcome a huge obstacle in the parent-child relationship.

I leave the house and meet Josh at the end of the block.

"How are we going to get past without tripping the alarm?" I ask.

Josh smiles, hands me the drill. "It doesn't work. It's for show." He points to the alarm business name. "They've been out of business for several years."

I shake my head and mutter, "Rookies. Cover your eyes." Sometimes people think a flashy sticker will work. For a normal burglar, probably. Normal burglars, though, probably don't break into building-supply offices.

I drill into the keyhole—the shrill sound of metal on metal screechy and loud. *Really loud.* I don't stop, though, until I can feel the bit hit something. Curls of metal drift to the floor.

Josh hands me a screwdriver. I wiggle it until I hear the pins and springs fall out, then go back and drill again, repeating until the screwdriver turns, acting like a key. "Open sesame," I say.

Josh sweeps his hand in front. "After you."

We walk down the narrow corridor and kick in a flimsy aluminum door to the main floor of the supply house. The place smells like mechanic oil and metal, a faint whiff of oil-soaked sawdust.

Mottled light seeps through greasy garage doors. It's like piecing together a puzzle—giving shapes to the shadowy figures, finding the nuance in the spectrum of grays. Lights from big trucks stretch through the high garage-door windows, caressing the walls, a light show for a moment until the trucks pass, the darkness wrapping us in its million grays again. The office is upstairs—a glass room perched like an aquarium, with a view of the warehouse and building yard.

I listen.

Metal siding bangs and howls with gusts of wind. Cars rip along Highway 50, muffled and distant. There's a soft hum somewhere—maybe a generator.

We walk up the stairs—rubber soles tapping on metal.

That familiar sound of kids going up and down bleachers. But softer. Softer.

The office door is locked.

I take out the screwdriver to open it, but Josh just bashes in the glass with the drill. It's that windshield glass. A web of cracks forms—glinting. Pretty. An intricate design of Swarovski shards.

Josh shrugs. I flick him in the temple. "Patience."

"Yes, Yoda," he says, and fans his fingers on the outside of his head.

I unscrew the doorknob and pop it in. It thuds on the thin carpeting, a soft singing-bowl-like hum hanging in the air.

No safe.

It takes all of two minutes to find the bank bag with four piles of cash—wrapped tightly in deposit slips. I sometimes wonder if anybody else in this world watches cable. One *To Catch a Thief* show is enough to teach these people to deposit their money. I hand Josh the bills. He takes out the spray paint and signs BABYLONIA on the glass. "They have to replace it anyway," he says.

On the way out, we tape up the manifesto.

I like to think of somebody showing up, opening the manifesto, and *knowing* that they've been robbed. It's better than them just entering and seeing it. It gives them time to anticipate it, think about it, dread it. And wonder who else knows.

Conviction replaces ideals. Now black-white world.

39

Sanctuary 3:30 Comma Coffee

I CRADLE A CAFFEINE blaster in my hands. "Decaf?" Josh asks.

I shake my head. "I fell off the wagon. I'm just so tired."

He sits next to me. We're in the back room waiting for others to show. "Do you sleep? After?"

I shake my head. "I just don't sleep anymore at all. You?"

"Yes and no. At first, when I get home, I crash, like my body needs to turn off. Then I wake up an hour or so later and just lie there—"

"—replaying it all in my head. Going over and over the scene, hoping that—"

"—we didn't miss anything."

I bite into a blueberry muffin with crumble topping, sipping on my coffee, wondering why the *Nevada Appeal* didn't print our manifesto. Why Seth didn't. Maybe we're old news. Maybe they don't get it—why this is so important.

It's not about us. It's about Mrs. Mendez and Luis Sanchez. It's about Caleb and Comba and all the guys who think it's okay to kill.

It's about justice—without a price tag attached to it.

The room crams with kids from school. "Wow," I say.

"This tournament is crazy unpredictable," Javier says. "It's too hard *not* to bet."

"You all get your coffees?" I ask.

A couple of kids groan.

"Listen. Go buy a dollar cookie or something. Like we really need to be booted out of here because you're cheap."

By the time everybody's settled, a calm enters the room. I clear my throat and begin with the reading of the day.

> *What am I? I am zero—nothing. What shall I be tomorrow? I may be risen from the dead, and have begun life anew. For still, I may discover the man in myself, if only my manhood has not become utterly shattered.*

"Yeah. I don't get that one," some kid says. "I'm just here to place a bet."

I roll my eyes. No poetry. How can they *not* know they've all got the capacity to be something great—to start again—to be part of something way greater than placing bets and losing money?

"Okay, ladies and gentlemen." I look in the crowd of faces. "Sweet Sixteen. Big deal. Big upsets. Nothing weird today. Too many bets—straight up, money-line them, or bet the spread. And *please*, unless you're twelve, don't come to me with a parlay. I'm not in the mood for wiping up snotty tears Friday night. Saturday I'll open up Sanctuary for Elite Eight. We're going to Grandma Hattie's. Eight o'clock a.m. All in person. No call-ins."

"Eight? Fuck. That's *not* human. My *one* day to sleep in." Tim's parents make him go to sunrise services at the Catholic church Sunday mornings. Brutal.

I shrug. "It's up to you." I wink. "Think of it as tithing for a cause."

"Yeah. Some cause," some guy says. "More like a money suck."

"You guys know the stakes. Am I right?"

There's some mumbling.

I write everything down. This tournament has been especially fun because only two front-runners are still in the tournament. An amazing ride. So how can they *not* understand that we will rise from the dead, start life anew? And with U-Dub, we'll have our resurrection. It's serendipity.

Nim waits until last. "I want to place a bet." He's cracking his knuckles. I can hear the pop of synovial fluid between his bones and cringe. I *hate* that sound.

"Go ahead. Just not with me. We're done, Nim."

He leans in, so close everything goes a little blurry. If it weren't for the fact he shares over ninety-nine percent of his genetic material with me, I'd swear he was Saint John's seven-headed blue beast.

"Enough," I say. "Just go away."

"You're *nothing*," he spits. Thousands of spittle dots of bad breath soak into my skin. I half expect it to sizzle. I'm probably going to have to run to CVS for Clearasil or some emergency skin-care product that removes Beelzebub's acidic drool.

That's a product that would raise some eyebrows. There's probably a decent market for it somewhere.

"Nothing," Nim repeats.

Yeah, Nim, I heard you the first twenty thousand times.

"Then *why* do you keep coming to me?" I ask. I lean in. "I *saw* you there cheering Caleb on, kicking Luis Sanchez. I know who was there that day."

Nim pales and grimaces; his seven heads return to his one big, dumb head. Even his helmetlike waves of hair have come ungelled. "My word against yours." His voice wavers. He clears his throat. "All of our words against yours."

"Just remember." I glare. "Just remember who *nothing* is."

Nim leaves, Medusa trailing behind him like she's some kind of parasite and Nim's the host.

Josh hands me my caffeine blaster refill. A bitter coffee

aroma clings to the furniture in the room. I feel like I'm suffocating. "Hey," he says. He turns my face to his. "What was that about?"

I bite down and clear my throat. "Saturday?"

"Are you thinking what I'm thinking?"

"He's on the list." Anger bubbles up inside me.

"I've kind of got plans." He flashes me tickets to the Aloha Dance.

"Oh." My heart sinks. I think it's skipped a beat. I'm supposed to be Josh's plans. "Sorry. Of course. I mean . . ." I shove my books into my backpack, palms slick, hot. I've seen Josh talking to Sadie, Marilyn's friend, in the hallways. Of course he's going to want to have a real life outside of what we do.

"So?" he says.

"Another day."

"I don't mean *that*." He smiles. "*That's* a given. I mean this. Will you go with me?"

I pause. I've just been asked to a dance. I expect, any moment, for lightning to crack in the sky and the world to turn to ash.

"So?" Josh asks. "Man, you'd think it'd be easier to ask you to a dance since, well, we do lots of other stuff together." He laughs. A flock of sandy hair flops into his eyes. "I am feeling totally lame right now." He wrinkles his nose. "Um. Hello? Protocol here would be a response—verbal or otherwise—to put me out of my misery and make me feel like less of a jackass."

"Oh. Okay," I say.

"I'm waiting."

"That's it. Um. Yes. Okay," I say. "A dance."

"Okay," Josh says. "So it's a date."

"It's a date."

This is probably the first awkward silence we've had, and I'm not sure whether I should high-five Josh or kiss him or shake his hand or . . . whatever. What's the procedure for a platonic Hawaiian dance date? Or is it platonic?

He breaks the silence. "Then we can sack Nim's house for every last penny."

I smirk, back on comfortable ground. "Okay. Done."

Slipping into unmapped territory. Predictability gone.

40

"MARILYN? HELP!" I CALL her after Sanctuary, and she squeals.

"I *knew* that you and Josh had a thing. I mean, *hello*, all he's done since he got here is follow you around. He's *adorable*."

After we've decided that Josh looks best in green because it makes the flecks of green-gold in his eyes stand out, and his sandy-brown curls curlier, and the little scar above his left eyebrow sexier (how a color can do that is beyond me, but when we're talking, Marilyn has me convinced as well), Marilyn calls in reinforcements and we plan a Friday emergency Hawaiian shopping trip. "What are you going to look for?" she asks.

"I don't know." How many options are there for Hawaiian?

"You're so perfect for a Hawaiian dance theme. God,

I wish I had your skin."

Where's that coming from? I wonder who people see when they look at me.

Thursday's games had two more upsets. I had to deal with a couple of near-tears phone calls late into the night. Josh and I are ripping it up.

We. Can't. Lose.

Four more games tonight, breakfast tomorrow, and we slide into the Elite Eight.

When we come out ahead this weekend—with the bets we're going to place—we'll end up banking almost twelve thousand dollars.

Twelve thousand dollars.

Most kids don't make that in four years of part-time work.

That's enough for Luis's family *and* Mr. Mendez . . . enough to get Mr. Mendez back on his feet, to get him to set up his restaurant. To get Moch out of la Cordillera.

It's enough to give to Clinica Olé and Brain Food. This is our chance to make a big splash—not just some dinky donation.

Twelve thousand dollars.

I'm so busy spending our money that I don't even see Seth's paper until we're in first period.

Babylonia Backfire? Local Businesses Lay Off Workers Without Papers

Cash Reward for Babylonia: $3500

Babylonia backfire? I read the article—once again, filled with supposition. *Are* businesses firing undocumented workers?

By the end of the school day, it's hard to get excited about shopping. But with Marilyn's infectious girl thing going on, I soon forget about Babylonia and a rise in homelessness, and focus on fabrics.

I'm trying to shove my hips into some kind of shimmery mermaidlike dress that, on the model, flows in silvery-blue cascades, making her look like she's from the lost island of Atlantis.

"You okay in there?" Marilyn asks. She, Sadie, and three others I don't know really well are trying to find me something Hawaiian.

"I don't think Hawaiian means being some kind of amphibian mutant," I say. I inhale, exhale, then peek from behind the dressing room door. "Help. I'm stuck."

Marilyn feeds me dresses. When I try to protest, she interrupts. "Just try." It's embarrassing and wonderful at the same time.

After trying on approximately ten thousand ensembles from Bermudas and Hawaiian button-up shirts to sarongs and ridiculous dresses, we find *the one.* Though I'm not convinced a dress is *the one* out of desperation, lack of alternatives, or just plain exhaustion. But when I try it on, it is *the one.*

"Oh my God, that's it!"

"Isn't it a little dressy?" I ask. It's a halter dress with a smocked top that goes into a full skirt.

"Oh, no way," Sadie says. "Just keep your hair down and wear flip-flops. It's too perfect. Perfect. Can you put a flower behind your ear, like here?" They all surround me, tugging, pulling, until it's decided my hair will be put back in a clip with a purple flower. Going to the accessory shop becomes the most urgent thing on our to-do list.

After we find a clip and it's been decided, democratically of course, that I need a real flower in my hair, we buy glittery body lotion, swipe miniature perfume samples from Sephora, then collapse in the overheated Starbucks in the mall. We talk about where we're going to dinner, who's double-dating, and who's going to get lucky.

I clear my throat. I *so* want to ask for kissing tips. I've Googled and bookmarked every kissing tip on the planet. There's a deluge of information on circling tongues, sucking lips, nibbles. But I'm not sure where to begin.

I hope Josh kisses me.

"Hey. Earth to Mike. What about you and Josh? Have you?" Marilyn says, eyebrows dancing on her forehead.

"Have we?"

"Made out? Or more?"

I shake my head and feel my face turn furnace hot.

"Do you want to?" Marilyn asks.

More than anything. I nod.

The girls oooh and aaah. . . . "Okay. This is what you've got to do."

And it's like Google information duplicated—with contradictions and tried-and-true techniques. The best tip I get out of it, though, is "Don't hold your breath." I wouldn't have thought about that.

"Let's all meet up at the dance," Marilyn says. Sadie and the gang all nod in unison. It's kind of fun, this sense of solidarity. Maybe it's a girl thing. We'll all be uncomfortable in dresses together.

Lillian's gonna have a fit. Anything that has to do with high school dances she automatically relates to a sex fest and insta-pregnancy. As if wearing a corsage is like having unprotected sex. I sigh. Maybe she'll have night duty at the clinic. Maybe she won't even see me dressed up.

Friday's games are madness—Sweet Sixteen had more upsets than any other year. Saturday morning for Elite Eight bets, we have to leave Grandma Hattie's because there are too many of us. We have to drive over to Fuji Park. This is getting ridiculous.

Back at home, I call Leonard. "What are your totals for the U-Dub game?"

"One hundred and seventy-five."

I nibble on my lip. They're doing well, really well, on the road. And Ohio State is rocking. Neither team is playing a defensive strategy, but 175 is a pretty high score. "Eleven-to-ten odds?"

"You got it."

We can double our money if we bet it all here. I think about it. "A thousand. Over." Josh is gonna be fueled when I tell him about the extra money. "What else?" I ask.

"I've got U-Dub as four-point-five favorites."

I smile. "I'll take it. Four thousand." *We'll win.* I don't doubt this. It's like me saying I have two eyes and ears. A fact. *We can't lose.*

"You can cover this?" Leonard asks.

"I've never *not* been able to cover a bet."

"You're talking five grand here, Mike. That's not something I'll blow off."

"Leonard, you don't blow off twenty bucks. What? You're gonna break my legs?"

"You think this is a joke?"

"Since when have I ever considered any of this a joke?"

We slip into one of those cliché movie silences, and I hope one of us will have something earth-shattering to say.

"You want to be treated like a client, I'll do that. So this is when I give you payment incentive, Mike. I'm not going to go after your grandma or family or any of that shit. That's Italian Catholic Jersey *Sopranos*, and let's get real. I'm a Norwegian Lutheran from North Dakota who spent half my life getting my ass kicked by those Italian kids. I eat lefsen, for God's sake."

"So what's the payment incentive, Leonard?" I ask, and am pretty intrigued.

"Information, Mike. You never know how much somebody knows about you. And the information I've got about you and your little boyfriend is the kind of shit you don't want everybody knowing about. So I expect payment."

I can feel the tectonic-plate movement and crevasses opening up in the world. Yep. Earth shattered. "I don't know what—"

"Don't mess around, Mike. You're a lousy liar. So?"

"Uh-huh," I croak.

"You placing this bet?"

I nod.

"Mike?"

"I'm here, Leonard."

"And?"

"Place the over-under. One thousand. Over. Four thousand on the spread. Over. We've got it covered." My whole body tingles. The stakes just got higher. We're on the edge, ready to jump, and I can't wait to feel the rush.

Wanted: Outside to match inside. Please.

41

THE REST OF SATURDAY FEELS
like a time vacuum. Lillian gardens. She's not leaving. She'll
be here when I get ready.

Help!

I need to talk to someone about going to a school
dance. Like this would be a good time for Lillian to get all
involved—just tell me I look nice. I don't even know how
to dance. I think about my mom. What would she be like?
These past couple of months, it's like the memory of her has
invaded me. I want to know her, what she was like. What
was her favorite color? Dessert? Did she peel her apples or
eat them with the skin? Does it matter?

I don't know who to ask.

I wish the school counselor could pass out a hand-
book of what to feel during which occasions—like a
reference guide—because I feel like I'm soaring, then

flailing. I can't find solid ground.

I start to get ready.

I look up at the bathroom ceiling. Water marked and stained. It's hard to imagine Mrs. Mendez way up there, beyond. I'll have to look for her when I'm not sitting on the toilet.

Tears well in my eyes, and my chest aches. She'd know what to do—to help me with my hair. I probably should've gone to Marilyn's. That would've been nice. Just to have some company.

We've got another thousand for Moch's family that we're going to stuff in the mailbox after the dance. Tonight and tomorrow . . . we're going to win big.

Big.

I swallow back the feeling of guilt I have because, in a way, it's starting to feel like Babylonia and the stealing and the betting have become more for me than for justice, like my politics are secondary to the thrill.

This is for Mrs. Mendez. For Moch. Luis. This is for Clinica Olé. Brain Food . . .

I see it like a mantra. I say it until I almost believe it.

I put on the dress, put on some makeup, and, as instructed by Marilyn, Sadie, and the others, pull my hair back, putting one of Lillian's purple geraniums in it. I'm as ready as I'll ever be, which is not at all.

I sit in the bathroom, my feet shoved into cute-but-not-too-casual flip-flops. Subtle, according a magazine article, sparkly silver nail polish on my fingers and toes.

"Mike?" Lillian knocks on the bathroom door. "Josh is here."

"Coming." But I feel like my butt has been cemented to the toilet.

I peek out of the bathroom and around the corner. Josh is wearing a pair of khakis, brown sandals, and a bright-green Hawaiian shirt. His hair flops in front of his eyes, like the usual, but I can tell he's used a little gel to keep the curls from going haywire.

He's sitting on the half-reclined rust-colored recliner. I hope there isn't some greasy tuna-fish stain on it or something. He sips on diluted Kool-Aid.

"Hi," I say.

"Wow." Josh stands up. "Wow."

"You're lovely," Lillian says.

"I love the dress. It's like a Monet—the water lilies. Wow."

"I really like your shirt."

I like your shirt? C'mon.

Josh smiles, his crinkly-eyed, half-moon smile.

"What's going on tonight?" Lillian asks. She eyes my dress.

"Hawaiian dance," I say. "Just to do something different."

I can hear her brain screaming *sperm, insemination, reproduction, condoms!*

She smiles—like for real—the kind when her eyes light

up. I don't see it very much around here and can't help but smile back. Pretty soon we all look like a bunch of smiling nincompoops—goofy grins, shuffling feet, flushed cheeks.

"Shall we?" Josh holds out his arm.

"I'd love to."

"Wait . . . wait just a second, please!" Lillian grabs for her camera. "Last three pictures."

It's a camera with actual film, which says a lot about the fact I haven't given her ample photo ops.

"Can I have a copy?" Josh asks.

"I'll bring this roll down to get developed tomorrow."

Part of me loves feeling humiliated by a parental figure—something I haven't experienced on a regular basis before. *Lillian wants a picture of us. Together.*

Lillian holds my hand in hers. "*Estás preciosa.* You look so much like your mother right now."

The words hit me, sucking the air out of me. I bite down on my lip.

"What time?" Lillian asks as Josh escorts me to the door.

"Midnight okay?" Josh asks.

"Please," I mouth to Lillian.

She nods. "I'll wait up."

"Thanks, Lillian."

After a kind of weird, not-sure-if-this-is-a-date Thai dinner in which I drop my fork three times and have an unfortunate flying-chopstick incident, we show up to the dance and take the obligatory posed picture with Josh's arms wrapped around me, hugging me close to him. There's a balmy seascape painted behind us—the art club's project because, I can see in the sand, thousands of miniature skulls. I have to laugh.

We walk into the gym followed by Nimrod and Medusa. Nimrod's wearing a barely there loincloth. Medusa's wearing a bikini top, a grass skirt, and an empty smile. She does this stiff, awkward, beauty-pageant elbow-elbow, wrist-wrist wave to some friends across the room. "That is a direct result of *Toddlers and Tiaras.* She could sue for the cerebral damage caused by excessive hair spray."

Josh's shoulders shake from laughter. "She wasn't—"

"Yep. From the time she could wave, she's been wearing a crown."

Josh stares down at me, running a fingertip across my collarbone. "You are so pretty," he says. I'm glad the lights are low, because I think I might be melting.

The music kind of sucks—no Johnny Cash, of course. We find a table way in the back corner, away from the crowd. The student council and dance committee do this weird choreographed dance number with Polynesian drums and lots of grunting. There's a minute of silence for Caleb.

Some girl thinks he died and starts to bawl until they explain to her it's just to think about him getting better. Trinity chokes on a sob, then is held close by her new boyfriend. How she convinced a minor-league baseball player to come to a high school dance is beyond me.

Just as the minute ends, Seth takes the microphone and says, "I'd like to say a few words about Luis Sanchez." Seth takes out a piece of paper. "I didn't know him. He was a freshman. But I talked to his family and they told me some things about him. He played clarinet. He loved baseball, especially the San Francisco Giants. His favorite player was Renteria." Some kids start to whistle. Hiss. Seth clears his throat and says, "If anybody has any information regarding his beating, please contact the Carson City police."

I swallow.

Why don't I tell? Why didn't I say anything almost a month ago?

He finishes, saying, "That minute. I was thinking about Caleb. Yeah. I like Caleb and hope he gets better. But I was also thinking about Luis. Some kid I'll never get a chance to know because somebody beat him up with a baseball bat. Think about it."

Seth—the school conscience. Maybe Seth should be a man of the cloth—do some missionary stuff and teach people what it's like to have integrity, to walk the walk.

I feel sticky-hot and realize I have way more fun when we're just being us. Seth comes by, clicking pics on his camera. "Camera man, writer, editor—this is a one-man show," he says.

"Thanks for saying that about Luis," I say. "That took guts."

He sits next to us. His date, Jeanne, pulls up a chair, too. "What you said the other day in Creative Writing. That took guts."

I shake my head. "I don't know what I said." Everything's kind of blurry these past few weeks—memoirs and Mrs. B, Babylonia and *PB & J*.

"'Distorted mirrors. Filtered memories. Everyone's guilty.' It got me thinking, you know. How I write this stuff but, I dunno. Like it's not enough. I've got to get loud—like Babylonia loud."

I nod. "So now you're doing the paparazzi red-carpet thing?" I try to laugh. Keep it light. I can feel Josh tense next to me; his smile doesn't reach his eyes.

Seth shrugs. "The superficiality of it all kills me. But I need more funds. This sells."

"Loincloths sell?" I ask. "Hardly *PB & J* material."

"Yes. The problem of the press—needing money to get loud."

Jeanne leans over and says, "Well, I *like* to check out what everyone's wearing."

Seth groans.

"Call me superficial. Mike, I *love* your bracelet. Are those dice? Wow, and your dress! You look gorgeous."

"Thanks." Seth takes a picture of Jeanne looking at my bracelet.

They move on, walk through the crowd, take pics. The DJ puts on the chicken dance.

"You ready to go?" Josh asks.

"Yes." I exhale. "Anywhere."

Josh smiles. "I've got a surprise. C'mon." Marilyn and Sadie oooh and aah at us while we're trying to make our big escape. We manage to get into about a half dozen photos and avoid being pulled onto the dance floor to flap our arms like wings.

"I thought we'd *never* get out of there," Josh says, opening the car door for me. I slip into the passenger seat and feel butterflies rise up my belly.

"I've never actually gone to a dance before. It was kind of—"

"Lame. Yeah." Josh laughs. "But it's an excuse to get dressed up, do something different. We kind of have a pattern of, well, activities. Nice to break from tradition. For a bit." He winks.

"It is," I say. Even I believe I'm pretty tonight.

As soon as we drive up to the house, I know what we were going to do. The familiar buzz of excitement fills my chest, making me feel like me again—not the Michal everybody else sees. Everybody except for Josh. I feel a tinge of disappointment until Josh pulls out cotton gloves instead of the typical surgical ones. "Mrs. Brady spends the weekends up in Tahoe. Every weekend. The place is ours. Let's steal in style tonight."

He hands me a gorgeous Mardi Gras–type mask and

boosts me through the laundry-room window. He spray-paints cameras as we go through each room.

We take our time.

He throws down a blanket and brings out soft, gummy cheese from the refrigerator, spreading it on thick-crust French bread. We eat on the floor in the glittering dining room—a palace just for us.

I'm not sure what's worse, though—the weird cheese or awful wine. I attempt to swallow them down, bite by bite.

"Maybe we can go have breakfast at Denny's after this," Josh suggests, tossing his bread into a plastic bag he brought. "We don't want to leave our DNA here." He laughs, holds my hand; and we wander through the shadows of the house—sparkling chandeliers winking in moonlight, inaudible footsteps moving across thick carpet. My water-lily dress swishes, the hem sweeping across the floor. I listen to the house embrace us. We become the sounds of the house—the way it breathes, the way it lives.

"Close your eyes," he says, guiding me into a room. It smells musty—familiar. "Now!" I open my eyes. We're standing in the middle of a giant library. It doesn't take long to find a stash of money in a hollowed-out Bible. It's the only religious book in the office and the only one that looks like it doesn't have an inch-thick coating of dust on it. We don't trash the place. It's like we know exactly where to look—like the house is leading us to its treasure.

Josh slips a CD into the stereo and turns it on. Gavin

DeGraw's "Belief." He lights candles, turning the library into what could potentially be considered Carson City's biggest fire hazard.

"May I have this dance?" Josh bows and holds out his hand.

I slip my hand in Josh's. We've taken off our shoes. He pulls me close and we sway with the music. I lean my head against his chest and inhale the pine-fresh scent. He's wearing a little cologne today. Not too much. Undertones of cedar and nutmeg. He pulls me closer and I listen to the rhythmic thudding of his heart instead of the whispers of the house.

That's why I don't hear the footsteps in the hallway, the turn of a doorknob, the click of the hammer of a gun being cocked.

42

"DON'T MOVE." HER FRAIL arms hold the gun up, pointing at me.

Obviously.

I'm an easier target.

Every sense of mine is on hyperdrive. I smell Josh's cedar-nutmeg cologne, now becoming sour with sweat. I smell dusty book covers and moldy paper, peach-scented cream and hair spray.

Outside the wind picks up. The house wheezes with the howl of the wind; windows chatter; shingles screech as they're being ripped off the roof. This is the kind of house I love, and for a moment it was mine. It's the kind of home that screams back at the weather—comes to life with anger and defiance. Branches from a tree claw across the siding. Thick desert raindrops pound at the windows.

I hear shrieking now—all sounds coming from the old woman's mouth. "I know who you are, you little bastards!"

"Please," Josh says, his voice wavering. "Please don't shoot."

"You sit down. You don't move. I'm calling the police." She pauses, staring at Josh. Her cloudy blue eyes squint from behind thick glasses. "Are you that kid? That Ellison kid? Is that who you are?"

Josh's hands tremble.

"You little shit—eating dinner at my house, asking for a grand tour. Shame on you." She looks down at the empty Bible. Her voice trembles. "Shame on you. I don't ever forget a voice."

She moves toward the phone on the desk, picking it up from its cradle with quaking hands. Just as she looks down to dial, Josh plows into her, knocking her against the bookshelves behind the desk. An avalanche of two-hundred-year-old encyclopedias rains down on them. Josh stands up, knocking his forehead on a shelf.

"Oh my God," I say. "Oh my God. Oh my God. Is she okay?"

Her crumpled body lies in a heap on the floor like a biology classroom skeleton. I push books aside and lean my head against her chest—rattling with uneven breaths.

"Oh my God."

A thick pool of blood forms below her head from where she bashed it against the corner of a sticking-out world almanac. Josh brings me a towel from the bathroom, and we prop her head up on a pillow on a pile of ice.

"What else do we do?" I ask.

A welt runs across Josh's forehead. He sits across from me. "Does she need CPR? Oh God. I panicked. She knew who I was. She was dialing nine-one-one. Like what was I supposed to do?"

"We've gotta go. Call for help. Like now." I take out my phone.

"Not from that. They'll trace you. A pay phone."

We run through the house holding our shoes in our hands, slipping back through the laundry window, out onto the street. Rain pelts my skin as if it were trying to burrow into me, keeping me in a state of forever cold. We splash through puddles, bare feet striking the gravel outside. A thick piece of broken glass cuts into the sole of my foot.

We drive to the Old Washoe Station to call 911. Rain drizzles down in a misty sheet now, the thick drops replaced by thousands of tiny spatters, like walking through a cloud.

"Please, please. Please get to her as soon as you can. She's bleeding. A lot." I think I'm screaming. I lean my head against the thick glass of the booth.

"Can you repeat that, ma'am?"

"She's hurt. Really bad, okay?" I give her the address again.

"May I ask who's calling?" the operator asks.

"Babylonia," I whisper, and hang up the phone, tears spilling down my cheeks.

Josh buys towels at Walmart. We huddle, shivering in his car, the heat cranked up to ten thousand degrees Fahrenheit. He wraps my foot in gauze. "What have we done?" he asks. "What have we done?"

How do you fix the unfixable?

43

JOSH LEAVES ME AT HOME just before midnight. Lillian has fallen asleep on the recliner. I put the afghan on her and watch her sleep for a while. Her head leans to the side, jaw slack.

She actually waited up for me.

Then I limp to my room and spend the night praying for a call, a text, a smoke signal, carrier pigeon, Morse code tap on the window—*anything* from Josh.

Sunday passes.

No call.

We lose.

We lose. I watch the game on mute, not able to handle the squeaky basketball shoes, whistles, and pound of the ball. U-Dub wins. By three points. Total: 179.

We lose the over-under and the spread. We lose.

Vaporized hope.

Five thousand dollars.

Gone.

And Josh hasn't called. Leonard has. Three times.

Monday is Senior Ditch Day. So I get up to go to school. I don't know where else to go. I'm not the only lame senior here. Seth is here along with a handful of others. Mrs. Brooks brings us doughnuts, coffee, juice, and fruit.

There are only ten of us in class. No Josh. So I kind of have to participate. Even Moch is here. "What are you doing here?" I ask.

"Mike." Moch smiles. "I can ditch *any day.*"

Mrs. B laughs. "Yeah. And one more ditch, Mr. Mendez, and you won't be graduating. Understood?"

Moch nods. "Understood."

I feel like Mrs. B and Moch have some kind of student-teacher mentor thing going on. Maybe she's his lifeline.

Mine is Babylonia.

Was.

Mrs. B asks the class about the dance.

"It was fun," I say, trying to pass my nonenthusiasm off on being exhausted, not the fact that I'm probably going to prison for the rest of my life.

"You looked really pretty," Seth says. "You've been looking different lately. I guess. I dunno."

It's called the Home Invasion Diet. Steal from people and watch the pounds slip away.

"Thanks," I say, feeling my cheeks get hot. "So did Jeanne. She's nice."

"Yeah. When she gets away from the dragon lair for more than an hour at a time. I kept expecting her to turn into a pumpkin."

We all laugh.

We talk about the dance as if it were important—some kind of indispensable rite of passage watching the most popular kids in our class wear shiny, plastic crowns.

I almost killed a woman on Saturday, so this conversation feels pretty empty.

"Read the news?" Mrs. Brooks hands us the *Nevada Appeal* front page story.

Babylonia Leaves Local Philanthropist in Coma

"Maybe she's like the others," Javier says. "What do they say? Twenty-first-century slave owners?"

"Maybe," Mrs. B says. "But who will know if she dies? She'll never get a chance to tell her side. You want to risk someone's life for a *maybe*."

Mrs. B's words are like razors, slicing across my abdomen, my chest; every part of my body stings with the truth.

We could be wrong. A sick feeling floods me. A bad feeling. *We were wrong. I think we were wrong.*

Moch passes the paper back. Mrs. B has brought in a

few for all of us to look at. I stare at the headline, skimming the article. The words blur, then come into sharp focus again. Maybe, maybe if I can change the words, it won't have happened.

Maybe.

"*PB & J* didn't get that scoop." Seth shows the front page with Tarzan and Jane caricatures, the headline:

Hawaii According to CHS

The class laughs.

Mrs. B says that Police Chief Dominguez got the name of every kid at the dance, probably to narrow down the suspect pool.

"Great," Moch says. "I'm officially a suspect because I choose to abstain from school gatherings where people dress up like retired old people in Florida. *Mierda*."

"Language, Mocho."

"Sorry."

"I'm with you then, Mocho," Catalina says. "I wasn't there, either. Should we just turn ourselves in now?"

Moch smiles at Catalina. "Nah. Let's let them sweat it out for a bit. Make them work to find us."

"Deal."

The class talks, eats, does what normal classes do. Mrs. B tells about the time she was in the Peace Corps. She talks about teaching English all over the world until she settled back into Carson City.

I stare at the headline. The hollowed-out-pit feeling in my stomach fills with fire.

Was the dance just an alibi? Maybe I'm just an alibi. For Josh. Nothing more.

At lunch, Josh is waiting for me in the hallway outside of the library. "Roast beef." He holds a Schat's Bakery bag up. "Coke. Homemade pecan cinnamon roll."

I swallow down the huge knot that's worked its way from my stomach up my esophagus, filling my mouth with anger and sadness and confusion and disappointment, wondering if every horrible human feeling known to man has to be experienced in some twisted rite of passage and all at the same time. I'm an emotional time bomb.

The welt on Josh's head has gone down and is now a bluish-green color. "Please," Josh says. "I could use some company."

I sit next to him. His eyes are red, dark circles underneath. The smell of the food makes me feel nauseous, so I just sip on the Coke. We can give the food to some poor kid who's been exposed to the cafeteria food all year.

"I stayed at the hospital all night and yesterday," Josh says.

I nod.

"Just outside. It's not like I could do anything, go inside or anything. But I just needed to be there."

"You didn't mean—" I start to say. "It was an accident."

"She could die, Mike. And I'd be the one who killed her."

"She's not gonna die."

"So when she wakes up—"

"We'll figure it out when she wakes up. Okay? She's. Not. Going. To. Die." This has to be a fact now. No odds or probabilities or looking back. She. Will. Live.

We have placed our bets.

"I need the money," I say.

Josh peers over the rim of his Coke can. "I left it in an envelope, in their mailbox. I didn't know what else to do. I just don't know how to make things right."

Open heart, insert knife. A white-hot feeling of pain seizes me.

"But you *can't* just do that. You have to tell me about that kind of stuff. Call me. Text me. Send me an email. It's as simple as saying, 'Hey, Mike, by the way, I'm giving five thousand two hundred and twenty-three dollars away.'" It feels like somebody's wrapped his fingers around my trachea, closing in on it tight.

"Would you lower your voice?" Josh says. "Plus what else were we going to do with it?" Josh asks.

"We lost," I say, lowering my voice. "We lost the bets."

"How much?"

"Five thousand."

"*Five thousand?* What the—are you out of your mind?" Josh paces back and forth.

"Out of my mind? *Out of my mind?* I'm not the one throwing money at a family to get over my Daddy Warbucks guilt. Guess what? Mrs. Mendez *will never come back.* And your family—"

"My family what?" Josh's scar is white-hot. His eyes narrow. "What?"

Every word that comes to mind is poison. I clench my jaw.

Josh seethes, speaking in a forced whisper. "You just do it so you can be seen." He holds his hands up, doing obnoxious quotation marks when he says *seen.* "You work so hard to make sure everybody knows you're above everybody else, but at the end of the day, you just want to fit in. Guess what, Mike." Hearing *Mike* rattles me. "You can't buy yourself friends or respect. Your three-hundred-dollar boots don't make a difference to anybody out there. *Anybody.*"

The ugly words bounce off the walls, hitting me over and over again. It feels like I've been punched so hard I can't breathe.

I pull my knees to my chest and cradle my head against them. I take off my glasses and press on my lids, seeing the crackle of light behind them.

"Okay, Trust Fund. I don't suppose you have five grand lying around?" I'm really hoping Josh is doing this for the game of it and actually can access thousands of dollars from some secret bank account set aside for his yacht when he turns eighteen.

He glares at me and shakes his head.

"I'll take care of it." I stand up, throwing my backpack over my shoulder, trying to keep the nettles out of my heart. Josh watches me in silence. I feel like I've been pricked by a pin and deflated, become a two-dimensional paper doll, creased and folded, ready to be thrown in the trash.

The bell rings.

He doesn't move.

I turn my back and walk away.

On my own. Better this way.

44

LEONARD HAS LEFT FOUR
messages. I call him. "I'll get the money for you. By tonight.
Late." And hang up before he has a chance to go into some
kind of *Sopranos* speech. I've checked my accounts. I have
to pay out nearly five hundred dollars this week to my winners. Five hundred I would've had, had I not bet it all.

One basket. *One basket* and we'd be fine. We wouldn't
be fighting. We'd be collecting almost four thousand dollars
from Leonard and would shrug off the botched over-under
bet. ONE SHOT. Two points. Luis's family would have
money. Moch's family would have money. Brain Food,
Planned Parenthood, the Boys and Girls Club . . .

Five thousand five hundred dollars.

Damn damn damn stupidstupidstupidstupid.

Lillian's at the clinic. Outside, it's a regular spring

afternoon. Kids are playing with a flat soccer ball that thuds when it gets kicked and wobbles just a few feet. The neighbors are cleaning out their yards, getting ready for spring planting. Five thousand five hundred dollars.

I stand outside Lillian's bedroom, leaning my head against the door. *Maybe she's got something. I'll pay her back.*

"I'm so sorry," I say, walking in the bedroom. I start with the dresser drawers, making my way through her room like I would a house on our list. I look under the mattress, behind the headboard, in the not-so-secret panel in the back. I run my fingers along the base of her bed frame. I look behind the mirror on her dresser and run my hand along the base of the dresser, too. Nothing.

Her closet is impeccable. Three pairs of shoes from Payless—brown, black, and blue—all in a row. Practical. Inexpensive. I think about my shoe collection, Josh's words, and cringe. *Focus.* In the back of her closet, there's a shoe box, tucked behind some ancient Christmas ornaments. I pull it down and open it up. I flip through her Mexican passport, staring at the picture of the girl in the black-and-white photo. She looks so young. She looks like me. There are some letters—in Spanish—Mom's birth certificate, a medallion of a saint. I hold it up and look close, squinting to see which saint. Saint Jude. I'll have to look it up, so I pocket it. I can use all the help I can get.

I'm about to put the shoe box back up when I notice

there's a funny bump on the lid. I pull away at the loose cardboard and find a savings account book. I do a double take. It has my name on it. I flip through the book. Every month, since I was born, she's deposited between twenty-five and fifty dollars. I now have nearly eight thousand dollars. Money Lillian's saved for me for college. Money she's *not* spent on herself to buy shoes.

A knot of sorrow fills my throat. I placed my bets without having all the information. "I will pay you back," I whisper. I hold the savings book in my hands—its pages worn and fuzzy at the sides. Seventeen years of saving for me, my future. "I'm so sorry," I say.

My phone beeps again. Leonard. I listen to the message. "Tonight, Mike. Or things are gonna get ugly."

I'm the last to slip through the door before the bank locks up. When I withdraw the money, the teller doesn't even blink. She just says, "Do you want to close the account?"

"No. Can I leave ten dollars in it? For now?"

"Sure. Buying a car?"

"Yeah," I say. "A car."

She smiles and hands me the money. "Drive safe."

I drive up to Reno, tapping the money, Lillian's money, against my thigh. I rub Saint Jude between my thumb and forefinger, wondering where I'll get the money to pay Lillian back, thinking about the games this week. I just have to bet smarter.

Two points. One shot. One. Stinking. Shot.

After I leave Leonard's place, I stand outside. A nearby parking lot is filled with men hanging out, looking for a day's work. I look at my watch. Way too late. And I don't have anything to give them.

Lying. Hiding. Falling. Nowhere to land.

3D living overrated. Too late now.

45

AT SCHOOL, IT'S LIKE JOSH
and I don't know each other—don't even live on the same
planet. How can he *not* wonder about Leonard? How can
he *not* be worried that I'm in deep shit and he's just sitting
pretty, going to tuxedo fittings after school for another tea
or whatever?

After school, I end up at Moch's house.

Moch is standing outside on a crooked ladder, fixing
the screen. He's wearing jeans and a T-shirt. His hair isn't
slicked back; he's not wearing sunglasses. He almost looks
normal—like a regular high school senior stuck fixing his
parents' window on a Thursday afternoon.

I can't sit still. I can't think.

Mr. Mendez gives me a giant hug and hands me two
Cokes; I pass one up to Moch. He wipes his head with his

forearm, cracks open the can of Coke, and takes deep gulps, his Adam's apple bobbing up and down. "Pa takes the bus up to Reno in the mornings. Right now it's like every business, contractor, and industry in Nevada has gone licit."

"Licit. Good word."

"Not always," Moch says.

"I'm sorry."

"What for?"

Everything.

That should be my six-word memoir: I'm sorry. I'm sorry. I'm sorry.

He climbs down the ladder and sits on the bottom rung, finishing off the last of his Coke. "It's hot. Too hot for March. Gonna be a dry summer. Lots of fires, I'm guessing."

I shrug and shiver. I don't feel the warmth, just a piece of ice. I sit next to him in his lawn chair, sipping on my Coke. Cold sweat prickles the back of my neck.

"Where've you been?" Moch asks. "You don't come by much."

"Just busy, I guess."

"Ellison? You two together or something?"

"No." It sounds so final and my voice catches.

Moch nods. I can't tell if he looks relieved or disappointed or is slipping back into monosyllabic Moch.

"Staying for dinner?" Moch asks.

I look at the trailer house. It's a was home. Its past

smells and tastes and sounds lost under a blanket of death and sadness. "I dunno," I say. Moch goes into the house and comes back out with two more Cokes.

The Coke fizzles; perspiration beads on the can. The sun lowers in the sky. The air cools. We sit together, listening to neighbors fight, TVs on full blast, the boom of somebody's bass, the sound of a baby crying. Barefoot kids run up and down the street chasing lizards and beating them with sticks. A lizard scurries across the lawn, and Moch whispers, "You'd better hide, little dude."

Boredom kills. Literally.

I inhale. The neighborhood smells deep-fried, dusty. It's a tumbleweed haven.

Moch takes a big drink and hiccups when he comes up for air. "I went to that doctor's house. I had a gun."

It takes a second to digest what he's said. I rub my arms. I try to read Moch's expression in the shadows. He pauses, tapping his fingers on the can, drumming an aluminum rhythm. I listen.

"He was alone, sitting outside reading. I saw him there *alive* and *reading*. Like he had no right to be there at all. I walked up to him, gun in my pocket. He saw me. He didn't run or cry or anything. He asked me to sit down. I did. You know, I was so ready to kill him. He knew I was going to kill him, too. It was like he had been sitting there, reading in that stupid fucking porch swing, waiting for me to come.

"I asked, 'What are you reading?' You know what he showed me?"

I shake my head.

"*The Gambler.* ¡*Joder!* So I couldn't kill him because he was reading your book. How's that? So I got up to go. He said, 'Why didn't you do it?'"

"I say, 'Once more I looked around me like a conqueror—once more I feared nothing.' Yeah. I quote from *The Gambler.* And he's like, 'You've read it?' But he doesn't say it in a surprised way like some *pendejo.* He says it like he wants to talk about it. 'Yeah,' I say, 'it's this book my friend always quotes from, so I picked it up.' It's like we're in some kind of book club. I couldn't believe it. I have this gun. Ready to kill him. And now I'm about ready to sit down for tea and scones and a book talk, and it hits me. The whole thing hits me and I'm just blown away because I don't know what to hope for outside of these tattoos and all the other shit I'm caught up in. I don't know what I'm fighting for. I don't even know who I'm fighting.

"So my legs give out on me, and I collapse on his lawn and cry and cry and he comes over and hugs me like some kind of *joto.* And we cry together. All because of *The Gambler.*"

Moch runs his arm across his nose and finishes off his second can of Coke. The sky is blotchy purple, the first stars shining.

"What are you hoping for?" I ask.

Moch crushes the second can and holds the two together like cymbals, clacking the aluminum, making a tinny, ringing sound. "I've been working on that—to figure that out—real hard, you know. I'm even doing homework and shit—so I can maybe graduate. Get out of here."

"And?" I ask. Maybe he can give me a tip. Something to hope for beyond surviving the week. How quickly things change—I'm him, he's me.

Does he see that?

The lizard genocide has come to an end; the neighborhood kids have been called in for dinner. A pizza delivery truck drives by, honking at a couple hollering at each other in the street.

Dinnertime.

"I'm going to Indiana," he says.

"Indiana? When? Why?"

"We've come into some money." Moch stares at me.

I look away.

He continues. "Pa has a friend, Gary, who rebuilds motors in old cars and then sells them. He's going to train me. Who knows? Maybe I'll find myself a nice little wife there—go green, you know." He winks.

"I'll marry you, Moch," I say before I realize what I've said, and my whole body turns that purplish-red-right-after-the-sun-dips-down-behind-the-horizon color.

He wraps his arm in mine, his copper skin over my can't-decide-what-to-be skin I have going on under a spray of a thousand freckles. He leans over and gives my cheek a kiss. "Thanks, Mike. But you deserve more. You're going places."

Like prison. But I don't say that, because then I'd be the big disappointment all around.

"What about your dad?" I ask.

Moch exhales. "I don't know. But I know I'm not doing him any good around here."

"The restaurant?"

"Some dreams die."

"You'll do good there, you know?" I swallow back my embarrassment. "I mean. You'll be good at building motors—or anything."

"Yeah. I figure I've managed these *cabrones* for the past two years." He points to the la Cordillera tattoo on his arm. "I'll probably be able to manage building some motors and starting a *licit* business." He picks up my cans of Coke. "Recycling."

I grin. "So not only will you have a licit business, but you'll also save the world."

"Something like that." He winks.

"What does the gang think?"

Moch puts his forefinger to his lips. "They don't know."

"I'm glad."

"Me, too."

I get up to go. "See you at school tomorrow. Tell your dad thanks for the Cokes, okay?" I walk to my car, feeling a little better about Moch.

Moch smiles, though the sadness in his eyes remains. "Mike?"

"Yeah?"

"Whatever you're doing, whatever you're up to, it has to stop. You know that, right?"

If it were anybody else, I'd play dumb—put on my bookie face and say the right thing. But not with Moch. "It'll stop," I say. "This weekend."

Moch stands and stretches. He heads inside. I watch him go up the lopsided front porch stairs and kick on the wobbly steel. Something else for him to fix before he goes.

Moch found the path I lost.

46

Sanctuary 4:30 Mills Park

WE GATHER AT THE SKATE
park. "Place your bets, guys," I say, pulling out my betting
book, scanning the crowd, hoping to see Josh. I lost that
bet, too.

"Mike, aren't you forgetting something?" Javier asks.

"Yeah, Mike. C'mon, you're gonna totally mess with
my luck," Tim says.

I look at the group. "What?"

"A little *Gambler* to set the mood?"

"Oh. Yeah. Okay." I inhale, and only one quote comes
to me.

> *Oh, you self-satisfied persons who, in your unctu-*
> *ous pride, are forever ready to mouth your maxims—if*
> *only you knew how fully I myself comprehend the*

sordidness of my present state, you would not trouble to wag your tongues at me!

"Well, that was a downer. Geez, Mike, what's your problem?" Tim laments.

"C'mon, guys. Lay off." Seth has come to make his biannual bet. He never misses March Madness Final Four or finals.

"You bummed about BYU?" I ask.

He shakes his head. "Nah. I was banking on Arizona."

"Good choice," I say.

They place their bets. I act normal, like some lady's not almost dead because of me.

Mission accomplished.

But the mission kind of got blurry. I wonder if this is how the Crusades began—a couple of conversations about why my religion is better than yours, then a few hundred years of slaughter. Just a giant misunderstanding.

Mrs. Brady is out of critical condition and is semi-conscious. As far as I know, though, she hasn't said anything about Josh—about us. The governor is going gung-ho, pleading through the media for information regarding the dangerous duo Babylonia. We've gone from sainthood to Judas with the flip of a coin.

Because of her, I'm thinking about all the houses, all the robberies, doubting us, what we did.

Maybe we were wrong all along.

How did right and wrong get so hazy? How come I couldn't see this coming? I lie down on a bench, the sun long set, the cold seeping through my clothes, skin, until I can't tell where the bench ends and my back begins. I listen to the skateboarders' whirring wheels, the scrape of the bottoms of boards across concrete jumps, the clatter of boards when they flip.

"You'll get pneumonia," Josh says, draping his jacket over me. A faint smell of nutmeg clings to it along with the familiar fabric softener and pine. He sits at the end of the bench. I keep my eyes closed. He talks. "I had to give them the money. I just had to do something. I panicked and felt hopeless. I'm so sorry."

I lie there, my back frozen, my front warm from Josh's jacket. I can't speak to him, though, because he left me when I needed him. Big-time. He left me to deal with Leonard. It's like my voice box has frozen, too.

"My dad fired them," Josh says. "Mr. Mendez and all the others. The investigations, the feds looking into Ellison Industries' employment records. He fired them all. About twenty that I know of."

I already knew. Mr. Mendez is riding up to Reno every morning to look for work.

"I found out last week," he says. "Dad was talking about it to his lawyer. His lawyer said it was time to stop *thinking outside the bun.* So my dad totally lost his cool then, you know. Telling his lawyer that he was a racist son of a bitch, blahblahblah. And his lawyer said, 'With all due respect, I'm not the one employing them.'"

More rich guilt. Scoop it on.

You still left me.

"I went to Leonard's. I was going to give him the title to my car," he says. "But he said the debt had been paid. What did you do?"

The ice starts to melt. A tear trickles down my cheek. I hate that I'm crying, hate that he matters. Even when he shouldn't. Not anymore. "Turns out I had a trust fund," I will myself to say. "I need to pay it back somehow." The cold bites into my fingers and nose. "I've lived with Lillian for years and I don't know anything about her. That's pretty sad."

Josh moves and sits down on the grass in front of me. He pushes my bangs out of my eyes. I can feel his breath. Cinnamon Trident. "I didn't mean that stuff I said to you. I was freaking out and—"

"I'm sorry, too," I say. And mean it.

"We'll get the money. One last job—one last bet. And we're done."

"Done," I echo.

"Yeah. Maybe we'll have to start going to pizza and the movies like normal teens."

"High cholesterol is sounding like a pretty good option right about now," I say, finally opening my eyes to look at him.

He kisses a tear from my cheek. "We're going to be fine." He has that perfect smile again—making me feel like everything's under control. Like he really has a solution to all this. It's like he's back in that world where Babylonia is untouchable, where Babylonia is right.

"I can't find my bracelet," I say. "I don't know where it is. The last time I remember having it was showing Jeanne at the dance."

Maybe we were wrong. But I can't bring myself to tell him. Not now. I have to believe this last hit will be right. I look up to the sky, the first spray of stars coming out.

Josh is quiet. "It could've fallen off anywhere—at school, at the dance . . . anywhere." He scratches behind his left ear. The corners of his mouth fight to smile, then win out. But the smile doesn't reach his eyes. "Anywhere," he says in a flat voice.

"Anywhere," I echo, and lay my head back down again.

Wanted: lost bracelet, message from God.

47

SETH INVITED US OVER FOR
the games. His parents have a massive basement that smells
a little funky but is private enough to give us our space.
They pump us with ginger ale and snack foods. His brothers and sisters watch, too.

I called Leonard and bet a little over two thousand on
U-Dub, money-lining it the whole way—the money I have
left over from Lillian's bank account. I'll need to pay off my
clients—the winners. I don't have any extra cash to do that.
So we'd better win. We *have* to win.

Bet what you can lose. What if I can't lose anything?
I'm feeling a whole lot of sympathy for Nim these days.

The VCU Rams and Huskies tip off, the Huskies in a
sludge start. By the end of the second quarter, they're behind
by twelve. God, their tongues are practically dragging on

the floor. The party goes on. Seth is pacing back and forth, his fifty-dollar bet looking like money thrown down the toilet.

And I'd swear to God his brothers and sisters have multiplied. More blond-headed, clean-cut kids come in, wrestling for space on the remaining bean bags.

The teams are back with their coaches—slick, gelled hair and thin ties in Armani suits. They pace the sidelines, shouting, screaming. The Huskies' coach has a red vein that bulges on his forehead.

I'm trying to visualize the two worst conversations on earth I'm going to have to have. One: telling Lillian that I emptied the savings account; two: telling Police Chief Dominguez that it's all my fault.

"C'mon, c'mon, c'mon, c'mon." I'm kneeling before the TV.

Somebody throws a jujube at me and says, "Move out of the way."

"Sorry." I blush.

Josh, for the first time I've ever met him, is still. Frozen to the couch cushion with a half-eaten pretzel in his hands. His eyes narrow. "C'mon, U-Dub Huskies. Win. This. Fucking. Game."

The basement gets quiet.

Josh looks at the wide-eyed faces of Seth's sisters and says, "So sorry. Excuse me. Sorry."

The Rams have the ball and are practically playing

with the Huskies, tossing it around the three-point line, all too confident. Then something happens. Something magic. You can see it in Gutzman's face. He's in the zone—totally in command of the court, his silver high-tops a shiny blur on the screen. Gutzman rushes the point guard—who pauses, just at the wrong time—steals the ball, and tosses it to Grisemer, ready for the cherry pick.

Fire.

The Huskies work the court, pulling in from behind, pressuring the Rams' offensive—moving from zone to man-to-man defense, pretty much camping on the Rams' butts.

Rams call time-out. Twenty seconds on the clock. The Rams are in possession of the ball and up by one. They come back, make a quick two pointer, then do a full-court press, pushing the Huskies' offensive.

Gutzman takes the ball and there's this moment, this pause; I think everybody sitting in the stadium sees it. He stops, the time racing to zero. But he stops, takes the extra second, fakes right, then dribbles, gliding by the Rams' defense—as if the Rams were doing the boulder-in-the-hallway test. They can't touch him.

Gutzman tosses it to Grisemer, who sinks the ball, getting fouled in the meantime.

Two seconds on the clock.

Grisemer stands on the free-throw line and swishes the first.

Tied.

The stadium has gone mad—electrified. We can practically feel the pounding of feet, the thunderous stomping.

"One more. One more," I whisper.

My eyes go blurry when he sinks the second shot. We're all jumping and screaming—my voice feels foreign, hollering so loud. This is a sign.

Everything's going to be okay.

Everything.

One more bet. One more hit.

48

Investigators Get First Big Clue Leading to Identities of Babylonia Burglars

"DID YOU READ THE PAPER?"

Josh asks.

I stare at the glow of lights from the alarm clock: 6:14 a.m. I've been awake since three a.m. "In case you didn't remember, we're always a day behind, so I *do* know what the weather forecast for yesterday is."

"Well then. That gives us a day before Lillian finds out."

"Finds out what?"

"They found your bracelet."

I look down at my naked wrist and feel like I've been impaled on Satan's pitchfork.

"At Mrs. Brady's house."

"Oh." Now all the air has been sucked out of my world.

"Okay," he says. "Who saw you wearing it?"

I rub my eyes.

I've been wearing it for a month. Everybody and nobody.

"Has anybody ever *noticed* it, though?" Josh asks.

Jeanne.

"We've got to talk to Seth before—"

"Need a ride?"

"I can meet you there."

"Need coffee?"

"Yes."

"Get dressed. I'm outside waiting—double shot of espresso, three pumps of cinnamon dolce."

"Okay."

We get to Seth's just after seven o'clock. The sun has risen over eastern Nevada—bright orange rays like fire creeping through the valley.

His family is piling into the van—ready for church. I don't see Seth. Maybe he's gotten out of going to church with everyone. We wait until they leave.

Who'll be the first to call in the tip for five grand?

Probably Nim. But he doesn't read the newspaper. I have my doubts he even reads. And he'd never pay attention to anything I'm wearing. At all. It's been a lifetime since Nim was my greatest nemesis. It's like that old life was swallowed up by something much bigger than me—something better.

Something worse.

We knock on the door. Seth says, "I'm *not* going. I've *told you a thousand times*." He throws open the door. "Oh. Hi. Come in." He rubs bloodshot eyes. "I was just thinking about you." Today's *Appeal* is lying next to him on the table.

"Imagine that," I say.

"Imagine that."

I try to keep my eyes from the front-page article. The description of my bracelet. The reward.

"So. Babylonia, huh? Have you come to spray-paint my house?"

I'd laugh if I didn't feel like I was choking on air. I inhale and exhale, leaning over, hands on knees, trying to catch my breath. Maybe I should be a fish—grow gills, slip into dark murky waters where I can drift around unnoticed in algae swamps.

"What have you done?" Seth asks.

"I don't know anymore. It just seemed—"

"We need a chance to make this right," Josh says.

"How are you going to do that?" Seth asks.

Nobody had to know about us. Babylonia would've become a Carson High legend, something future generations would've tried to repeat. Now we'll be voted "most likely to be on Interpol." All because of a lost bracelet and Mrs. Brady. She wasn't supposed to be home.

Josh is pacing like a caged tiger.

Nobody has to know about him. Will Seth keep quiet? About Josh?

We won a chunk in the Final Four. We have just *one more game*. The NCAA final. But how can I explain it to Seth? How could he understand? If we can just do one more hit—one more house—to pay back Lillian and leave a little extra for Luis and Moch. Counting the cash we had for our bet and win, we've now got almost four thousand dollars. I need $3,700 more. Then we can cut our losses. It's all about knowing when it's time to stop. Just one more hit, one more bet, and we're done.

"Look at this," Seth says, and turns on the TV—the local news. We're everywhere. WANTED: Babylonia. WANTED: Fugitives of the law. WANTED: Near-assassins. Seth shows us all the articles he's saved on Babylonia, bookmarked blogs.

We skim through articles. Three casinos have been fined thousands of dollars for doctoring employee files. There are shots of dozens of men and women standing in the lot near Leonard's—blurred faces—waiting for day work. "What did you expect would happen? Did you even think this through?"

How can you think through infinity?

"We just need one more day," Josh says.

Seth looks at us. "Why?"

Because . . . I don't have a real answer why, why I think tomorrow will be any different from today. But tomorrow feels like it's millions of miles away. Tomorrow is a lifetime away. Today is our last chance.

Today is Josh's only chance. Mine's already been blown.

I stare at the *Appeal*. Seth looks at me. I can't read his expression. I say, "Have you ever, I don't know, been given a chance to do something, really *do* something? For the first time in my life, *now* mattered. It was all about now. Hope. Purpose."

"High school isn't forever," he says.

"Tell that to me four years ago," I say. "We need today. Just one more day. Please." My mind races to give Seth a reason. "I have to make things right. Set things straight. Please."

Josh and I go to the Cracker Box, but I can't stomach the smell of the greasy potatoes, so we end up getting a coffee and sitting outside. Josh tosses me a "last chance to buy" yearbook flyer.

We're on borrowed time. Who knows who else saw my bracelet?

I think about the yearbook. A stupid thing to think about, really. It's a collection of moments, memories: edited experiences. It won't include the time Mick Hill put Bengay on some new kid's jock strap before baseball tryouts sophomore year. Or the time the wrestlers threw a bucket of spit on Sarah Jennings after she broke up with *the* 152-pound state champ.

I stare at the yearbook flyer. The cover has a picture of the Berlin Wall being torn down. No Borders, No

Boundaries. Open up the cover to see pages filled with a generic high school experience, one without Garbage Disposal, la Cordillera, and Babylonia. *No borders, no boundaries.*

Where will I be in the yearbook? Where was *my* experience?

Our lives edited, erasing the truth.

49

now, this very moment in time?

I told Seth I'd lived now. Each second counted. Every time we entered a house, my whole nervous system caught fire. Like winning the money, watching the games—it was like being there, being part of something so much bigger than me. What was now for? Mrs. Mendez's memory? Charity groups? Acceptance? Admiration? Power? The chance to be kissed? Yep. I want a whopping, standing-in-the-rain, sweep-me-off-my-feet-and-make-me-sing-hallelujah kiss.

World peace.

Nah. I'm not Miss USA.

Right now, I'd take five thousand dollars over world peace, which says a lot about the kind of person I am.

What do I hope for?

U-Dub seems so far away—like a mirage, a lie, something I made up. I'm aware that, odds are, tomorrow is gone. I've traded all my tomorrows for today.

Think like a bookie; find a way to make the spread.

I don't know what bet to place—how to make it so things can at least even out, so that we all don't lose.

Somebody has to win.

I turn my phone off. Leonard's really pissing me off.

And every kid in high school wants to bet on tomorrow night's game. I've turned my betting phone off, too. Tomorrow's just for me, just to make things right.

I head to Josh's and my meeting place, turn off the car, and lean my head on the steering wheel.

It feels different. Not enlightened or political or righteous. Desperate. We've become what Police Chief Dominguez said we were. "A couple of punks on a joyride." But I can't help feeling the rapture—a prickling sensation pumps through my body.

I practically self-eject when Josh taps on the window. Josh's face, gap-toothed smile, crinkled hazel eyes, flushed cheeks, is on the driver's side. He's holding up some wilty-looking white daisies wrapped in bright purple cellophane. I roll down the window. "Hey," I say.

"Hey. I thought you could use these. Stopped by the Seven-Eleven, and they were the only ones left. They're, well, kinda dying."

"They're beautiful," I say, and resist hugging them to my chest. "Thank you, kind sir."

"Shall we?" Josh asks, opening my door, holding my hand in his, leaning down to kiss it.

"We shall," I say. "After you."

We make our way through the sagebrush, working our way to the homes that border the Bureau of Land Management property.

"You know, most burglaries are committed during the day," Josh says.

"Which show did you get that from?" I ask, zipping up the dark blue Pet Scoop uniform, pulling the gloves on tighter.

"The internet, actually," Josh says. "Ready?"

Always.

"Ready?" he repeats.

"Ready," I say. This one's for Josh. This one has to be for him because—I swallow down the bile that's worked its way up my esophagus.

Josh hands me a shovel and we walk down the street, black garbage bags slung over our shoulders. The driveway is clear. We scan the windows while we shovel up dried dog crap. It doesn't look like Nim or his dad have shoveled the lawn . . . ever. "Got a fresh pile over here!" Josh hollers, scooping.

"Fly-infested foul feces . . . Can't think of anything else."

"Fly-infested foul feces. Open sesame! Enter."

I look up and see the living room window is wide open—no screen. Just a wide-open window.

"Nice," I say.

"Double nice," Josh says.

"If they leave the window open like that, then . . ." I walk to the front door and twist the handle. "This is just too easy."

Josh and I lock eyes. "How many minutes have we got?" he asks.

"Nim will be done pumping iron and shooting up his weekly Equipoise dose in about twenty minutes. I don't know where his parents are."

This is big-time risky. Too risky.

"Plenty of time."

"Plenty."

"Mask on."

"Mask on."

"After you." Josh opens the door and waits for me to enter, closing it gently behind us.

It smells more like dog crap inside than out. We both check our feet. Nothing. We steal, yeah. We kind of trash the house, trying not to break things, but it's inevitable, really, during a robbery.

I listen. Wind chimes tinkle outside. Somewhere there's the sound of music, but it's so faint, I can't tell if it's inside or out. I listen harder—lullabies. Definitely has to be outside.

This is a mute house—the kind I hate the most. There are no moans or creaks, no sighs. It's a house that doesn't talk, doesn't respond to the seduction of the wind or the pounding of the sun. It's the kind of silence that keeps the world outside. It's a lonely soundless place.

Josh taps my shoulder. He holds up ten fingers twice.

The downstairs is clean. We don't even find a change pile.

Josh points upstairs, and I follow behind. The third stair creaks. The banister is loose. The music is like that garbage you have to hear when you're on hold, but it feels kind of nice to have sounds to accompany us. Maybe there's hope for this place to become a home after all. Maybe it will come alive.

Maybe there's hope for the entire family to become humans.

Maybe.

In the walk-in closet there's a jewelry box filled with all sorts of jewels that would, no doubt, bring in loads of money. But we don't do jewelry. We can't risk selling on the market, getting recognized, getting caught.

Will Lillian turn me in?

I don't suppose she'd suspect something weird if I cut a gaping hole out of her day-old newspaper.

I push past strands of pearls and delicate gold chains with diamond pendants. Taped to the back of the jewelry box is a key. We look for drawers and find, behind the now turned-over box, a tiny music box. We open the box up—a fuzzy cranking sound the background to the shrill belllike chime of "It's a Small World" in an amped-up, 120-decibel music box.

The ballerina twirls—her plastic face and red-painted lips in a perma-smile. Her once-white tulle tutu has a tear. The motor cranks her around and around. I scoop up the money and slam the box shut. My hands are trembling when I pass the cash to Josh. "I hate music boxes," I say.

"Creepy shit."

It's a world of laughter, a world of tears.

I shiver.

Josh holds up ten fingers. We have one room left to search. Nim's room looks like a trophy case. Shelves are covered with gold trophies for football, baseball, wrestling, and every other sport he was ever in. Plaques, medals, and ribbons paper the walls. The air freshener plug-ins do little to mask the stench—testosterone, musty gym socks, and a clove after-scent. I practically gag.

We search through drawers and under Nim's mattress, and I'm so glad we wear gloves. If a CSI unit were to come in here with a purple light, they'd see that the whole room is probably covered in semen. We find almost six hundred dollars tucked in the most obvious hiding places. Josh points to the dirty laundry basket and I shake my head. I'll only go so far.

He laughs, points to the bedside table drawer and to the

hallway. He holds up five fingers and goes to the door while I rummage through the drawer.

At the bottom I find a carefully bubble-wrapped photo.

It's from that day camp where Lilian sent me the first spring I came to Carson City. In it, we're all staring at the camera with goofy, missing-teeth grins. We must be facing the sun because everybody's squinting except for Nim.

He's staring at me. There's a crooked, faded red heart around my picture. He had a crush on me. He was the meanest person I'd ever met. But he *liked* me.

If I had known, would that have made a difference? Made me happy? Felt like I belonged?

My head hurts, temples throb.

Breathe.

I swallow back regret. "Thank you," I whisper, pulling the picture out of the frame, folding it up, putting it in my pocket next to Saint Jude.

Josh raps on the door. He holds up a zero sign with his fingers.

I nod and I follow him out the front door.

We get back to our cars and climb on Little Car's hood, leaning back against the windshield. Wispy clouds drift in the cobalt sky. The afternoon heat has waned, leaving us with the first taste of the desert-chill evening; the sweet smell of blooming lilacs perfumes the air.

I chose today. Sure, I erased yesterday and lost tomorrow. I've blown it with U-Dub since they don't, not that

I remember, have a little box on the application form to check if you're a convicted felon.

But I chose today.

I *choose* today.

If it weren't for Mrs. Brady, everything would be perfect. We'd still be Babylonia—the name people whisper because we are *doing* something. We stepped off the sidelines and became the game.

Don't look back.

The only proof they have is my bracelet, *my* bracelet. That and the note I'll leave, placing my last bet with Seth. I'm counting on him to make this right.

"This isn't going to end well," I finally say.

"Why does it have to end?" Josh asks.

Josh is still living the fairy tale. His eyes are closed, a spray of thick chestnut lashes on his cheeks. A smile curling up the edge of his lips. I slip my hand in his and squeeze, deciding to live the fairy tale, too. Just for him. Because all I've got is today.

Don't look back. Make it right.

50

I LISTEN TO THE SOUNDS
of our house—our home. Funny I've never done that before.
The front screen rattles when a gust of wind comes up. The
floorboard outside my bedroom door creaks just a little.
The east windows moan in protest to the darkness—the
sunless night. Lillian's breathing is raspy when she sleeps—
like every breath is a struggle.

I like the sound of my home.

The phone vibrates. Seth's name flashes.

"Hello," I say.

"Mike?"

"Yeah."

"For real?"

"For real. But there's a catch, okay?"

He's quiet, then says, "I'm not sure about this."

"I need to count on you, Seth. You always do the right thing. You have to be the anonymous tip. Five thousand dollars. You could use the cash next year at college."

"So it was really you?"

"What?"

"Babylonia?"

"Yep," I say. "That's pretty obvious, isn't it?"

"And *only* you." He emphasizes *only* because he knows that I'm editing the truth—something we've all become masters at. It's like the crib-note version of the past two months.

"Yes."

He's silent. My throat is dry. I stare at the wilted-looking flowers on the cactus and splash them with water, then drink down a glass. How is it possible to kill a cactus?

"What's the catch?" he finally asks.

"You've got to make the call"—I look at my watch—"tomorrow morning. Early. Before anybody else gets a shot."

"I'm in. What's the catch?"

"You need to place a bet with this guy I know. The bet I'm about to give you." I give him my bet, then hesitate. "I've left something else for you. It's in your bushes. In a plastic bag. You can take it to the police."

Seth's quiet. "What is it?" he finally asks.

"A bat," I whisper. "It should have evidence on it or something. There's a note explaining everything."

"Are you coming back?" Seth asks.

"Yes. I just need to see one thing before I'm locked up for all of eternity. Really."

Seth forces a laugh. "You won't be locked up for all of eternity."

"Hope not. So?"

"Deal," he says.

"Deal," I say.

He doesn't hang up.

"Mike?" he says, then gets quiet again. "Ahh, never mind." He hangs up the phone.

I leave Lillian a note on the coffee table and look around the shelves for a better place to put the second note—the one with all the truths, my confessions, my memoirs. The bank book. The one only for her. I owe her at least that much.

I go to her gardening area—a little shed she got at Home Depot. She's bought more geraniums to fill in some patchy spots. You'd think she'd get tired of planting the same thing all the time. I push them aside, the little plastic name stick dropping out.

Geranium "Salome."

There's a laminated page from an old Martha Stewart catalog.

A perennial geranium, "Salome" produces large, bright-lavender flowers streaked with magenta in summer and showy, chartreuse foliage that remains bright all season. It makes a charming trailer for borders or pots. Perennial geraniums, or cranesbills, are long-lived, easy-to-grow plants whose foliage often changes colors in fall.

They're for me. They've always been for me. She's taken care of me for seventeen years—put all her energy into pruning and weeding and making sure I flourish.

Maybe I was who she wanted all along.

I write one more memoir: I love you, too. I'm sorry.

I go to Lillian's room and kiss the door, repeating the words I just wrote. "I love you. Please take care of yourself." My voice catches.

I need to hang out for a few hours—just lie low. I tap in Moch's number, calling in all my last favors. "Hey."

"Mike, you're fucked."

"You noticed?"

"The bracelet. Yeah."

"I need a few hours this morning—just to crash." Funny how I've been betting away my days—now it's all about time.

"Meet me at American Flats."

"Thanks, Moch."

"Then what?"

"Then it's the morning, sun rising, and all that eternal march of time stuff," I say, hanging up the phone.

I've got to get to Leonard, to tell him about Seth. By

the time I'm there, though, my name will be all over the news—his leverage gone.

Josh will be safe.

Lillian will be taken care of.

It's all in Seth's hands now—Seth and Gutzman.

Championship game. One bet. Last chapter.

51

MOCH SPENDS THE NIGHT
with me. We play cards. We calculate how many aluminum
cans we would need to live off recycling.

We talk about Mrs. Mendez, Babylonia, Josh. About
Luis. We talk about Gary in Indiana and hope. What hope
he's found—what I've lost. And it's all okay because losing
hope is pretty cool in its own way. Losing hope means I
actually had some to begin with—something *now* and not
a few months from now.

We talk about guilt and shame and six-word memoirs.
I fall asleep listening to him talk about mango sunrises
and his mom's chili-pepper temper. Then the sun rises, as
expected. Moch gives me a giant hug, pulling me close to
him. "*Te quiero, hermana.*"

My heart soars.

◆

"You're a popular girl," Leonard says. The TV is on behind him—my senior picture being flashed everywhere in Nevada, California, Utah, and Arizona, like a felony Amber Alert. There's news about Mrs. Brady's recovery. She's out of her coma.

She doesn't remember anything.

The images of me, Mrs. Brady, the hospital, Caleb, all flash like some 1970s cinema-intermission subliminal messages.

You messed up.

You messed up.

"Today's a big day. Your friend can cover the bet?"

I nod.

"I've heard that before."

"It's covered."

He pulls out a handkerchief and wipes the sweat off his forehead. Fans are on full blast but only serve to blow around hot air.

"You could invest in some air conditioning," I say.

"Bad for the environment."

"We'll win."

"A bookie-turned-gambler who doesn't even know it. You're so sure about it, aren't you?"

I nod. "Because I can't lose this one," I say.

"Where are you going?" he asks.

"Where they'll find me," I say. "Running from the

law just isn't my thing."

"It's a shame—wasted talent."

"Nah. I'll have something to keep me busy in prison."

Leonard salutes me as I leave, the early-afternoon sun glinting off the clumpy asphalt. It's got to be at least eighty-five, and it's not even April. I push damp bangs off my face.

I sit in the driver's seat and put on Johnny Cash full blast. I'm about to kick the car into gear when Josh jumps on the hood, pounding it. "What have you done?" He rips open my door and tries to yank me out. "What have you done?"

"It's done," I say.

"No. It's *not* done. You can't do this to me. Leave me here after I found you. You can't *do* this." He kicks the back of my car.

"Why'd you go and do that?" I say, getting out and running my hand along the dent. "It's just Little Car."

Josh grabs my shoulders. "They came. Asked questions I wouldn't answer. Dad has a lawyer; they're all looking for you. *I've* been looking for you, but you left me—just disappeared. We're in this together."

"I'm not going to do the whole *Romeo and Juliet* thing. They'll be easy on me. I have no record. You'll be okay."

Josh shakes his head. "No. This is *not* okay. You can't leave me again. And . . ." Josh clears his throat. "I'll never leave you again."

I sit back in the car and close the door. "I'm going now.

To Great Basin. Kind of like a pre-grad gift because it looks like I'll end up graduating in prison. Anyway, after the great road trip, I'm turning myself in to the police. It's not all that dramatic. I just need to say good-bye, and this might be my last chance to do it."

Josh runs around the car and sits next to me in the passenger seat.

I shake my head.

He takes my hand in his and repeats, "You can't leave me."

"Stalker," I say, and try to hide a grin. "I could totally get a restraining order."

He laces his fingers in mine. "Together. Great Basin. Police. *Together.*" He buckles his seat belt and inhales. "This car gonna make it?"

"Doubtful." The motor chugs, sputters, and wheezes. "I will always testify I did it on my own."

"And I will do the same."

"It seems we've come to an impasse," I say.

"Nah. I'll convince you. We've got about an eight-hour drive, right?"

"Maybe six—maybe seven." I tap the dashboard. "Depends."

"I *never* get tired of talking."

"You'll fall asleep in about ten minutes."

"Wanna bet?"

"How much?"

"How much you've got?"

I open my wallet and tip it upside down, nothing comes out. "That's it. A full tank of gas. A twenty-dollar gas card. And me."

"Ahh, then I guess we'll have to make the bet more interesting."

Color rises to my cheeks.

"Well, let's go."

"*Fear and Loathing in Great Basin.*"

Josh catches on to the reference and smiles. "Road trip. Good-bye, past. Hello . . ."

"Jail," I mutter.

52

"WE CAN AFFORD CHEESE-
burgers," Josh says.

"We've been on the road an hour, and you're already hungry."

"What? We're supposed to fast, too?"

I shrug. "Fine. Cheeseburgers."

"Two Cokes and fries."

"What about gas?" I say.

He pulls out thirty dollars. "My allowance."

"I think, considering the situation, we should probably go through the drive-through. I'm a person of interest, you know."

"Totally." Josh winks.

I roll my eyes.

"Okay. Ask them for a crown, though."

"A crown?"

"Two! Two crowns."

"Two."

"Hey. If we have time, after Great Basin National Park, do you think we can get married in Vegas?"

I laugh. "No."

"So you don't want to marry me?" Josh asks.

I shake my head. "The whole conjugal-visit thing doesn't really sit well with me. Plus maybe I'll meet somebody in the can."

The guy passes us our order with two crowns. Josh kisses salt off my fingers.

"You're a tease," I say.

"Nah. Just waiting for the perfect, first-kiss moment."

I shake my head, look at the gas gauge and Nevada map. "I think we'll make it to Austin before we have to gas up."

He holds up a fry. "Cheers," he says.

"Cheers."

We both tap Little Car on the dashboard. "To Austin," I say.

She burps and we drive away.

This has been her first road trip—open road, open windows, guzzling gas. I can see the gas gauge move toward empty. *Criminy.*

"We've still got a quarter tank," Josh says.

"Let's gas up and see what happens."

Josh nods. "Use the debit card to gas up. Just to stay out of sight."

I swipe the card. It doesn't take. I swipe it again. The man speaks over the intercom. "Can't get a reading. Can you please come inside?"

"Fuck," Josh says.

The next gas station is far enough away that we'd run out before we got there. I feel like someplace this far removed will be safer. I just need to get to the Great Basin National Park.

"Let's go," I say. "We'll buy some Pony Express souvenir. Something to commemorate the greatest road trip ever taken by . . . me."

"How many road trips have you been on?" Josh asks.

"This one," I say.

"Same here. My family's more of a first-class ticket kind of family. Where's the fun?"

I smile. "Let's go in. It'll be fine."

I hand the man my card. He nods, his nose buried in a *Fishing and Hunting News.* "How much you want?"

"Twenty," I say. Behind him, the game's already in halftime. I stare at the score. Huskies are ahead. My stomach flutters.

Maybe we can listen to it on the radio. I turn my attention back to the man.

"You like basketball?" he asks. He's young—way younger than he looks at first glance. His red, curly beard covers an acne outbreak like Grizzly Adams meets failed retinol. He has bleary eyes—bloodshot, dazed. He smells fermented—like he's slept in the same clothes for the past year.

I shrug. "It's okay. If you can get past the squeaky shoes."

"Squeaky shoes," he grumbles, and swipes my card through the machine—a sprinkle of crumbs stuck in the wiry hair.

I gas up the car. When I go back inside, Josh has piled key chains, snow globes, patches, and a couple of stickers on the counter. He's still wearing his Burger King crown. "Pick your poison," Josh says. "What do you want?"

"What's the cheapest?"

"C'mon, Mike. Just pick one. Don't think about the price. I owe you a gift."

The guy watches us. My stomach knots. I glance at the game behind him. Third quarter has begun. Our eyes lock. His eyes change—like something's clicked in his brain—a connection has been made.

I shake my head at Josh and smile at the man. "Ready?"

The register dings—one of those old, coffee-shop registers with numbers on tabs that rotate. He scribbles on the receipt and hands it to me, just as he pulls out the gun, pointing it at me. "I think you two oughta sit down. You're worth about ten grand now."

I read the receipt: *Gotcha!*

53

I STEP BACK AND TRIP OVER
a Corn Nuts display—bags of nuts raining down. Josh
jumps to help me and then there's this loud bang. Deafen-
ing. An acrid sulfuric, ammonia smell fills the air.

My head hurts. I've banged it against the windowsill. I
touch it. Warm blood on my fingertips. Everything's blurry,
my vision's blotchy. I touch my face; my glasses have fallen
off. "Josh?" I say. "I can't find my glasses."

He comes to me, placing my crooked glasses on my
nose, a spray of blood on his clothes.

"Oh my God. He shot you," I say. "You're bleeding."

Josh shakes his head. He looks from the man back to
me, then places his hand on my stomach—bright red blood
covering the palm of his hand. "Michal."

My head feels like somebody's drilled into it—piercing

pain in my temples, a dull throbbing near my neck. "My head. It hurts," I say. "I'm fine, though. Really."

Josh grins, relieved. He wipes his nose and laughs. "Don't scare me like that. Please." He gets some disinfectant and Band-Aids from the shelves. His Burger King crown sits crooked on his head.

Everything's kind of slowed down. There's a weird burning in my stomach, but it's not like gunshot-wound burning or anything like I expected gunshot-wound burning would be. More like . . . I don't know.

I feel a little woozy, but not so bad. I'm shot, after all. I look down at the bright red blood on my shirt. "Where's Grizzly Adams?" I say.

"I hit him over the head with a Pony Express snow globe. I panicked. He shot you, and you were there, lying in these—"

"Corn Nuts," I say. "Sheesh. Talk about silly." I manage to wipe a couple of packs off. "Is he okay?" I ask.

"Yeah. He's breathing. He's not even bleeding," Josh says. "C'mon, Michal. We've got to get to the Great Basin. Your destiny awaits." He holds out his hand. "Michal?"

THE END

"NOW THIS SUCKS," I SAY.

Josh helps me sit up by the glass door. It's covered with yellowed flyers and advertisements. Apparently everybody between Fallon and Austin has lost their cat. Grizzly Acne moans from behind the counter and farts—filling the store with a rotten-egg smell—worse than the gunpowder. He moans again and snores. Josh has tied him up with about ten yards of duct tape.

The lights outside sputter on in a soft yellow glow. The sky looks like raspberry sorbet. "It's pretty."

Josh flips the OPEN sign on the door to CLOSED. He kneels next to me. "You're bleeding so much." His hands fumble on gauze and napkins. He finally pulls off his shirt, balling it up and shoving it on my stomach.

I flinch.

"I'm sorry. It's just the blood. There's so much." He leans over and kisses my forehead. "I'm going to make a call, okay? I'll be right back."

The cruisers appear like they were a mirage. But a crummy one, since mirages, on general principles, are supposed to be good and happy and filled with tropical fruits, muscular guys in turbans, and stuff like that. The cars rip along a shimmering strip of tarry highway—the loneliest road in America—between two billboards: THERE'S PLENTY OF ROOM FOR GOD'S CREATURES NEXT TO THE MASHED POTATOES and NEVADA: LEADING THE COUNTRY IN BEING JUST EAST OF CALIFORNIA. THAT AND BROTHELS (FLIP A BITCH . . . 5 MILES BACK). I'm not gonna go all *Great Gatsby* about the billboards because they're not a symbol of anything at all.

Nothing is.

The cruisers come to a screeching halt in the parking lot, tires kicking up loose rocks from the half-melted asphalt, modern-day Keystone Kops with wailing sirens and clumsy, fishtail stops. When the burnout smoke settles, the cops pile out of the cars, guns drawn, crouching behind the opened doors of the cars.

I pull back the corner of a flyer advertising hand-knit Snuggies to get a better view. Four cops. The lanky one has midnight skin and talks into a radio. The next car over, two cops roll to find better cover. Albino maintains her position behind the car door. They've got to be using phrases like "clear the area," "set up a perimeter," "Starsky and Hutch will take the back while Ponch and Jon hold the front."

Well, everything but that last phrase, anyway.

Josh is wearing his golden Burger King crown. It sits lopsided on his head. He kneels next to me, cupping my face in his hands.

Sweat drips down my temple. I'm so cold. But my hair sticks to my forehead and the back of my neck. I'm not what Josh would consider mirage worthy.

I never have been. Not for him.

Josh pushes my bangs to the side. I touch Josh's cheek with my hand and shiver.

He's managed to pile blankets on me—musty, red-checkered blankets he must've gotten from a closet or a back room or something. I didn't even notice he'd gone.

One of the officers talks through the megaphone. "Michal Garcia. Josh Ellison. We know you're in there." He says my name wrong—like Michael, not like Mee-kal. Whatever.

Grizzly must've called the cops when I was tanking up and Josh was on a Pony Express shopping spree. He'll get the reward money and be a big hero now. I hope there's a camera, though. A camera that filmed it all.

It's not like we'd rob a convenience store.

Ever.

Josh breaks open a window and screams, "Where's the fucking ambulance? I called for an ambulance!"

"Who won?" I see confetti on the screen. "It's hard to see much through these glasses." I try to take them off but can't lift my arms.

Josh takes off my glasses and dabs my face with baby wipes. "Michal?"

"Who won?"

Josh turns and looks at the screen. "U-Dub," Josh says, his voice trembling. "It doesn't matter."

"It's okay now. Everybody's going to be okay. We won. The game's over."

"No. Nonononono, Michal. It's not over. The game's not over."

I close my eyes.

"Michal?" He leans over, his lips press on mine—soft, slightly open. Cinnamon Trident, salty tears—sweet and gentle. He cups my face in his hands. "Michal?" He chokes, leaning his forehead against mine. "Please don't go."

I open my eyes.

Josh's face is a little blurry. I try to move my hand up. He pulls it out from under the blanket, kissing my fingertips. I shiver. It feels like somebody injected ice water into my spine. "Please," he says. "I love you."

My stomach's on fire, as if somebody made me swallow dry ice—a crippling blister-cold sensation. I feel the way blood drains from my body, leaving me. At first it pumped out fast. Now it bubbles. Slow. Sporadic, leaving me hazy, drowsy.

Josh wraps his arms around me. He leans forward and whispers a song. I can't hear the words. I can just feel them—their rhythm in my ear, the pounding of his heart.

Mrs. Brady's out of her coma, on the road to recovery.

We won the money to pay Lillian back.

Moch is going to be okay.

Lillian loves me. *Lillian loves me.*

And so does Josh.

I'm vaguely aware of the police breaking down the door, screaming for Josh to get on the floor.

"Where's the ambulance?" Josh asks. "Michal?" Josh leans over. "Michal, can you hold on until the paramedics get here? Can you do that? Where's the fucking ambulance?!" His screams echo in my mind.

Calm down. It's okay. You're going to be fine.

But he can't hear me. Or I'm not talking. I can't feel if my lips are moving—everything's become so still.

Josh is lying next to me, his face pushed to the crimson tiles with rough hands. Tears drip down his cheeks mixing with the sticky dark floor—slippery, smeary gray. The color is gone now. Except for Josh's eyes—bright green.

Don't cry. It's all okay now.

It's not like in the movies where everything flashes before you—scenes of regret or happiness. It's like becoming a fish—slipping underwater.

Josh frees his hand, reaches it out, lacing his fingers in mine.

It's so clear. I am wanted.

ACKNOWLEDGMENTS

IF ONLY GETTING A BOOK out there was as easy being as a wizard standing behind a curtain, or clicking your heels in snazzy red shoes. . . . This book is in your hands because of a slew of people who worked incredibly hard to make sure it got there.

Thanks to the phenomenal team at HarperCollins and Balzer + Bray, including: Caroline Sun, Olivia deLeon, and Emilie Polster—publicists and marketing director extraordinaire. *Huge, giant, never-ending* thanks to Renée Cafiero, who has to be the most brilliant mind in copyediting south of the North Pole. To Michelle Taormina in Design, who created a breathtaking cover. Sara Sargent, for seeing this through. And finally to Alessandra Balzer and Donna Bray for taking a chance on an unconventional western.

This book would be nowhere without the exceptional

insight, editorial eye, and patience of my editor, Ruta Rimas. Thank you so much!

I have the fortune and privilege to work with the best agent south of the North Pole as well. Thank you, Stephen Barbara, Super Agent, without whom my odd ideas wouldn't get very far.

Thank you to the amazing children's writing community and my critique group.

I'm so grateful for my friend Gwen, who not only let me hide in her house for days on end to work on this novel but also offered full-on catering and twenty-four-hour coffee service. You're a writer's secret weapon.

I thank Dad and Rick for being the most gentle giants I know.

And if there *is* a wizard behind a curtain, it's my husband. Cesar lost me to a world of online gambling and crime for much of 2010 and 2011. Thank you for your patience and support and patience. I'm back!

ABOUT THE AUTHOR

HEIDI AYARBE GREW UP IN NEVADA AND has lived all over the world. She now makes her home in Colombia with her husband and daughters. She is also the author of *Compulsion*, *Compromised*, and *Freeze Frame*. You can visit her online at www.heidiayarbe.com.

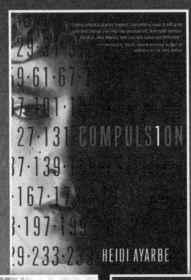